# DOUBLE-EDGED BLADE

## JIM SCORZELLI

Tate Publishing & *Enterprises*

*Double-Edged Blade*
Copyright © 2010 by Jim Scorzelli. All rights reserved.

No part of this publication may be reproduced, stored in a retrieval system or transmitted in any way by any means, electronic, mechanical, photocopy, recording or otherwise without the prior permission of the author except as provided by USA copyright law.

Scriptures taken from the Holy Bible, Today's New International Version®. TNIV®. Copyright© 2001, 2005 by Biblica, Inc.™ Used by permission of Zondervan. All rights reserved worldwide. www.zondervan.com

This novel is a work of fiction. Names, descriptions, entities, and incidents included in the story are products of the author's imagination. Any resemblance to actual persons, events, and entities is entirely coincidental.

The opinions expressed by the author are not necessarily those of Tate Publishing, LLC.

Published by Tate Publishing & Enterprises, LLC
127 E. Trade Center Terrace | Mustang, Oklahoma 73064 USA
1.888.361.9473 | www.tatepublishing.com

Tate Publishing is committed to excellence in the publishing industry. The company reflects the philosophy established by the founders, based on Psalm 68:11,
*"The Lord gave the word and great was the company of those who published it."*

Book design copyright © 2010 by Tate Publishing, LLC. All rights reserved.
*Cover design by Amber Gulilat*
*Interior design by Joey Garrett*

Published in the United States of America

ISBN: 978-1-61739-188-0
1. Fiction / Christian / General
2. Fiction / Christian / Suspense
10.09.15

# DEDICATION

Lovingly dedicated to my dear wife, Joanne,
who prayed me into the faith.

# CHAPTER 1

Joel targeted the .22 caliber pellet gun on a nearby streetlight and squeezed the trigger. The explosion of plastic and glass split the night air and echoed across cold, black buildings. At first, Joel thought curious neighbors might rush to their windows in response, but a quick scan of upper floor windows convinced him no one considered the crashing sound unusual in this bleak and dying section of the city. Blanketed in darkness, he felt invisible. And powerful.

He holstered the pistol in an inside pocket of his black leather jacket then zippered it against a stiff February breeze. A lone snowflake melted on his frosty nose. Even with his collar turned up and long wavy hair tucked against his neck, the icy wind found its way to his shivering skin. Despite the discomfort, he kept a watchful eye on the street and sidewalks as far as he could see in all directions. It was past midnight, and only an occasional car sped by. No one dared walk the dismal block.

Crouched in the niche of the electronics store entrance, Joel smiled at the thought that he was becoming an important member of the Blades. Tonight he was the trusted lookout while others took anything of value from the run-down store. *This is only the beginning*, he thought. Someday, he would be Derrick's second-in-command and maybe even have his own gang.

Suddenly, an engine roared to life. "All right!" said Joel, as little gusts of vaporous breath followed each word. Three seconds later, screaming tires propelled the car in reverse out of the alley. It made a quick turn, barely stopped, and then raced away, spitting smoke and bits of asphalt in its wake.

Joel jogged toward the car. "Hey...hey...wait up will ya?"

But moments later, he was alone in an unfamiliar section of the city, surrounded by silence and foul-smelling exhaust. "Man!" said Joel as he kicked a beer can. The metallic *clank clank clank* cut through the frozen air. Any sound was better than the awful silence.

Joel had ridden with the Blades, who had purposely driven to Greenpoint on the north end of Brooklyn, so no one would recognize them. But now that he was alone and on the street, far from familiar territory, and with some pretty rough neighborhoods between him and home, the gang's notoriety had become a curse. He slipped a hand into his jeans pocket and felt the switchblade. Between that and the pellet gun, he should have no trouble defending himself.

Joel shoved frozen hands in his jacket pockets and started walking. Anger chased his thoughts around. *How could they leave him like that?* They knew he was outside waiting for them. Had an alarm gone off? He hadn't heard one. Something must have spooked them so bad they didn't have time to pick him up. He couldn't blame them if that was the case. The thought took the edge off his anger, but still he fumed.

He mentally mapped out the way home. The shortest, most direct route would take him through Skull territory—a dangerous journey even at this time of night. The Blades had a run-in with that gang once in a neighborhood that was considered neutral territory. The brief clash had amounted to nothing more than throwing beer cans and insults at each other; both gangs had someplace else to go and weren't looking for a fight just then.

Slightly smaller than the average fifteen-year-old, Joel knew he was no match for any group that stumbled upon him. He would have to disappear in the shadows and stay on high alert every step of the way. Even if he was careful, there was still a chance he would run into someone lurking in the countless black crevices on every block.

Mile blended into lonely mile as Joel approached the business district. Long rows of shabby store fronts gave way to three- and four-story office buildings, which in turn, became twenty- and forty-story monsters. Traffic picked up as the earliest commuters trekked into work.

It was still dark when Joel reached the clock tower downtown. Roughly the halfway point of his journey, from here his neighborhood was maybe an hour away. But he would soon have to go through a section of proclaimed Skull territory where rotting, abandoned stores and old office buildings were likely hideouts for gang members. His only hope was that they were all sleeping off whatever alcohol or drugs were taken the night before and wouldn't notice a lone figure invading their streets.

Joel ambled down a side street that would eventually lead to the Brooklyn Queens Expressway—a safer bet for a while until it turned away from his destination. After the first block, he realized most of the streetlights had been knocked out. Chills tickled his neck as he strained to see into the shadows on both sides of the street. His own footsteps were the only sign of life here.

Something made him stop. He turned and faced an old stone church. A chain-link fence surrounded it; its gate was held shut with a massive lock. Joel tried the lock anyway—you never knew when people were conveniently careless—but it was secure.

"Huh," he said aloud. "Guess God doesn't like visitors this time of night."

Joel's eyes followed the contour of the building up to the steeple. At the very top, black against the moonlit sky, he saw the cross. It seemed far away and cold. A shiver rippled through his body.

A click returned his gaze to the street ahead of him. Maintaining a wide-eyed radar search, Joel continued walking. He heard another click, closer this time, coming from the narrow ally between the church and the neighboring building. Was it a footstep or a drop of water? Suddenly, a dog started barking. It had heard something too. His body stiffened, and he quickened his pace to a slow jog, quickly swiveling his head.

As the road curved to the left, Joel came upon two large groups of boys converging on a corner parking lot. He dashed beside concrete steps leading up to an abandoned building and cautiously peered over the top step. A lone streetlight cast its stark beam on the space between the two groups, spotlighting the asphalt stage. From this distance, he couldn't make out who the two gangs were, but he dared not move any closer. He would be quickly disposed of if either gang considered him an enemy. As he watched, several boys brandishing crude weapons exploded from the alley behind him and rushed past. Joel instinctively ducked into the shadows, but the boys' eagerness to join the fray had made them oblivious to his presence.

Joel crouched low and peeked around the steps, grasping the cold concrete. The two groups had drawn closer, forming intimidating battle lines. Each side cursed at the other and gestured with weapons of pipes and clubs. A single shot cracked and, like a race-starting signal, it set the warring gangs into frenzied motion.

The two gangs merged into each other. Short blades flashed briefly as they caught the glaring streetlight. Spiked two-by-fours and heavy chains swung relentlessly. Metallic clanking mixed with dull thumping as the weapons found their mark. Another two shots rang out in rapid succession. Shouts of the assailants blended with sickening screams of the beaten and stabbed. Joel had never been this close to a full-blown street fight before. Although something inside wanted to join in the battle just for the excitement, he didn't know who was fighting or why, so he settled on being a spectator.

Above the din of conflict, Joel heard faint sirens. The wailing grew louder, and he strained his ears to pinpoint their approach. Two police cruisers soon rounded the curve and stopped abruptly just a few feet from Joel, their blue pulsating lights stabbing at the night. Another two cars appeared simultaneously on the far side of the battlefield. Even before the police officers could emerge from their vehicles, the battle disintegrated. Its combatants scattered in all directions. Some limped away under their own power while others stumble-ran as they clung to fellow gang members. Those who were badly wounded tried to crawl away, but were quickly rounded up by the police. A couple of boys lay motionless on the street, dead or dying.

Having seen enough action for one night, Joel quickly moved into the black alley behind him. He backtracked in a wide circle of several blocks before heading toward home so that he would be well outside the "drag zone" where the police combed for straggling gang members and possible witnesses to the fight.

Finally, Joel made it to his own neighborhood, Dutch Hill. Here there was a better chance that anyone he met would be relatively friendly, or at least a known enemy he could deal with. He passed row after row of two-story apartment buildings where the government, he had been told, paid most of the rent. The buildings were in various states of disrepair. Peeling paint and rotting wood formed a neighborhood pattern, and many of the common entrances had no door. Comfort bathed him as he strolled through this familiar territory.

Joel instinctively jumped over the badly cracked fourth step on his way up to his second floor apartment. He slipped the key out from a secret pocket he had sown inside his pants, unlocked the deadbolt, and cautiously opened the door; you never knew what was waiting for you behind a closed door. He moved silently inside, locking the door behind him.

He scanned the small living room faintly lit by a streetlight over the far side of the street. On the coffee table were a dozen

beer cans, an empty Tequila bottle, and several empty glasses. There were two different brands of cigarette butts in the ashtray. His mother had entertained a guest or two. The last time his mom had a party, he had to sleep on the couch.

Thankfully, Joel found his bedroom unoccupied. Without bothering to undress, he threw his jacket on the floor and himself on the bed. "Man, what a night," he mused. "Well, at least with Mom sleeping it off, I won't have to go to school again today. Cool."

---

"Not cool."

Abner floated in a corner of the bedroom unseen by mortal eyes. He was disturbed by Joel's ailing soul, a soul continuously sickened by his harmful desires and the unsavory influence of those he called friends. Abner swooped close to the bed, within inches of Joel's already sleeping form. He wished he could stroke the boy's hair, perhaps providing physical comfort; but, of course, in his present manifestation that was quite impossible. It was enough that he could feel the boy's powerful but restless spirit.

Father Himself had assigned Abner to watch over Joel, to help him avoid the Evil One's snares during this crucial time of life. He found it to be a daunting task, but one he would give his life to, if it were possible for angels to truly die.

"Joel," he whispered to unhearing ears, "no matter what you do or where you go, whatever comes against you, I'll always be close by. But your choices are your own. Your journey is of your own making. I pray you will tread carefully."

Abner suddenly looked up and focused on a point beyond the sky. He was being summoned. Joining a sunbeam that was just entering the room, he traveled to his destination in less time than a thought crosses the human mind.

# CHAPTER 2

Joel's eyes blinked open. The small clock on his nightstand displayed 11:04. He was still tired, especially after his ordeal the night before, but he was never able to sleep more than six hours. Sleeping was such a waste of time anyway. After a long stretching yawn, he rolled out of bed and then silently walked past his mother's bedroom and into the kitchen.

Three roaches darted across the floor as he entered their domain. Scarcely noticing, Joel swooshed open the refrigerator and grabbed a Coke. He reached into an open breadbox on the counter and pulled out a handful of chocolate chip cookies. Munching on the cookies with Coke in hand, he walked back down the hallway and peeked into his mother's bedroom. Satisfied that there was at least one lump under the covers, he slipped into the bathroom across the hall and opened the medicine cabinet.

Joel fingered a cluster of amber prescription bottles until he found what he was looking for: *No Doz*. He poured out a small handful of pills and dumped them into his pants pocket. As he closed the cabinet door, he glanced at his image in the dingy mirror. Brown, sunken, and slightly bloodshot eyes stared back at him. Dark, bruise-like crescents under his eyes contrasted sharply with his fair skin tone. "Humph," he said. "Dead man walking." He didn't know where he'd heard the phrase, but it sounded cool. He widened his eyes and then smiled at the menacing image. Back in his bedroom, he slipped on his leather jacket, felt that the pellet gun was still in its place, and then stealthily left the apartment.

---

The Blades' headquarters, the second floor of an abandoned apartment building, was a mile away from home. Some of the Blades, those who were able to skip school, were already there when Joel walked in. A stolen kerosene heater warmed the sparsely furnished room. Fifteen-year-old "Mickey the Matchstick," nicknamed by Derrick because of his thin body and shocking red hair, lounged on two pallets padded with a rotting striped mattress. True to his nickname, Mickey had a quick, fiery temper. The Wilson twins, relative newcomers, sat next to Mickey. Eddie, Derrick's second in command, sat backward in one of the two wooden chairs, resting his arms and head atop its back. Randy, a lieutenant, sat in the other chair. Three newer members huddled on the floor around the heater. It was a well known rule that your standing in the gang determined, among other things, your choice of seating. Derrick had, of course, reserved the best seat for himself: a large, well-padded lounge chair situated prominently at one end of the room like a king's throne. A scarred round table squatted in front of him.

Joel approached the "throne." Derrick's long black hair tightly pulled back into a ponytail, steel-gray eyes, and square, lightly bearded jaw gave him the look of a true warrior. With one leg draped over the arm of the chair, the seventeen-year-old gang boss pushed a button on his six-inch switchblade, and the spring-loaded blade shot out from the end of the handle. He clicked the button again, and the deadly weapon quickly retracted. He extended and retracted the blade again and again while staring off into space.

Joel stared at the gleaming, incredibly sharp blade. It reminded him of the initiation ritual that he and every member went through. First you had to steal a switchblade while being watched by a full member. It had to be a good quality blade, at least four fingers in length. Then, you had to keep your hand flat on the round wooden table for five minutes while Derrick and other senior members played a frightening game of mumbly-peg with your own knife and your hand as the target. If you moved your hand, even slightly, you were out. If you screamed or cried without being hit, you were out. They had told him the story of one boy who suffered a stab wound right through the center of the hand and lost the use of two of his fingers. Joel rubbed the scar on the fleshy area just below his pinky. He was cut clear to the bone during his initiation.

As a full member, Joel had the right to speak his mind, but it was never a good idea to anger Derrick. He would have to choose his words carefully. He said, "How come you didn't pick me up last night? I had to walk all the way back."

Derrick scowled, "We couldn't take any chances with that racket you made knocking out the streetlight. Besides, you knew where I was. You shoulda come to me. I can't go around like some taxi when I'm hot, man."

"I know that," said Joel with a boldness he didn't feel. "Just don't leave me there next time."

Eddie chided, "What's the *matter* little boy? Scared of the dark? Did you cry for your *mommy*?"

Amid sinister chuckles from other gang members, Joel lost his composure. He slammed his body at the side of Eddie's chair so hard it tipped over, spilling its ill-prepared occupant onto the dusty floor. The laughter grew, but Eddie quickly recovered. The tall sixteen-year-old lunged at Joel, pinning him against the wall with one hand on his throat. Joel tried to kick his opponent away, but Eddie simply stepped back and out of reach.

Joel felt his face fill with blood, and he couldn't breathe. A throbbing began in his head. He grabbed Eddie's arm to push it away but with his feet barely touching the floor, he had no leverage. Kicking, pulling, grabbing; nothing he could do lessened Eddie's vise-like grip.

"All right you guys, cool it," Derrick casually commanded.

Eddie immediately released his grip and in the same motion yanked Joel down to the floor. He returned to his seat, grinning and slapping hands with fellow gang members. Coughing hard, Joel tried hard not to cry. He had been beaten in front of his leader and friends—a sure sign of weakness. But crying was the absolute worst thing he could do. If even one tear dripped out, he might get kicked out of the Blades for good, or, even worse, have to live with a label that would make him wish he had been kicked out.

Joel wiped his face with his sleeve, then picked himself up and flicked his hand at Eddie in a gesture of contempt.

Eddie jumped up, eager to mix it up again. "You want another piece of me, punk?"

Derrick sat up and pointed the blade at Eddie. "Hey, you want a piece of *me?* Lay off him, Eddie. It don't do no good killing each other."

Joel felt a lump in his throat whenever Derrick stuck up for him. It was like having a big brother look out for you. No, it was even better than that. It was like the general of an army taking your side. And nothing could hurt you when you had that kind of protection.

"Hey kid." Derrick motioned him over. Joel liked it when he called him that. It reminded him of great men in history—Billy the Kid and Captain Kidd.

"Yeah?"

"What did you bring me?"

Joel knew exactly what he meant. He searched around in his pants pocket for the No Doz pills and pulled out all but two. He might need those for himself later.

"Here. My mom uses them when she has to get up early."

"All right. Go sit down."

Derrick popped three of the pills, shirt-pocketed the rest, and addressed the gang.

"Okay boys, gather round. I've got a plan that's gonna take some teamwork and special instructions, but if we pull it off, we'll be sittin' pretty for a long time!"

The boys pulled in close, excitement growing in their faces. Derrick put on the guise of a master storyteller.

"It so happens that Randy has just landed a job at a video store over on Fulton Street. And it seems they really *trust* their employees to watch over the cash register when the boss is out."

Some of the older boys let out a low giggle, and it spread to those who hadn't yet grasped what Derrick was leading up to. Derrick watched the reaction of his followers. He grinned as he unfolded a rough floor plan of the store.

"Here's what we're going to do on a Friday night when the store has the most money..."

Derrick's plan to rob the video store was a bold but simple scheme that involved staging an auto accident in front of the store to get the manager and any customers outside while Eddie helped Randy clean out the cash register and the safe. The backup plan, if the first diversion didn't work, was to start a fire in the back room to empty the store.

When Derrick finished giving the details, everyone started talking about their own ideas and what they would do with the money or how much it might be. Joel was especially eager to hear about his part in this latest adventure. He was trusted now, trusted enough to be in the thick of the action.

Raising his voice a bit over the heated conversations around him, he said, "Hey Derrick, what do you want me to do? I could be in the accident, or I could sneak to the back room and start the fire if I have to. Maybe grab a few videos while I'm back there. What do ya think?"

Derrick momentarily turned away from his officers and said, "You're the lookout when we make our move."

"But…but I don't want to do that. Let Mickey do that. Or the Wilson brothers. They never did that before."

"You're the best lookout we got, man. I can't take a chance on those amateurs." He turned back to his officers.

Joel raised his voice a bit more, hoping he wouldn't sound disrespectful. "C'mon, Derrick. I wanna do something else…not that stupid lookout job again. I wanna have some fun for a change…"

Derrick didn't hide his anger. "You *will* do that job, or I'll let Eddie hang you on the wall till you squeal like a baby. *You got that?*"

All conversations stopped at the unexpected outburst. Joel looked over at a grinning Eddie, who made a fist and punched his open hand several times.

"Yeah. I got it. No problem. I'll be the lookout."

It was late afternoon by the time the meeting broke up. On the way out, everyone was slapping hands and backs, proud of themselves for being a part of an ingenious plan. But Joel walked home alone and furious.

When he was out of earshot, he said aloud, "I can't believe it! I'm gonna be the stupid lookout again!" He kicked a beer bottle on the ground so hard it stung his toe. He had been with the Blades for over a year now and it occurred to him that he might never do anything except be the lookout while everybody else had fun. He thought of joining another gang, but how? What if Derrick found out? Would the other gang protect him? Probably. But he would have to start at the bottom again. Of course, he was pretty close to that now anyway.

Joel came to a familiar intersection. If he kept going straight, the road would eventually take him to his neighborhood. After a short pause and without really thinking about it, he turned left toward Skull territory.

As Joel walked further down the street, early darkness of winter enveloped him. As was his practice for maximum safety, he stayed in the middle of the street just in case. Doing so would buy him a few precious seconds if he were attacked. A few streetlights started to flicker on, but most had been knocked out. The alleys between three-story buildings on both sides of the street formed black canyons. Unspeakable things could happen there, witnessed only by street rats and the occasional drifter. Joel thought it was strange that even though it was only early evening, there was no one on the street. Either people didn't live near by or something kept them inside.

At the next intersection, Joel passed a bar on the left and a drugstore across the street. A dim *"Open"* sign flickered in the black window of the bar, but he could see no one inside. The drug store was open too, its light bathing the sidewalk through a large window, but when he glanced inside as he passed, Joel saw only an old man slowly sweeping the floor. Across the street, directly ahead, was an abandoned store, its front windows covered with plywood. One of the panels had been pulled away from the building just enough for someone to crawl through. The outline of a Skull spray painted across the plywood was unmistakable. Joel had stumbled on a hideout.

A terrible fear seized Joel. *What am I going to tell them when they ask what I'm doing here?* He knew they would not believe he was on their turf on friendly terms, that he was thinking about joining their gang. The Blades certainly wouldn't.

Realizing he had made a mistake, he turned to go back and was blocked by three boys. One was smaller than him and the other two taller. All three wore black leather jackets, variously decorated with small chains, silver brads, and swastikas. Large silver Skull pendants hung from their necks. The two older boys' heads were shaved.

The inevitable question came quickly. "What are you doin' here, *punk?*"

Joel was not as afraid as he thought he would be. He held his hands up and said, "Look. I'm unarmed." It was a lie. He still had the pellet gun hidden inside his jacket, but there was no reason to show it yet. Surprise might be his only advantage.

"I just wanted to find out more about you guys, ya know? Do you guys, like, accept new members?" His words felt lame even as he spoke them.

The two older boys laughed wildly. The smaller one glanced at his elders and then laughed too. It was clear he was just a novice and hopefully wouldn't fight well. Joel felt his face redden. This was going very badly so far.

Joel sensed the one who spoke was the ranking member among them. The leader made a quick motion with his hand and immediately the three surrounded him and kept moving in a circle.

One of them said, "So you want to join up with us? You think you're *man* enough little punk?"

Another chimed in, "You ain't nothing! I wouldn't even let you lick my boots clean!"

Joel had to keep turning his head to see where any two of them were, but there was always one behind him. It was an effective tactic, and Joel felt whatever confidence he had drain away completely. He had no choice now but to even up the odds.

Even as he reached for the pistol, they were on him. He hit the frozen pavement hard as one of them yanked the gun out of his hand. Two of them held him to the ground face up while the leader held up the pistol.

"So you're unarmed, eh?" He shoved the gun hard against Joel's face. "Then whaddaya call *this*, you piece of crap?"

Joel had never felt the depth of fear that gripped him now. He could not move or speak. His heart pounded against his chest and throat.

The leader kneeled down and put his face within inches of Joel's. His breath stunk of alcohol and cigarettes.

"Ya know," he said softly, "the Skulls have certain rules. You'll have to learn them if you want to join us. One of them is no *lying!*"

He shouted the last word as he hit Joel in the face with the gun barrel. Joel screamed.

The novice said, "Yeah. No lying," as he kicked him in the side.

Joel desperately hoped he would pass out from the intense pain. The one who held the pistol looked it over more closely.

"Huh. Just a little pop gun. Couldn't kill a bird with this thing." He looked down at Joel as if he were a puddle of vomit. "You call this a weapon, little boy? Where'd you get this... from your little sister? Huh?"

The other tall one got up and kicked him hard in the ribs. A searing explosion shot through him. "Answer him, *punk!*"

Just then they heard a siren in the distance. "Shh," said the leader.

The three stood motionless as the siren got louder. Joel was grateful for the reprieve, but there was nothing he could do to take advantage of it. If he tried to run, they would quickly catch him and beat him for the attempt to get away. He had no choice but to lie doubled up in agony holding his ribs, and wait for the punishment to begin again. Maybe, he thought with increasing hope, someone had seen what was happening and had called the cops. He would welcome even them right now. The siren grew to a peak then trailed off as the vehicle moved out of the area. Joel's heart sunk. He knew there would be more pain. For the first time in his life, he wondered if he would die. And for the first time, he wanted to.

"P... please," Joel sobbed. "No more. I... I won't ever come back here again. I promise."

The leader ridiculed Joel's plea. "Did you hear that, Danny? He's never coming back to bother us again. Oh, I feel so much safer now!" He moved closer to Joel, his voice dripping with hatred. "That's right, you'll never bother us again, but not because you'll never come back. The truth is you're never gonna *leave* here... alive!" He stood and addressed the others. "Pick him up, boys. Let's have some fun with him back at the bunker." He pointed the pistol at Joel's head. "Maybe we'll have a little target practice!"

Joel did not have the strength or conscience of mind to resist. There was only severe throbbing in his side and face. He felt a trickle of blood seep into his mouth. All else was a dim cloud.

As they picked him up by his jacket, the younger one said, "What was that?"

Everyone froze in the silence. Danny grew impatient. "Ah, you're just hearing th…"

"Shhhh! There it is again," he whispered. "Don't you hear it?"

They could all hear it now—slow, methodical footsteps steadily becoming louder. They each let go of Joel's jacket, dumping him on the street like a rag doll.

"Where's it coming from?" said the leader in a hoarse whisper.

"I don't know," Danny gasped. "Maybe the alley or around the block. I don't know. Sounds like a bunch of 'em."

"This ain't right. Something's wrong," said the leader, less sure of himself. "How many… how many you think there are?"

"No way I'm gonna stick around to find out, man. Let's *go!*" said Danny.

The younger one pointed at Joel, "What about him?"

Danny said, "Leave him here." He shot a thumb in no particular direction. "They'll get him." He tugged on the leader's sleeve. "C'mon, Karl. We're *outta* here."

Karl swiveled his head, trying to look in all directions at once. "I don't get it. Where *are* they?"

Danny was already on the move down the street. "No time, man. C'mon!"

The three broke into a dead run.

Joel heard the siren in the distance again. He closed his eyes. Barely conscious, he thought, *Please let them find me.*

He didn't see the ambulance roll to a stop minutes later, or the emergency medical technicians rush to him, quickly check his vital signs, then gingerly but swiftly scoop him onto a gurney and into the ambulance.

---

Abner watched the ambulance speed off with its precious cargo. Father God had compelled a fearful neighborhood resident to look out his window and dial 911. He then sent a dozen angels to stage the invisible onslaught. Joel was safe for now, but Abner knew he would need to find the path the Father intended for him in order to be truly protected. He prayed reverently that he would be successful in helping Joel, and that he would be able to defeat the evil forces that surrounded his charge—evil that sprang from the heart of both human and spiritual beings.

## CHAPTER 3

Derrick watched through a cracked and smudged window as the last of the Blades exited the building. *About time.* He walked into what was once an eat-in kitchen and pulled the last can of Budweiser out of a cooler half filled with water. He moved the heater closer and then plopped onto the lounge chair, letting out a long breath. He shook his head. "Man, what a bunch of losers," he said aloud. "I'll never get anywhere if I have to depend on them."

Derrick fingered the sharp edge of the can opening and then took a long swig of lukewarm beer. He stared across the room and once again coaxed the Dream to dance before his mind's eye. In it, he had all he ever needed: power, money, girls, cars, and a huge home. The mayor of New York City came up to him and shook his hand. He didn't know what he was being congratulated for, but he was sure it had something to do with keeping the city "safe" from criminals and being in control of everything. Then he saw himself in a large corner office on the top floor of the Empire State Building overlooking the city. *His* city. He had his feet up on a desk overlooking the expanse of concrete and glass while judges and high-ranking police officers stood against the walls waiting for his next order. Meanwhile, huge bags of money were brought in by dangerous, shadowy men who mutely went about their business of stockpiling wealth. *His* wealth.

Derrick smiled to himself as the vision melted away. *Someday. Someday it'll be real.* Beer can in hand; he walked back into the kitchen and pulled out a large manila envelope between the defunct electric oven and the adjacent cabinet. In the envelope were bills of various denominations. He counted the cash for the fifth time that week.

*Five thousand five hundred and twenty dollars.*

The money came from everything that the Blades had stolen, or cash from anything that was sold. It was a fair enough deal, he thought. As the gang leader and mastermind of all robberies, Derrick took what he needed for his immediate expenses and then gave out half of whatever was leftover to the gang members present. They didn't know how much money was taken in on any given job and were happy to get anything at all. Weekly "paydays" kept everyone interested in the gang's activities. The rest would be used to finance the Dream.

Derrick carefully poked the envelope back in its hiding place and unexpectedly thought of his father. Tommy Wicker was the definition of a burned-out blue collar worker. Twenty-five years' dedicated service at the Armstrong Asbestos Tile Manufacturing Company got him nothing but a severance check, lung cancer, and a lawsuit that never happened. Tommy died before his suit against Armstrong got off the ground. Shortly after his father's funeral two years ago, the house went into foreclosure and Derrick had been homeless ever since.

Derrick sat on the floor, leaning against the cold oven door. He remembered his mom, who died a few years before his dad. She was shot by an undercover cop chasing a drug dealer and died on the way to the hospital. No charges were filed against the police officer, but the city paid a modest compensatory sum to his father. Too bad all of it went to lawyer's fees, private investigators, and who knew what else.

Derrick took another long mouthful of beer. *That's not gonna be me. That's for sure.*

---

Pus, a black and hideous demon, floated near the brooding Derrick. The simmering rage and emotional pain streaming into him from the human's powerful spirit was much more pleasurable than the occasional outbursts so many exhibited when he was able to make them feel frightened or angry. Usually, those emotions subsided as understanding or—he nearly choked on the thought—*forgiveness* took over.

Pus had worked ceaselessly over many months to cultivate Derrick's notion that he was a great leader in possession of superior fighting skills. Gradually, he instilled the Dream to solidify the lie that he was destined to claim leadership of the city. He had built up visions of a future filled with fame and prosperity and convinced him that he had power over those who would oppose him. He knew it would be a simple matter for him to act according to those perceptions of himself. Lately, he had focused on providing pure hatred for those boys who wouldn't perform or heed his command. He whispered to Derrick's inner mind, "Those kids are not even giving you all the money they collect. They're cheating you every day. How dare they?"

---

Derrick muttered, "Stupid kids," as he threw the half empty beer can across the room with such force it cracked the wall. "*I'll* teach them to cheat on me!"

Pus couldn't contain himself any longer. The sharp emotions spewing out of Derrick fed the demon, puffing him up. Delirious with a fresh infusion of sweet evil, Pus floated into an open drain in the basement of the building laughing uncontrollably. "Teragon will be well pleased with me when he sees how easily I can control this one!"

Pus rubbed his slimy, gnarled fingers and peered into the antechamber of Teragon's domain. Usually, a warrior demon stood guard, its yellow, bloodshot eyes searching the chamber entrance for the slightest opportunity to slice an intruder to pieces. This time, however, only a couple of fat little drones were on duty. They were sleeping, and Pus easily tiptoed by, giggling at their fate when Teragon learned of their lack of discipline. A crooked fang slipped out of his mouth as he grinned at the image of Teragon's rage when he told the sub-ruler about the drones' infraction. He giggled again and then quickly muted himself so as not to awaken the underlings and thereby save them from disaster.

Pus was well acquainted with the protocol required upon entrance into Teragon's court, although he hated doing it. "Great and mighty Teragon, your humble servant desires only to serve you. What is your pleasure, Most High Priest of the world above and the world below?"

The cavernous chamber was nearly as dark as deep space. Teragon slowly rose from his throne of blood-red marble at the end of a wide, column-lined aisle. He held a staff adorned with live snakes and wore a crown fashioned of a single blackened bone. Directly in front of the throne was a wide steaming caldron of molten rock. Pus once saw Teragon toss a tactless drone into the caldron simply for giggling at the wrong moment.

His voice thundered. "Who is it that dares enter my domain?"

Pus loathed this game. Teragon knew all his underlings perfectly well. A privilege of power and position, Teragon preferred to constantly remind his subjects of their inferiority. Pus was not ready to buck the status quo. "It is I, Most Dishonorable One,

Pus. I come with news of a great victory over a human soul. If it pleases your Lowness, I will tell you of my progress."

"Ah, Pus. Come forth."

Pus slipped closer to the throne, cringing as he approached. He knew Teragon's calm demeanor could quickly turn to scorching wrath at the slightest provocation, and he had the scars to prove it. He stopped just at the far side of the smoldering cauldron, its sides glowing faintly from the intense heat. Knowing his place, he waited to be addressed.

"So," Teragon roared, "what have you done to promote wickedness and misery on earth?"

Pus licked his fang with a slimy tongue. Suddenly, even his easy control over Derrick didn't seem quite good enough for his Overlord. In his mind, he began concocting a self-aggrandizing lie that would seem more acceptable to Teragon, perhaps peppered with reality so it would pass for truth. But if it wasn't convincing enough…

"Speak, you bungling speck! How dare you waste my time? Would you invent mythical stories thinking to amuse me?" Teragon hurled his staff, snakes flying everywhere, just as Pus ducked behind the cauldron.

"Sire! Please, kill me now if it would give you pleasure," said Pus from behind the great pot. He peeked over its edge. "But then I would not be able to continue to cause great havoc for you and our great and mighty leader, Baal-Zebub himself." Gaining confidence little by little, he stood halfway, but still remained ready to dodge another onslaught at any moment. "I have one called Derrick Wicker in the palm of my hand. I have encouraged him to be angry and frustrated, cheated and vengeful. He is learning how to use evil as a tool to further his desires. He can be of great use to us. Just think of how much favor you would gain if…"

"*Silence!*" Pus cringed. "I know of this human. He is an easy catch, scarred as he was by fortunate events of his past. But I am after a bigger catch, a more meaningful one that I can offer as a sacrifice to our Beloved Lord. Do you know the boy, Joel Somers?"

Pus finally had something to brag about. "Why, yes, of course. I know all those who…"

"*Quiet*, imp! It is the boy I want, and any collateral damage you can incur along the way. But the boy, Joel, is the prize. Bring him to me, and I will reward you well."

# CHAPTER 4

Joel suddenly awoke in a brightly lit room. *Am I in heaven?*
He tried to lift his upper body, but the stabbing pain in his side forced him to quickly lie back down and wait for the throbbing to subside. He brought a hand to his face and discovered the gauze bandage on his cheek. Pushing on the dressing, he felt the pinching bulkiness of several stitches beneath. The thought about being in heaven quickly vanished; there was no doubt he was still in the world he knew.

Near the bed, a small glossy statue of a woman looked down at him with her palms pressed together. She wore a white scarf and a long, light blue shawl. He was captivated by her frozen expression of concern. As his eyes focused and as memories of the night before flooded back to him, he realized he was in a hospital room.

Joel had been in hospitals before; he had his share of stitches, broken bones, and wounds. But this room was unlike any he had seen. His was the only bed in the small room. The wooden table and chair nearby were the only other furniture. A thick book sprouting thin colored ribbons lay on the table. On the far wall was a picture of a bearded man with a long staff, curved at the end, tending sheep. The man had a glowing ring around his head. On the wall above the bed was a cross. The man in the picture was nailed to the cross by his hands and feet. He had a sad expression, as if nobody cared what had happened to him. A woman who was dressed very much like the statue, white scarf and all, hurried past the open door.

*What kind of hospital is this?* thought Joel. As if in answer to his question, a tall pale-faced man walked in. He wore black pants and a matching shirt with a stiff collar. Beneath the collar was a white band.

"You're awake. Good," he said and gestured toward the bed. "May I?"

Joel didn't really know what he was asking, but he shrugged his shoulders, and the man sat down on the bed. He slowly propped himself up on one elbow, trying hard not to show the searing pain in his side.

"My name is Father Scala. I'm a priest. You were pretty badly broken up when they brought you in last night. I've got a few questions for you, but I'm sure you have some of your own. So fire away."

Joel thought the man looked friendly enough. Priests didn't lie, did they? He said, "Where am I?"

"This is Saint Mary's Catholic Hospital. You were taken here last night when you were found and couldn't be identified. What's your name, son?"

Joel wasn't sure he should give any information about himself just yet, so he ignored the question. "When can I go home?"

"We can't let you go until we know more about you. Your name, where you live, that sort of thing." Father Scala paused a moment. "Have you run away? Is that why you don't want to tell me your name?"

"Joel Somers. And I'm not a runaway."

The priest smiled. "Okay. If you don't mind, we'd like to call your parents so they know you're safe, and to pick you up when it's time to go home. What's your phone number?"

The prodding was starting to annoy Joel. "So when do I get to go home?"

"Would you like to tell me what happened to you?"

Joel looked away. "No. It's none of your business anyway."

"Listen. You have two cracked ribs and some pretty nasty cuts and bruises on your face. It appears that you have been in a fight. I think it's safe to assume sooner or later it will happen again. And you may not be so lucky next time. Next time it could be much worst. You could be stabbed, shot, or even killed."

"I've got friends. They'll protect me."

"Like they protected you this time?"

Joel was silent. The priest was right. It was the way Derrick had treated him that drove him to Skull territory in the first place. He couldn't push the thought out of his mind that nobody wanted him and nobody cared about him. His lip quivered, and he tried hard not to cry. Father Scala put a hand on his shoulder. Joel twisted away.

"There is a better way, Joel. You have a loving Father waiting for you to turn to him."

"Oh yeah? I ain't got no father. It's just me and my mom, and we do all right."

"I mean that you are a child of God. He loves you very much, you know."

Joel shot back, "God does *not* love me. If you loved your kid, would you treat him like this? Why don't you just leave me alone?" He slammed his body into the bed, burying his face in the pillow. It was a painful move, but it made his point.

Father Scala was taken aback by Joel's angry outburst. He opened his mouth to say something, then stood and quickly left the room.

---

The hospital had notified Joel's mother, Catherine Somers, and she picked him up a few hours later. She hardly spoke to him until they were in the car on the way home. As she pulled out of the hospital parking lot she snapped, "So what happened to you?"

Joel slouched against the door. He hadn't looked at her until then. Her gray-blonde hair was carelessly tied in a loose bun, her pale blue eyes moist and bloodshot. He was angry, but he wasn't sure why. "Nothing. What's it to you anyway?"

She dabbed her cigarette out in the ashtray, tapping it a little more than necessary. A cloud of blue-white smoke exited her mouth as she spoke. "You were fighting again, weren't you?" Her hand approached the stitches in Joel's cheek, but he slapped it away.

"Lay off me, will ya?"

"Someday you're gonna get hurt real bad, Joel. Maybe even get killed. Is that what you want? Do you want to just throw your life away? Do you know what that would do to me?"

Something was bubbling up inside Joel. He clenched his fists and felt his face tighten into a frown. His mother went on.

"And another thing. I got another letter from school yesterday saying you haven't been attending. It said if you keep this up they're gonna start some kind of legal action or something. I don't need that hassle. You just go to school and you stay there, do you understand me?"

Joel couldn't remember when he felt angrier. Without bothering to stop himself, he burst out, "So what about you? You talk about me throwing my life away... well look at yours."

"You hush! That's no way to talk to your mother!"

"Every time I see you you're either drunk or sleeping it off. You drink all the time. You probably had a drink before you came to the hospital this morning."

"That's none of your bus—"

"*Did you?*"

Silence filled the car. Catherine stared straight ahead. A car rushed by, and she glanced at the rearview mirror as if suddenly remembering she was driving. A tear trickled down her cheek, and she wiped it with a trembling hand.

Catherine brought the car to a stop at a red light and sniffled. "I...I can't help it sometimes," she whined. "Ever since your father left...it's just been real hard on me...and we're barely making it from paycheck to paycheck." She let out an anguished whimper and then continued. "Maybe I should just throw out all the bottles and not take another drink. At least for a while."

Joel mused aloud, "Yeah right. Like *that's* ever gonna happen. There's a better chance of me going to school every day than you quitting drinking."

Catherine looked at her son with a wry smile. "You don't think I can do it?"

"No way."

"Tell you what. If I stop drinking, will you start going to school every day?"

"*What?* You're joking, right?"

"Nope. What's the matter, don't think you're up to the challenge?"

Joel sat up. "Let me get this straight. I go to school all day, every day, and you're gonna stop drinking?"

She smiled. "Yep. That's the deal. Are you in?"

"I don't know..."

"You're not chicken are you? Afraid you can't live up to your word?"

"My word's golden."

"All right then." She put out her right hand. Someone behind them honked. The light had turned green.

"Mom, *go!*"

"Nope. I'm not leaving until we shake on it. Is it deal or not? You started this, don't forget."

"Man, you drive a hard bargain." The honking multiplied in intensity and number. "All right, all right. You got a deal." He grabbed his mother's hand and quickly shook it. "Just get moving, will ya? Everybody probably thinks we're stupid or something!"

Abner smiled. This agreement could certainly be a step in the right direction, but Joel still had a long way to go. Demonic schemes and the influence of the lost souls surrounding him still stood in his way. He sensed a difficult battle ahead, but one that he must win at all costs.

# CHAPTER 5

Monday at school: Joel couldn't think of a worse combination of day and place. After homeroom, Joel mindlessly strolled toward his math class. Every minute he spent in the hallway was one minute less that he had to spend in class. Mickey ran up alongside him.

"Hey man, what happened to your face? Were you in a fight?"

Before coming to school, Joel had pulled off the bandage so the ugly stitches would be in plain view. He figured he might as well get some mileage out of his run-in with the Skulls. Stitches were always a good way to show how tough you were. But it would be a mistake to let Mickey know the source of his wound.

"I just fell, that's all. What's it to you?"

"Nothing." After a moment he said, "Hey, that was some fight you had with Eddie the other day."

Joel ignored the junior Blade member. Mickey went on, "Eddie's out to get you, ya know. He's gonna cream you next time."

Joel stopped walking and scowled at Mickey. "So what? I coulda brought him down if I had the chance. He's lucky Derrick broke it up when he did."

"Yeah right. You were down, and you know it. He beat you good, man. Admit it!"

Before the next thought came to mind, Joel slammed Mickey against a row of lockers with his arm against his throat. "You're just too stupid to know when to shut up, you know that?"

Students began to gather at the prospect of a fight. Joel released Mickey, and he grabbed his throat, coughing. Between gasps, he said, "You think you're...so tough when Eddie's not...not around."

"Tougher than you'll ever be."

Mickey walked away backward while pointing at Joel. "You better watch your back, man. Someday you're gonna find out you're not as tough as you think." Then he turned suddenly, knocked a ninth grader down, and trotted down the hall.

---

Mrs. Avery, Joel's tenth grade math teacher, squeaked out an algebra problem on the chalkboard. But Joel's mind was nowhere near algebra. Several thoughts danced around in his head. Each one led to the next, and the next, until eventually the first came around again. They ran something like this:

*Why did I make that stupid deal with Mom?*
*She better keep up her end of the bargain.*
*I wonder what the Blades are doing right now?*
*Man, I'm bored. I haven't the faintest idea what this teacher is talking about.*
*Why did I make that stupid deal with Mom?*

A tap on the shoulder from behind broke the spiraling thought-cycle. A girl whispered, "Hey, get my pencil, will ya?"

Joel casually looked down beside his desk, picked up the pencil, and twisted around to return it to its owner. His heart jumped in his chest. Why had he never noticed her until now? Staring back at him with her hand out, she was the most beautiful person he had ever seen! She had long, straight, light brown hair, large brown eyes, smooth clear skin, and a cute little nose. Joel was so struck by her he completely forgot what he was doing.

"Well," she whispered impatiently, "give it to me!"

Joel looked at the pencil, then at the angel with her hand out to him. He realized his mouth was ajar and quickly clamped it shut. "Oh sorry," he said and gave her the pencil. She thanked him tersely and returned to her note taking.

Joel was absent so often he had never bothered learning anyone's name. Now he frantically ran through what he remembered of the names Mrs. Avery called while taking attendance. Was it Tabitha? Tracy?

He wanted to keep staring at her, absorbing her image, but in that same moment, he realized he had already spent way too much time looking in the wrong direction.

"Mr. Somers. Would you like to face the front now or did you suddenly turn into a pretzel?"

Muffled giggles filled the room.

Joel turned around and said innocently, "No. I mean, yes. Um, which question would you like me to answer first, Mrs. Avery?"

More giggles. Mrs. Avery was not amused. "You just sit still and pay attention. If you give me any more trouble, you can answer questions in the principal's office!"

Ten minutes ago, Joel would have gladly accepted her invitation. But he wanted to sense the presence of the beautiful girl behind him and maybe even sneak another look at her, so he said nothing. Was it Toni? Tracy?

For the remainder of the class, Joel's mind was still nowhere near algebra, but now he could think of nothing but the girl just a desk away behind him. He struggled to think of an excuse to turn around without getting into too much trouble, but with Mrs. Avery zeroing in on him every five seconds, he couldn't take the chance.

The next period was world history. For Joel, it was even more excruciating to sit through than usual. The nameless girl of his dreams wasn't in his history class, but he thought she might be in the same lunch period afterward. Again, his mind was laser-focused on her instead of the lesson at hand. He managed to evade the teacher's suspicion by making believe he was taking notes. In his notebook, he wrote different girl's names hoping it would jog his memory. He must have heard her name at some point. Tori? Tammy?

To his immense pleasure, she was in the same lunch period as his. But how would he get close to her, let alone start up a conversation? Talking with girls was definitely not his strong suit.

As Joel watched her take her lunch tray to a table, Brian Evans, one of the Blades' newest recruits, sneaked up behind her, yanked hard on her hair, and then ran away laughing.

"Hey!" she cried.

Joel sprang into action. He cut Brian off and stood in front of him. Brian was taller and more muscular, but he hadn't gone through the Blades' initiation yet, and Joel knew his standing as a full member in the gang gave him the upper hand. Thanks to the surrounding noise of a hundred conversations, he could speak loud enough to be fierce, but still not attract attention. "Brian, I don't think Derrick would appreciate a Blade acting like a coward. Blades don't go around picking fights with girls."

Brian was defiant. "Hey, I was just havin' a little fun, that's all. Who are you to tell me..."

"*I*, you snot-wipe, am the one who's going to get you kicked out of the Blades forever and make sure you never join it or any other gang as long as you live." He moved in close and spoke in a low, menacing tone. "You'll have no protection, and every gang member looking for a punching bag will be looking for you. *You got it?*"

"All right. I *got* it," said Brian, his face flush.

The two boys stared at each other for an instant, and then Brian backed away and trotted out of the lunchroom, almost knocking over a girl carrying her tray.

Joel beamed inwardly at his gallant rescue as he boldly sat down next to the girl. "He won't be bothering you anymore."

"Oh, so now you think I owe you or something? I could have taken care of that squirt myself. And don't you try anything either."

"Whoa! Chill out, girl. I was just trying to help. Next time you can just..." Joel realized the conversation was rapidly going in the wrong direction. He said, "Listen. I don't mean any trouble." He held out his hand. "I'm Joel."

She hesitated for a moment and then briefly grasped Joel's hand. "Tonya. *Charmed*."

Tonya! Finally the mystery was solved. Joel smiled. "You've got a lot of fight in you. A pretty girl like you should have guys fighting over you."

The words leapt out before he could stop them. *Where did that come from?* He wasn't sure how Tonya would take the come on and whether he should duck or just get up and walk away.

Tonya gave a devilish smile. "I haven't heard *that* line before." After an awkward pause, she said, "Listen, do you want to eat lunch outside? There's a picnic table over by the parking lot nobody uses, and it's not too cold out today. There're too many people in here anyway."

"Sure," said Joel. He felt like he was in heaven.

---

Over the next several weeks, Joel and Tonya spent their lunch periods together every day. She told him about her father, who was out of work and drank most of the time, and her mother, who worked two jobs and was hardly ever home. She had no brothers or sisters and hated being at home. Joel realized he and Tonya had a lot in common. Both felt they were unloved and unwanted, and both were pretty much left on their own.

Joel and Tonya were eating lunch at their usual meeting place at the edge of the parking lot. Joel felt he could trust Tonya well enough to tell her about the Blades, without giving her too many details about its members or activities. Tonya was fascinated.

"You mean, you're all, like, best friends, hanging out together, and sticking up for each other, no matter what?"

Joel winced at the memory of Derrick abandoning him the night they robbed the electronics store and his run-in with Eddie the next day. "Yeah, something like that. Sometimes we have, you know, little disagreements, but mostly we're like family." Joel thought of the strained relationship with his alcoholic mother, then added, "Better than family."

"That is *so* cool. Are there any girls in the Blades?"

Joel was pretty sure girls would never feel at home in the Blades, but he didn't want to discourage Tonya. "Well, not yet, but maybe someday. Besides, aren't there any girl gangs?"

"I don't know. Maybe I could find out about them. Anyway, it sure would be nice to be able to talk to other people, you know, like us."

That made Joel smile. He couldn't believe how quickly he and Tonya had hit it off. It was as if he had always known her, even though they had met just a short while ago.

Tonya smiled too. "So, are you guys doing anything fun tonight? It *is* Friday, you know."

Suddenly Joel's mind went reeling in another direction. Friday! This was the night the Blades were going to rob the video store! He would be the lookout while Derrick stole a car for the first phase of the plan. He remembered he was supposed to cut the rest of his classes after lunch and meet at the gang's headquarters to go over the plan one more time. He wasn't sure how Tonya would react to the planned theft, and besides, the less she knew, the safer it was for her—and him.

He said, "Oh, tonight? I don't know. We'll just get together and do stuff. Maybe I'll talk to Derrick to see what he thinks about letting girls in." The bell sounded, signaling the start of the next period. "Well, listen, maybe I'll call you Saturday to let you know how it went."

As Tonya and Joel departed, God looked sadly upon them, knowing they were each blindly rushing toward certain disaster. He loved them both dearly, and it would be a simple matter for Him to steer them away from the dangers they would soon face. But that same unfailing love would not deny them the experiences that would strengthen and prepare them for the greater hardships to come.

# CHAPTER 6

"'mon, Jack," said Derrick. "You shouda been there by now."

Jack, one of the Blades' longtime members, had stolen his older brother's Jeep Wrangler and was driving toward the video store. He had gotten his license a week ago, but had actually been secretly driving for over a year. Joel was in the backseat. The plan was to play "chicken" with an oncoming car, causing it to swerve out of control and hopefully crash. Joel's job was to jump out after the near miss and signal Eddie and Randy when the right time came to empty the cash registers. Then, if the store didn't clear out, he was to start a fire in the back of the store.

Derrick said, "We have to get to the video store by six o'clock. Randy says that's when most people have rented their movies, and the cash registers are full."

Jack said, "But why don't we just hit it at night? No fuss, no witnesses. We just stroll in, take our time."

Derrick smacked the back of Jack's head. "Did you learn that in *moron* school? Tell you what, you just drive, and leave the thinking to me. At night, they set the alarm system and put all the register money in the safe. That's when they *expect* to get robbed. This way everything's there for the taking. No alarms and no safe to deal with. By the time they figure out what happened, we'll be long gone."

Joel liked Derrick's way of thinking of things. He wondered if he would ever be smart enough to be a gang leader like him.

Before long Derrick said, "Okay, the video store is just after the next light. When we pass the light, you hit the next oncoming car."

"What, are you crazy? *A head-on collision?* That wasn't the plan. I'm not doing it, man."

"You're a real wimp, Jack. You know that?"

"You can say what you want, but I'm not crashing my brother's car. He'll kill me for sure!"

Derrick grabbed the steering wheel and twisted it just enough to swerve into the opposite lane. "Here we go!" he yelled.

Jack struggled for control of the wheel, but to no avail. He was no match for Derrick's adrenaline-powered strength. Joel was mesmerized by the unnatural scene unfolding before him. A car was coming straight for them with no let up in speed, no instinctive swerving to avoid the unthinkable. As the cars drew closer, Joel kept hoping he would wake up from the slow-motion nightmare, but this was shockingly real. Jack screamed in terror while Derrick let out a yelping war cry. Just before impact, Joel put his head down between his knees, closed his eyes, and waited to die.

Agonizing seconds later, he was slammed hard against the back of the front seat amid the explosion of impact. The jeep spun around and then stopped abruptly, hitting another car, finally coming to rest facing the opposite direction. The driver of the other car maneuvered at the last second so that the two vehicles only careened off each other. Joel heard the horrifying sounds of multiple collisions, screeching tires, and blasting horns as car after car smashed into the growing heap of wreckage. It was all over after a few endless seconds.

Steam hissed out from under the Jeep's crumpled hood. A horn blasted continuously from one of the damaged cars, almost drowning out the shouts and screams of victims and onlookers. Joel's knees and shoulder ached, but nothing seemed to be broken. A drop of blood ran down his cheek. He wiped it with the back of his hand and then said, "Hey... you... you guys all right? Derrick?"

Joel leaned over the back of the seat and gently pulled Jack's head off of the steering wheel. Blood covered half his face. He was unconscious.

Joel shook him. "Jack, Jack... You okay? Wake up, will ya?"

Jack half opened his unbloodied eye. "Huh? What... what happened?"

Derrick managed to hang on, despite not wearing a seatbelt, and was relatively unhurt with just a small gash above his right eye. He roughly lifted Jack's head by his hair and examined his face. "He'll live," he said.

Then, like a general in the thick of battle, Derrick smoothly slipped into commander mode. "Okay, listen up, you two. The police will be here in a few minutes. Joel, you go tell Eddie to start emptying the registers, and then start a fire in the back room just to make sure everybody gets out." Jack dozed off. Derrick shook him violently. "We're moving out now, *Jack*. You got that?"

Jack groaned, "I don't... don't feel so good. Can't we just... just sit here for a while?"

Sirens split the air. Derrick's voice raised up a few notches. "Let's *move. Now!*"

Derrick had a panic in his face that Joel had never seen before. "He's hurt *bad*, Derrick!" Joel screamed with more boldness than he'd ever dared show before. "Leave him alone!"

Derrick shot Joel a sinister look, then with one stabbing motion, grabbed him by the shirt and catapulted him out the open Jeep door. Joel landed hard on the nearby curb. Derrick thrust a finger at him. "Get out there, and do your job!" Then he turned on Jack. "Are you gonna sit there and let them catch you, man? You know what that means? Jail time for sure. You want that?"

A block away, a police car turned onto the street, followed closely by an ambulance. Derrick jumped out of the Jeep, quickly looked in all directions, and then trotted away from an approaching police car.

Bystanders began to gather around Joel. A man tried to help him up, but Joel tore himself free and then pushed through the crowd and limped away as fast as he could. He ran down a side street, then doubled back. He had to see what was happening. Peering around a building, he scanned the scene. At least seven cars were involved in the crash. The metallic-sweet smell of steamed antifreeze mixed with the junkyard odor of leaking oil and gas. Cars coming from both directions had hit the smashed cars and then were hit by other cars unable to stop in time. Some were T-boned while others were hit head-on. Twisted metal and shattered glass lay everywhere.

A crowd of people had gathered near the wrecked cars. Just as Derrick had predicted, the video store emptied out as employees and customers ran into the street to try to help those who were either trapped in their cars or staggered about dazed and bloody.

Joel knew this was the moment to do his part. But doubtful thoughts froze him in his tracks. What if people were already starting to go back into the video store? Should he still go through with it? Just as he started across the street, two police officers entered the video store. A second later, Eddie ran out and blended in with the crowd of people. But where was Randy?

Half a block away, Joel saw that Jack was strapped to a gurney that was being gently slid into an ambulance. A police officer stepped up into the ambulance just before the EMT shut the door. Joel looked back toward the video store and caught sight of Randy walking out, followed closely by a policeman. His hands were cuffed behind his back. The officer put his hand on top of Randy's head and guided him into the backseat of the patrol car.

Joel had never felt such a sinking feeling of defeat.

"Hey kid, did you see what happened?"

The voice came from behind him. He turned and saw a police officer coming toward him. He must have seen the blood on his face, because he said, "Hey, you were in the accident. C'mere. I want to talk to you."

Joel never gave him the chance. He quickly dashed through the crowd, dodged two smashed cars, and then ran through a narrow alley before the officer even started to chase him.

# CHAPTER 7

Joel ran for what seemed like hours. Searing pain in his knees pulsed with each pounding stride. Tears streamed down his cheeks, but he didn't care. Nothing mattered. Not the video store theft, Derrick, the Blades, Jack's injuries, or Randy getting arrested. Nothing. Joel kept thinking how stupid the whole plan was. Who would force a car accident? How crazy was that?

Ten blocks later, Joel stooped over, hands above his knees, taking in great gulps of air. His body had become a trembling mass of spent muscle. Dusk was quickly giving way to a breezy, cold night, and he shivered, but not from the cold. The accident had certainly shaken him up, but after seeing what had happened to Randy and Jack, a tightening fear began to grow in his stomach. The police would soon know who was involved. And they would be looking for him and the rest of the Blades.

Joel ran a little further until he found himself in front of an old stone church. The glass-enclosed sign near the front steps said it was St. Michael's Catholic Church and that "All Are Welcome."

"That must mean me," he said aloud as he trotted up the steps. Cautiously looking around, he tried the door. It was open. He silently slipped inside.

After his eyes grew accustomed to the dimly lit interior, he entered a large foyer that opened out into a much larger room. Chandeliers hung from long stems anchored from the high arched ceiling. Along both side walls between stained glass windows hung pictures of men in robes, some of them with glowing circles over their heads. Joel cautiously walked down the center aisle, turning around several times as he gaped at the ornate surroundings. He had never been inside a church before, but instinctively knew there was something special about it. His mom had called it "God's House," and maybe, deep down, he had always felt God would be angry if someone like him wandered inside uninvited, and so he always stayed away. Now he had an uneasy feeling that he was invading God's territory, and for a fleeting moment, wondered if he would be punished for the intrusion.

At the far end of the room was a large table covered with a shiny green and gold tablecloth. Two nearly life-sized statues stood in cubbyholes built into the far wall. One was of an older man, the other of a young woman, similar to the statue he had seen at the hospital, except that she had a crown on her head. Both pointed two fingers up. Hundreds of small candles in red plastic cups near the front of the room were arranged in tight sloping rows. Several candles were lit casting an eerie glow on the walls. A waxy aroma filled the church.

It was silent as the dead of night and just as cold. Joel couldn't tear his eyes off the crucifix rising high on the back wall. It looked just like the one he had seen in the Catholic hospital. The man nailed to it had that same sad expression. Joel wondered what terrible thing the man had done to deserve punishment like that.

Joel surveyed the large, dank room and mused that this might be a good hiding place for a while. Maybe God will find him here and give him a break. But then again, it was so cold, dark, and damp, why would God want to come here?

A meager cough abruptly broke the silence. It echoed through the entire church, and Joel's senses went on emergency alert. He crouched low behind the front pew and carefully scanned every shadowy corner and crevice in the room, but could see nothing. He felt for the switchblade in his pocket. Although he was in no shape for a fight, he would if he had to. But if he could get away, it would be the best course of action. He alternated between looking around for another door and scanning the rows of pews for signs of life.

Then, in the corner of his eye, he saw movement. Something briefly rose above the back of a pew at about the middle of the church. Focusing intently on the spot, he saw it again. Someone was definitely hiding behind one of the pews. Joel kept low and made his way slowly down the aisle. He cradled the switchblade, ready to pull it out at the slightest provocation. If he opened it now, the loud *click* would pinpoint his location to his potential opponent, and he needed every advantage he could get. Fight readiness merged with curiosity. He had to know what kind of person would seek shelter in a church, as he had.

Joel almost reached the center pew when a man slowly sat up. He had a scraggly beard, shoulder-length disheveled hair, and dirty, ragged clothes. He knuckled the sleep out of his eyes and then noticed Joel for the first time. But unlike Joel, he wasn't startled to discover another person sharing his refuge.

The man spoke in a strong, deep voice that didn't match his appearance. "C'mere, son, I'm not going to hurt you."

Joel almost laughed at the prospect. "I wouldn't give you the chance. What are you doing here anyway? Don't you have a home?" Joel realized the answer to his last question even as he spoke it. The man gave a wide, toothy smile.

"Well, as a matter of fact, this is my home, for now. You got a name, son?"

"Joel. What's yours?"

"Name's Abner. Now you tell me, what brings a young fella like you to a place like this at this time of night? You in some kinda trouble?"

"Maybe." Joel didn't want to give him too much information; one of the most important street rules was not to trust anyone. He sensed no danger from the man, so he sat in the same pew, but still a good ten feet away.

He tried hard to think of a way to change the subject. If nothing else, it would end the awkward silence. He said, "Hey, this is God's house, isn't it? You ever seen Him here?"

That brought another wide grin to Abner's ancient, weathered face. "Not only do I see Him here and other places, but I talk to Him and listen to Him as well."

Joel shook his head. The old man was obviously either a liar or just plain crazy. "You talk to Him, huh? What do you two talk about? Who's gonna get zapped next?"

Abner looked down for a moment. "That's a mighty sarcastic remark coming from a young man. I wonder what terrible thing happened to you that would cause you to have such a bitter heart."

Joel thought of the condescending way Derrick and the other Blades had always treated him, about the battles with his mother, and the lack of any real friends. He had always believed the Blades were his only true family. But now the police were searching for him to put him in juvenile detention because of what the Blades had done. Of course, there was his friend Tonya, but lately she seemed to care more about joining a gang than being with him. Thoughts of being completely alone against the world haunted him. It took a great effort to hold back the tears.

"You don't know what you're talking about, old man," he said. "You're just a crazy old fool, that's all."

"Am I? I am a homeless man, grateful for the shelter of this church. You, on the other hand, have come here from the cold night desperately seeking to hide from something or someone when you should be safely at home. Doesn't that sound a little crazy to you?"

"What do you know?"

"I know you're alone."

"You don't know anything about me."

Abner grinned briefly. "No, I suppose not. But let me ask you this; do you have anybody who understands you? Anyone who really knows what you're going through and wants to make things better?"

Joel's mind raced to each person he knew—his mom, Derrick, Tonya—and came up empty. It became a little more difficult to hold back the tears this time.

"No. Not really," he answered weakly.

Abner slid down the pew toward Joel. He said, "I know someone who knows everything about you, who, in fact, knows more about you than anyone, even you yourself. He loves you very much and wants to help you."

Joel thought he'd play along. "Really? Who's that?"

"God."

Joel rolled his eyes. "Oh man, you almost had me with that fairytale. God loves me? I don't *think* so. Would you treat someone you loved the way I've been treated?" Joel didn't wait for an answer. "And what about you? God loves you too? If he loves you so much, why don't you have a place to live? Why did he do this to you?"

"God didn't do this to me. I did it to myself. I'm here, in this condition, because sin is in the world."

"Sin? You mean, like bad people?"

"Even good people can and do sin. Sin is, well, everything that God hates, everything that goes against what God desires. It's what separates us—all people—from Him."

"Why doesn't God just wave his magic wand, or whatever, and say '*Poof.* No more sin.'?"

Abner chuckled. "It's not that simple. You see, if God did that—which he could, if he wanted to—there wouldn't be a soul left to thank him for it."

"Wait a minute. Are you telling me I'm a sinner?"

"You are. Sin is inside of you. It's inside of everyone. A wise man once said, 'We are not sinners because we sin, we sin because we are sinners.' It's part of how we are made."

"I don't get it. God made everything, right?"

"Yes."

"So, God made us too."

"Yep."

"So if we're full of sin, then God made sin. It's all *His* fault!"

"No, God doesn't make mistakes. If we didn't know about sin, we wouldn't have known we need the Savior who promises that, if we truly believe in him, all of our sins—past, present, and future—will be forgiven."

"*The Savior?* Who is that?"

Abner raised a boney finger and pointed at the large crucifix. "Jesus Christ, of course."

Joel again stared at the nailed man. The sorrowful eyes seemed to stare right at him. He had heard that name used many times when someone was angry or shocked, but he had never thought that it was an actual person's name, much less a savior. Intrigued, he waited for Abner to continue.

"Jesus died long ago so that whoever accepted Him as their personal savior wouldn't have to suffer eternal damnation, but would live forever in heaven after their earthly life was over. But even before that happened, life here on earth would be filled with the joy of knowing that God can be depended upon to guide and protect us just like a loving father instructs and protects his children."

Joel wasn't too sure about what that last part meant, since he hardly remembered his own father, but he didn't question Abner about it.

Abner talked at length while Joel quietly absorbed what he had to say. Time rushed by unnoticed. At one point, Abner fell silent.

Joel asked him, "How come you know about all this stuff anyway? You don't look like a priest."

Abner chuckled and coughed. "Most of what I know about God, Jesus, and the Holy Spirit has been written down in God's own book, the Bible." Abner slid a Bible from the pew rack and handed it to Joel. "That, right there in your hands, is God's very Word. Everything God wants to tell us is in that book. Here, let me show you something." Joel handed the Bible back to Abner. He thumbed two-thirds through and then pointed at a verse. "Now listen to this: This is John 3:16, probably the most famous Bible verse in the world. It says, 'For God so loved the world that he gave his one and only Son, that whoever believes in Him shall not perish but have eternal life.'"

"So all we have to do is believe in God's Son, and we'll live forever?"

"That's what I've been telling you. Those are God's words, not mine."

"God wrote the Bible?"

"In a way. The Bible was written by many men over many years who were inspired by the Holy Spirit."

"What's the Holy Spirit? You mean like a ghost told them what to write?"

Abner laughed and then started coughing violently. When he finally composed himself, he said, "Not exactly. There are so many things that are just a mystery to us and will always remain so till we meet the Lord in heaven."

Joel was about to ask another question when a voice bellowed from the front of the church, "Hey… who's in here?"

The two instinctively ducked below the pew. Abner whispered, "That would be the Sextant. Right now, he's either checking each pew or he's calling the police." Joel peeked above the back of the pew.

"I don't see him."

"Then the police will be here in a few minutes. I would suggest we…"

Joel didn't wait for him to finish the sentence. With street-learned stealth, he quickly made his way to the door that he had come in and disappeared into the crisp night.

Abner left the church too. But unseen by Joel, he simply vanished from where he sat.

# CHAPTER 8

Joel returned to the Blades' empty headquarters as the first orange streaks of sunrise appeared in the eastern sky. He flopped down on the loveseat and fell into a deep sleep.

Someone kicked his foot. Without opening his eyes, he knew the voice that followed was Derrick's.

"Hey man, get up. This ain't no hotel! We got things to work out."

Joel rubbed his eyes and then scanned the room as he sat up. He could tell by the long shadows that it was late afternoon. Some of the older Blades were there, but none of the newer members. Everyone stared at the floor or the walls or out the window. No one spoke. Derrick threw himself on the throne fuming.

"I saw them take Jack and Randy," Joel said to no one in particular.

Eddie chimed in, still staring across the room at nothing. "Randy's boss grabbed him from behind right after he emptied the register. He didn't have a chance … they got him cold, man."

Joel's stomach was numb. "What about Jack? How bad was he hurt? Is he gonna... you know, make it?"

Derrick stomped his feet on the floor and shot up from the chair. "What are you, some kinda reporter? For all we know, he could be dead already. Nobody knows anything." He started toward Joel, but then circled around to address the rest of the group. "But I do know this much. Anyone... *anyone* who says anything about this is as good as dead! Don't ever talk about the video store or the car accident. You don't talk about the Blades either." He stopped at the loveseat facing Joel. "You got that?"

The group gave muffled expressions of agreement. Joel said, "Yeah, I hear you." He hoped Derrick did not catch the contempt he felt. Derrick continued to circle the room.

"Okay, this is what we're gonna do."

Joel was not in the mood to hear another one of Derrick's crazy schemes. The last one had failed so miserably. What made him think this one would turn out any better?

Derrick went on. "We gotta get Jack and Randy out before they talk."

Eddie's face twisted in fear. "We go in there and get caught, they're gonna know for sure we had something to do with this. What if they talked already, man? The cops could be here any minute." He nervously glanced out the window and then back to Derrick. "I don't think we should take the chance."

Joel looked hopefully at Derrick, but the leader's angry expression immediately vaporized any possibility that the risky plan would be called off.

Derrick lunged at Eddie, clenched his shirt with both hands, and half lifted him off the chair. "Shut up, you little wimp! Did you think we were just playing games?" Derrick dropped Eddie hard into the chair and turned to face the others. "This is a war, man. And we gotta fight hard to get what we want."

Eddie dived at Derrick, tossing him to the floor with a thud. Derrick quickly rolled over and kicked at Eddie's body until he released his grip. The last kick struck him in the face. Eddie staggered back while Derrick rolled a short distance and then sprang to his feet. Eddie quickly stood and faced his enraged leader.

Derrick said, "If you want to make the decisions around here, you're gonna have to take me down first. You think you can do that, little man?"

"I'm damn sure gonna try." Eddie flicked open his switchblade. Derrick did the same. They slowly circled, slightly crouched, ready to spring into action at the slightest provocation. Their eyes locked on each other.

"You know, you're not as tough as you think you are," said Eddie, turning the switchblade in his hand.

Derrick snapped his knife from one hand to the other and back again. It was an effective tactic to keep an opponent unsure of how to defend himself. He gave an evil grin and widened his eyes.

"You know what, you might be right. Why don't you see if you can prove it?"

He stabbed at the air as if to attack. Eddie instinctively jumped back. Derrick continued taunting him, another tactic designed to unravel Eddie's determination.

" You seem a little jumpy, Eddie. You sure you want to do this? You can back out now, and we won't say another word about our little disagreement."

The room froze. Joel watched with dreadful fascination. An unwritten rule of the Blades was there was no such thing as backing out. Once you start something, you finish it. One of them was going down, and Derrick had never lost a fight in his life.

Derrick's steely gaze and confident smirk contrasted sharply with the fear in Eddie's eyes and the occasional twitch of his lips.

Without warning, Eddie yelled a courage-gathering battle cry and charged. Derrick smoothly twisted, then grabbed Eddie's blade wielding hand and forced it upward. At the same time, he thrust his knee into Eddie's torso. Eddie gasped and rolled to the floor, but quickly regained his footing and sprang at Derrick again. Derrick easily stepped aside, and as Eddie stumbled past, he thrust the blade into his side.

Eddie shrieked. He got up on one knee and held his side. Blood began to trickle between his fingers. He moved his trembling hand just enough to see the wound, then looked, white-faced, at his attacker.

"You cut me, man. You cut me bad. Why'd you do that?" He slumped down to a sitting position and then curled up, wincing in pain.

"That's what you get for defying me, man. You took your shot, and you lost. That's just the way it goes." Derrick turned and slowly swept the blade around, still dripping with Eddie's blood.

"Anyone else want to express their opinion?" Every boy stood absolutely still, eyes locked on the deadly blade. Derrick wiped the blade off with his shirttail and clicked it shut. "I didn't think so."

As if to confirm Eddie's worst fears, Mickey cried out, his voice breaking into a higher pitch than usual, "Hey, two cop cars and another car just pulled up!" Derrick shot a look through the window then motioned everyone to sit on the floor.

Two of the officers, armed with shotguns, hastily got out and ran around to the back of the building. The two from the other police car stationed themselves on either side of the only entrance to the building. A man wearing a tie and jacket casually stepped out of the unmarked car and brought a bullhorn to his mouth.

"Derrick Wicker. Eddie Moran. And any others that are in there with you. The building is surrounded. We know about the video store robbery and the staged accident. It's over. If you give yourselves up now, it will go easier on you." He waited for a moment and then continued. "C'mon out boys. You can't escape. Don't make this any harder on you than it has to be."

Derrick put a finger to his lips and then motioned for them to follow him. Immediately, everyone headed for the secret exit that was created when the Blades first claimed the abandoned apartment as their headquarters. As if executing a practiced fire drill, each silently escaped down a ladder through a hole in the floor to the apartment below. They then slipped through a large hole where a bathtub used to be. In the basement, a missing manhole cover gave them access to the drainage system. They climbed down steel loops embedded in concrete to a three-foot drainage pipe. Stooping low, they ran in total blackness for a hundred feet through the pipe and then climbed up to a storm drain with a loose grate. Derrick silently moved the grate aside, climbed through the opening hidden by an abandoned car half a block away, and then he and the rest of the Blades scattered, crouching low between buildings. Joel glanced over his shoulder and saw that the police were just entering the building.

Questions haunted Joel as he ran: *Was Eddie going to live? Would he talk? Where could he hide now that the police knew about the Blades' involvement in the video store robbery?*

## CHAPTER 9

Joel found himself near the clock tower downtown. It felt like his whole life was falling apart. With Jack, Randy, and now Eddie in police custody, it was only a matter of time before they rounded up the rest of the gang. Every time a police car passed, he had to turn his head away or duck into an alley. Troubling thoughts kept swirling around in his head—like what it would be like in jail and how his mother would take the news that he had been arrested—and he realized he needed a place to hide and think. He would have gone home, but he didn't want to explain to his mother where he was the night before. Instinctively, he headed toward the sports arena a few blocks away.

As usual on a Saturday night, there was some big event at the arena. Joel wasn't interested in whatever sports or community performance was going on, but it was a good place to disappear for a while among the thousands of spectators. Besides, thickening black clouds and a stiff cold wind told him a storm might be coming in, and any place inside would be better than being out on the street.

    He easily scaled a ten-foot, chain-linked fence out of sight of the guards and blended in with a group of excited teenagers as they poured out of a bus and entered the seating area. The place was packed. Even many of the seats in the very highest rows were filled. What event had drawn so many kids here? Joel found an empty seat next to the aisle and sat down, hoping it was not previously occupied. It would be almost impossible for anyone to find him here. After a few minutes, he let himself relax and listened to a band playing on the stage below.

    Joel thought he'd heard every kind of music the kids played in school, but this was different. He soon realized what the difference was: the band was singing about *God*. He looked around the arena amazed that all these kids were into this kind of music. When the song ended, almost everyone stood up, clapped, and shouted. As the next song started, they remained standing and clapped to the beat.

    Although he had seen concerts on TV, Joel had never been to a live one before. Somehow, this was not what he expected. And he had never heard anyone sing about God or Jesus before. He looked around again. Were any of these kids in his school? He tried to see if he recognized anyone, but none of the excited faces were familiar to him. Where did all these kids come from? After the song ended, everyone sat down.

    Joel wasn't sure what was going to happen next. He wanted to leave, but when everyone sat quietly and focused on the stage, he decided to stay a while. If you didn't want to be noticed, just do what everyone else was doing. The lead singer introduced a man who walked out on the stage amid thunderous applause. After the crowd quieted down, the man began to speak.

    He talked about his own life and how, when he was sixteen years old, he used to be in a gang near this very sports arena. He said he drank alcohol, took drugs, and fought in gang wars. At one point, he had participated in a robbery, and the police were chasing him and his gang.

Joel sat at the edge of his seat, fascinated by the speaker. He couldn't believe it... this man had gone through almost the exact same things that he was going through right now! Joel imagined *he* was the man speaking and was telling his own life story. As the man continued to speak, Joel heard what could be his own future.

"A few years after joining the gang, I was in a big war. Stabbed in the side, I had a broken nose and three cracked ribs. I was taken to the hospital and, after they patched me up, to jail for my involvement in the gang's crimes. I was convicted of multiple counts of assault and battery, conspiracy to commit robbery, and disrupting the peace. I was sent to the state penitentiary for two to five years. While in the joint, I met a man who said he had given his life to Christ a few months before. I didn't know what that meant, but I wanted to know more. Why? Because this man was so content... no, more than that, he was so... alive! Whatever he did, whatever he said, you could just see the joy shine right out of him. I, on the other hand, was in a deep, dark hole of despair. I had nothing—no home, no money, nobody who cared about me, and no reason to live. But *this* guy was pretty much in the same boat as me, and he was all right with that; it didn't bother him a bit. It was as if he had found the secret to life that everyone was looking for but could never find. He had found such a peace and a comfort that it didn't matter what was going on around him. I knew right then and there, I had to have what this guy had."

A shiver ran up Joel's back. He wasn't cold, but it was a tingling sensation he had never felt before. He hung on the speaker's every word.

"I asked this guy—his name was Matt—I said, 'Hey Matt. What do you have that makes you so happy, even in a place like this?' I said, 'whatever drugs you got, I want some.'"

A flurry of laughter briefly swept across the audience. The speaker continued.

"So Matt says to me, 'It ain't drugs, man. It's Jesus!' And Matt went on to tell me about the problem with sin. About how everyone has a sinful nature from Adam on down that's built in. It's part of who we are. He said there was no way anyone could ever hope to get into heaven on their own because of our natural sin. Then he told me there was only one way that our sins could be forgiven. This man called Jesus had died on the cross a couple of thousand years ago so that, whoever truly believed in his heart that He had died for their sins, their sins would be forgiven and they would have eternal life after death. And not only that—as if that wasn't enough—but that anyone who trusted his life to Jesus would also have a peace that goes beyond all understanding here and now, in this life. And he said that I could have what he had just by sincerely asking for it. I said, 'Matt, I don't really understand everything you're saying to me right now, but I've got nowhere else to turn. I gotta have this Jesus.' And right then and there, in the state penitentiary, cell block F, cell number 219, at ten-thirty at night, I got down on my knees and gave my life to Jesus."

The audience exploded. Some stood and clapped, while others yelled or raised their hands, palms open wide. Joel simply sat in speechless amazement. It was a full minute before it was quiet enough for the speaker to continue.

"And so I put the question to you."

Joel thought the speaker was looking directly at him.

"Do you want the life that I have found? Not that all your troubles will immediately disappear, but that you will have an inner joy knowing you are loved and cared for by God in a way that is so much more than any human can give. Do you want to be guaranteed a place in heaven, where there is no pain or crying or anguish? If so, I'd like to invite anyone who wants to, to come down to the foot of the stage—right here, right now—to meet with one of our youth leaders, who will lead you in a prayer that will begin your new life as a follower of Jesus Christ."

Kids from every part of the arena, some with tear-streaked faces, started down the aisles toward the area in front of the stage. The band played a slow, soft tune that Joel had never heard before. It started with the words, "*Amazing Grace, how sweet the sound, that saved a wretch like me... I once was lost but now I'm found, was blind, but now I see.*"

Joel felt an excited flutter in his gut. He remembered what Abner had said about Jesus, and when the priest in the Catholic hospital had tried to talk to him about God but he wouldn't listen. From somewhere inside his mind, he heard the words, "*Go. This is your chance to change everything.*"

Joel felt himself stand, felt his feet begin the trek down the aisle, as if moving on their own. He turned and saw that the girl behind him was sort of crying and laughing at the same time. Those still seated were clapping, many with tear-filled eyes. The tingling sensation intensified as he joined hundreds of teenagers and a few adults right in front of the stage. He walked up to an older boy who gently placed a hand on each shoulder.

"What's your name?" he said.

"Joel. Joel Somers."

"Well Joel, are you ready to receive Jesus as your Lord and Savior?"

Joel did not hesitate. "Yes, I am."

"That's awesome! Now I'd like to help you pray for Christ to come into your life..."

---

Abner was intently watching Joel at that very moment. As soon as Joel finished praying, he threw up his hands and shouted, "Praise to the Lord! Hallelujah!" Even as he was speaking, a chorus of ten thousand angels singing their praises to the Father drowned him out. A scribe angel floated nearby and opened the enormous and ancient Book of Life. Excitedly, she found Joel's name, printed there long before he was born, and a placed an elaborate check mark next to it.

Laughing and dancing, Abner joined the massive chorus in their celebration. He was elated and relieved because no matter what Joel did for as long as he lived, or whatever happened to him, he was guaranteed to come to his heavenly home at the end of his earthly life.

Continuing Abner's thought, the Father joyfully exclaimed, "For he always was and forever shall be My child, whom I love."

And Abner burst out, "Amen and amen!"

---

Despite his underlings' best efforts to thwart the news, word of Joel's conversion had reached Teragon. Anger erupted out of him like volcanic vomit. With the back of his hand, he swiped the huge cauldron, spilling its molten contents onto several shrieking drones. Teragon's deafening scream trembled the air like crackling thunder. "*Who allowed this to happen?* Who will pay for this great loss, this disgusting turn of events?" He searched the room full of inferior demons with searing eyes. "*Well?*"

A cowering Pus slowly raised a shaking crooked finger. "My Lord, might I suggest that there was not anything any of us could do. It came about so suddenly, none of us had time to react, to try to discourage…"

"*Silence*, imbecile. You sicken me with your pathetic excuses." Teragon swept a pointed finger across the room. "Every one of you is guilty of treason against our Lord, Satan himself, and his kingdom. Your only redemption is to negate the so-called conversion of Joel Somers. Confuse him. Make him wish he had never called on the Son of our Enemy for salvation. Make him curse his God and die!" The room held its breath as Teragon deliberately made eye contact with each demon, planting individual instructions into their minds.

Finally, he commanded, "Be gone!" and the minions made a frenzied, confused exodus.

## CHAPTER 10

**B**arely noticing the chilled air, Joel walked home from the sports arena, his thoughts spinning in wild new directions. He still could not believe what had happened just a few hours earlier! After he went back to his seat in the arena, there was something new about him that he couldn't put a finger on. It was as if... he remembered when he was a little boy playing *army* with some of his friends in the neighborhood. If anyone got shot, they would have to lie on the ground while the others fought around him. After a few minutes, you would jump up and yell "New man!" then rejoin the battle. It was like that now. He felt like a new man starting out fresh. Nothing in the past seemed so important or troublesome. He had a whole new chance at life now, and it gave him an excited feeling inside, way better than when he first joined the Blades.

*The Blades.* What would they think about him becoming a Christian? He couldn't possibly stay in the gang now. What was he going to do if one of them asked where he had been or what had happened to him? Sooner or later, there would be a showdown in school or on the street. He knew he had better prepare himself for the inevitable confrontation. But how could he protect himself from them? From Derrick?

When Joel walked into his apartment later that evening, his mother was standing in the kitchen doorway with her back to him. She spun around and almost toppled herself.

"Joel!" she said much louder than necessary. Her bloodshot eyes narrowed. "Where you been?" she slurred, not bothering to take the cigarette out of her mouth. "I've been worried sick about you. You in some kinda trouble again?"

Although he had seen her in this condition many times before and had come to accept it as a normal side of her, somehow this time he felt genuinely sorry for her. "Mom, you promised not to drink anymore." It occurred to him that now he was under no obligation to go to school, since she had not kept up her end of the bargain. Unexpectedly, the thought embarrassed him.

"You don't talk to me in that tone of voice, young man. I am your mother. You tell me what to do. Not the other way around...I mean..." She staggered a bit and had to grasp the edge of the doorway to keep her balance.

"It's okay, Mom." Joel rushed to her. He put his arm around her waist and draped her arm over his shoulder to steady her. What was it one of the speakers in the sports arena had said? *Forgive others, because God has already forgiven you.*

"I...I forgive you, Mom."

She squinted at her son. "What are you talking about?"

Joel wanted to tell her all about what he heard at the arena that night, especially what had happened down by the stage, but not now, not with her like this. "Let's talk about it tomorrow, Mom, okay? C'mon, I'll help you get to bed."

Joel brought his mom to her bedroom, put her cigarette in the ashtray on the night table, and helped her lay down.

She sat up on one elbow, awkwardly fumbled with the cigarette, took a deep drag, exhaled, and said, "You're a good boy, Joel."

"Okay Mom. We'll talk some more in the morning. G'night."

Joel lay awake for hours. The tingling sensation that had started earlier in the evening had grown to something like the same excitement he felt the night before summer vacation starts, only stronger. It was as if a terrible weight had been lifted from his shoulders, and he was able to live carefree forever. As he replayed in his mind all the events that had happened to him over the last couple of days—the crash and robbery attempt, Jack in the hospital and Randy in jail, the police finding the Blade's headquarters—nothing could pull away the blanket of pure peace that covered him. Somehow, he just knew everything would work out. Now that God was on his side (or was it that he was now on *God's side?*), what could go wrong?

---

Joel's eyes burst open hours later. A shocking odor of burning wood filled his nostrils. It was still dark outside, but the nearby streetlight let in just enough light to see his door. He bolted into the dark hallway and saw a flickering glow coming from his mother's partially open bedroom door. Smoke wafted into the hallway. He burst into her bedroom. The curtains were ablaze and part of the night table was on fire. His mother lay motionless on the bed.

"Mom!" He jumped on the bed and shook her. *"Mom! Get up!"*

Joel was fast, but not strong. Even so, he managed to drag her off the bed and into the hallway.

Awake but groggy, the alcohol still slurred her speech. "Wha…wha are you doin'?"

"Your room's on fire, Mom! Couldn't you smell it?"

"Wh…what? My…room?"

Joel had no time to answer. He started to swat at the fire with a pillow, but only managed to fan the flames higher. The ceiling paint was already beginning to blister, and the bed sheets had caught fire. Never in his life had he felt so helpless.

Joel sprinted to the kitchen sink and began to fill a pitcher with water, agonizing over the precious seconds it took. Finally, he ran back to the bedroom, water sloshing on the floor along the way. He threw the water at the night table, now fully engulfed in flames. The fire abated for a moment, but then came back to nearly its full intensity. The corner of the bed was aflame as well as the headboard and the curtain on the other side of the window. The fierce fire was crawling along the ceiling, blackening paint as it went. Paint on the wall bubbled and then burst into flames, its hot flash bending Joel back with an arm over his face. His heart sank when he realized there was nothing he could do to stop the encroaching blaze.

Joel's mother had pulled herself up and was leaning against the wall in the hallway opposite the bedroom. She was crying, her hands covering her face. "What have I done? Oh God, what have I done?"

Joel grabbed her arm and pulled her toward the front door. Resisting her son's pull, Catherine threw open the hallway closet door, rummaged around the top shelf, and a moment later pulled out a small metal box with a built-in combination lock.

"C'mon! We've got to get out of here!" They ran down the stairs hand in hand, slipped halfway, and slid down the remainder of the steps. "You okay, Mom?"

She gave a quick nod then opened her eyes wide. "Mrs. Culpeper across the hall! We've got to let her know!"

Before Joel could stop her, she had dashed back up the stairs and began pounding on the door opposite theirs. "Mrs. Culpeper! Mrs. Culpeper! Get out! There's a fire!" She pounded frantically. "Mrs. Culpeper! *Please!* Can you hear me?"

Suddenly, she turned and ran into her apartment. "Got to try to call her…"

Joel raced up the steps after his mother. "Mom! *What are you doing?*"

When he reached the apartment, his mother was punching in Mrs. Culpeper's number from the kitchen wall phone. Flames were now licking at the hallway wall opposite the bedroom. Joel grabbed her by the waist and pulled her back out onto the stairway landing, phone and all. Mrs. Culpeper, well in her eighties, had opened her apartment door as far as the chain would allow and peered through the opening. In her usual frail voice, she said, "What's all the commotion out h...?"

Joel didn't let her finish. "Our apartment's on fire. You need to get out! Okay? Hurry!"

Joel's scream caused her to stagger back and then jump forward to slam the door shut. He pounded once on her door, "*Please*, Mrs. Culpeper. Do it *now!*" Then he helped his mother back down the stairs and out into the street.

Joel waited for Mrs. Culpeper to emerge from the building. A minute slipped by, then another. He could see diffused flashes of firelight through the front living room windows. The fire was spreading throughout the apartment. *Where is she?*

Five agonizing minutes later, Joel ran back into the building and up the stairs. The landing at the top was heavy with smoke. He glanced through the open door to his apartment. The hallway was a solid wall of fire and flames were stabbing into the living room. Joel pounded on Mrs. Culpeper's door while yelling her name, then he pressed his ear against it. Nothing.

Joel stepped back and threw his full weight against the door. Already tattered by a previous break in, it burst open, splintering the doorjamb. Mrs. Culpeper lay on her side in the living room next to a phone, its receiver held loosely in her hand. She was unconscious. He tried to pick up the elderly woman, but found he wasn't able to lift her full weight completely. He pulled her up by her armpits, dragged her through the open door and onto the landing. The intense smoke was now pouring out from his apartment. His eyes stung so much he had to peer through barely open eyelids in order to see. Joel shut his apartment door, but smoke still filled the landing. With each shallow breath, he felt the poisonous fumes scorch his throat and lungs.

Joel squatted and lightly slapped Mrs. Culpeper on the cheek. "Mrs. Culpeper, *wake up*," he said. "C'mon, we have to go," but it was no use.

Joel pushed away the thought that she might already be dead. Something shattered inside his apartment, and he felt the floor tremble. The fire was eating away at the walls, doors, and furniture in the living room, and would soon engulf the entire apartment. His lungs were starving for fresh air, and he felt his muscles drain of what little strength he had left. Terror seized him. *Is this how my life will end?*

Without a thought, Joel twisted and draped Mrs. Culpeper's arms onto his shoulders. Still squatting, he moved forward with her until he felt the top step drop off, then swung his legs around. With one hand gripping the elderly woman's arm and the other on the handrail, he began to drag her down the stairs, one agonizing step at a time. Mrs. Culpeper's hundred-pound dead weight constantly forced him down. Fighting the urge to escape the blaze behind him, Joel had to slowly negotiate each step. If he went too fast and lost control, he was sure they would wind up in a tangled heap at the bottom.

Finally, emerging from the doorway at the bottom of the steps, Joel shifted her weight on his back. His mother, still dazed and sobbing, helped carry Mrs. Culpeper across the street to safety.

# CHAPTER 11

Joel and his mother watched in stunned silence as the fire consumed the apartment. Two fire trucks, sirens blaring and red lights flashing, screeched to a halt near the building. Firefighters poured out of the trucks and commenced the practiced tasks of their profession. The white-helmeted chief barked orders while firefighters pulled out hoses and connected them to outlets on the side of the truck. Two men grabbed the hose nozzle and were joined by others wearing oxygen masks and armed with axes. Together, they charged up the steps to battle the ferocious flames.

An ambulance made its way through the maze of fire trucks and people, parking a short distance from the dying building. Three emergency medical technicians rushed from the vehicle and began treating the three survivors. Joel had a gash on his right arm, and both he and his mother were given oxygen. Mrs. Culpeper was carried on a stretcher into the ambulance, her nose and mouth covered with an oxygen mask. Her eyes were closed. In the past, Joel had thought of her as just a senile old woman who didn't know how to mind her own business. But now, without understanding why, he hoped she would be all right, and the thought that she might actually die twisted a knot in his stomach.

An hour after the firemen arrived, the battle to save the building was won. As part of the cleanup operation, charred and smoldering furniture was carried out of the apartment and thrown onto the sidewalk. Joel recognized the pieces of what used to be his desk on the sidewalk. Smashed video game cases lay scattered nearby. He remembered the incredible thing that had happened in the sports arena the night before and wondered when God was going to start taking care of him. Was God busy and couldn't get to the fire in time? Couldn't He have stopped it before it even started? Was there something he had forgotten to say or do before his new, protected life would kick in?

---

God knew Joel's thoughts, thoughts that matched those of countless generations before him who experienced similar losses and hardships. It grieved Him to see Joel, his mom, and Mrs. Culpeper suffer as a result of the terrible fire, but in His infinite wisdom and foresight, this tragedy was a necessary part of His perfect plan.

The Creator mused, "One day, Joel, you will know that in all things, I work for the good of those who love me, who have been called according to My purpose. Soon you will begin to learn more about Me, and about My plans for you."

---

A second ambulance had arrived and took Joel and his mother to a local hospital. There, they were given a quick examination to make sure nothing else was wrong with them. While his mother filled out forms, Joel sat in the nearly empty emergency waiting room. One elderly couple sat several chairs away and across the room a couple of older teenagers struggled with a whimpering baby.

The man he remembered as the fire chief approached Joel and knelt down beside him. His face was smudged with soot and he smelled like burnt wood. He said, "That was some rescue you made young man. That woman, Mrs. Culpeper, would have died if you hadn't pulled her out of the apartment building. Not to mention waking your mom up and getting her out of the apartment." He put a hand on Joel's shoulder. "You're a real hero and deserve some sort of recognition. What's you're name son?"

Joel opened his mouth to speak just as images of the video store robbery flashed across his mind. He was sure the police were still looking for him. Sheepishly, he said, "It wasn't nothing. I … um, don't really want any recognition, okay?"

The chief's eyebrows rose. "You sure? We don't come across heroes that often, especially ones your age. But if that's what you want…"

"Yeah, that's what I want."

The fireman squinted. "You in some kind of trouble, son?"

Joel shivered inside. It occurred to him that the chief could look him up in the police records to answer that question himself, if he had reason to. But, for the moment, it appeared he was being given the benefit of doubt.

He smiled and said, "No, nothing like that. I just did what anyone would have done. Like I said, it was nothing, really. No big deal. Ya know?"

The chief stared at Joel for a moment, then smiled and said, "Okay, I think I understand. Don't worry. No one will know about what you did." He stood to leave. "In my book, you're a fine young man. Someday, you'll make a name for yourself. You mark my words."

Joel watched the fire chief walk down the hall and out of the hospital. *A fine young man?* Just two days ago (was it that long?), he was involved in a video store robbery attempt. And now he was a fine young man? It was as if the person he was before had been replaced with the new person he was now. He shook his head. "But it was *me* who did those things," he said aloud. "I would have helped rob the video store if the police hadn't gotten Jack and Randy. And now...I don't know who I am."

When they were released from the hospital, a soft-spoken police officer, who seemed genuinely concerned, took Joel and his mother to a family shelter in a neighborhood that was unfamiliar to him. Joel had often imagined what it would be like to take a ride in a police car after being arrested for some crime he had committed. He never dreamed he would be taken to a place to live because he had lost his home.

The officer had said the shelter had been converted from a run-down grade school. When they arrived, they went first to the front office. Joel imagined the principal sitting in one of the inner rooms. If this had been his school, he would have known that office well.

A grandfatherly man with scarce white hair, and bulging gray eyes greeted them with a broad smile. "Welcome to the Grace Street Family Shelter. My name is Mr. Peterson. I oversee the place, so if there's anything you need, you just come and see me."

"Thank you, Mr. Peterson," said Catherine meekly. "We're grateful that you could put us up on such short notice."

"We always have a bed for anyone in need. The only thing I ask is that you don't bring any alcohol or weapons on the premises."

Joel looked at his mom. She had a pained, questioning expression, but said nothing. Then he slowly pulled out his switchblade and handed it to Mr. Peterson.

"Where did you get that, Joel?"

Joel glanced at his mom, but ignored her question. He watched as Mr. Peterson silently took the blade and placed it in a locked drawer behind the counter. It was as if a part of him had just been locked away and he wasn't sure how he felt about it. He was glad to give up a reminder of his past life, but how would he protect himself now?

Joel explored the shelter while his mother filled out papers in the office. The sounds of clanking metal and muted conversation led him to the cafeteria. Long rows of square plastic tables filled the room. Each table had bench seats attached, enough to fit three people on each side. On one side of the room was a serving area much like in the cafeteria at his school. It was lunchtime and the place was nearly filled with people shuffling along in line or eating at the tables. Many were women around his mom's age, some with small children, some alone. There were only a few kids that were his age.

Joel studied the faces of those who sat nearest him. Most of them stared blankly at the table as they mechanically consumed their food. One Asian woman, her face creased with age, wore a tattered coat, flimsy scarf, and a dirty knitted hat. She slowly looked up at Joel and smiled. One of her front teeth was missing.

"Young man," she said in broken English. "You work here?"

"No, I … um … I'll be living here for a while." Saying it made it real. A scary sickness attacked his stomach.

Joel had to get out of there. He turned and started down the hall that would lead to the front door, but that went right by the office where his mom, or someone else, would see him. He went in the other direction, past the cafeteria, and entered the sleeping area.

The large room, at one time the school gymnasium, was packed with rows and rows of cots topped with thin mattresses. Portable white curtains, like the ones he'd seen at the nurse's office in school, surrounded groups of some of the beds, while most of the others were out in the open. No one was in the room, and many of the beds were made. Joel plopped down on one of the bare mattresses. He felt his mouth contort into a frown as he fought back tears.

Looking up at the ceiling, he said, "God? I know you can hear me. Now that I know you're there, I'm asking you to get me out of this. I thought we were okay with each other now. Why did you let this happen to me?"

He rolled on his side and felt a hot tear drip across the bridge of his nose and onto the pillow. Did God really love him? Was the experience in the arena just a big show that didn't really mean anything? Where was God when you needed him?

Just then, Joel felt a hand rest gently on his shoulder. He thought it was his mom, but when he turned, quickly wiping his face with his sleeve, an older woman was bent over him. She had a wide smile and shoulder-length gray hair.

Joel sat up. "Who are you?"

The woman spoke in a slow, wavering but soothing voice "I'm a volunteer here at the shelter. My name is Mrs. Benton, but you can call me Miranda. I was passing by and happened to notice you lying there. I wondered if you were sick or needed something."

Joel was sure he had never met her and yet, when he looked into her eyes, it was as if he had known her all his life, as if she were his grandmother. He had the strange feeling that he could trust this person completely.

He finally found his voice. "I'm okay. Honest. I'm fine." He ventured what he thought was a silly question. "Do you know me?"

The woman sat on the bed. "No, I don't think so." She studied his face then said, "Have you stayed at the shelter before?"

"No," said Joel. "We just got here today."

"What's your name?"

"Joel Somers."

"May I ask what brought you here?"

"Our apartment burned down. We had no place to go, so a policeman brought us here."

"Oh my goodness, I'm so sorry. That must have been a terrible experience. Was anyone hurt?"

"No, I don't think so. They took our neighbor, Mrs. Culpeper, to the hospital, but Mom thinks she'll be alright."

"Well, I certainly hope so. But I'm sorry about your loss. You know, when I was much younger, our family lost everything we had—not from a fire—but because my father had died and we had no income. It was during a time when so many families were having difficulties because there weren't many jobs. I was sent to an orphanage when I was seven. But do you know what happened?"

Joel shook his head.

"After a while, it wasn't so bad. The Good Lord showed me that He would always be with me and would never turn His back on me."

Joel again wondered why God seemed to have turned His back on him. Maybe He only helped people who deserved it and left the rest of them to fend for themselves. He dropped his face, but Miranda gently put a hand on his shoulder and he looked up at her.

"You know, Joel, God is even better than the best friend you've ever had. He can help you in ways you never dreamed of. Like putting just the right person in your life right at the moment you need it. He is more powerful than anything, knows everything, and is everywhere. Do you know that he knows how many hairs you have on your head?"

Joel brightened up a bit and ran a hand through his thick hair. "Really? Wow!"

"Yup, that's right." She got up to leave. "Well, anyway, if there's anything you need, I mean anything, you just let me know. I work here every Sunday and Thursday. Okay?"

"Okay, I will."

Joel had heard similar words of comfort from adults before. But this was different. Somehow, he knew this was real.

## CHAPTER 12

That night, Joel slept fitfully on the thin shelter cot. His dreams were a mixture of remembrances and fantasies surrounding events that he had recently experienced. At one point, he found himself being chased by the police along a dark road, and although he tried to run at top speed, it felt as if he were trudging through mud up to his knees. Fear mounted with each agonizing step. Suddenly, Derrick charged at him with a hateful scowl, and he had to change direction. As he continued to run in extreme slow motion, he saw his mother off to the side. She was crying and pleading with him to do something, but he couldn't make out what she was saying. He turned and saw Eddie lying on the ground with one hand, holding his bleeding side. He slowly raised his other hand and pointed at Joel, saying, "Why'd you cut me, man?" They were the last words Joel heard him say.

Out of nowhere, Derrick grabbed him and shook him, screaming at him, *"What did you do? You're gonna pay for what you did!"*

Joel had no idea what he was talking about, but his fear intensified as Derrick became angrier and shook him more violently.

"Joel, wake up," said his mother, shaking him. Joel awoke with a start, then propped himself up on one elbow as reality seeped into his mind. Morning had come far too quickly.

"You okay?" said Catherine. "You must have been having some nightmare, squirming around like that."

"I'm all right." Images of the terrible apartment fire flashed across his mind. He swallowed hard against the lump in his throat. "Where are we going to live now, Mom?"

She looked at him with sad, moist eyes. "This will be our home for a while. They'll let us eat and sleep here until we can find another apartment, and they'll help replace some of our clothes. But…" She bit her lower lip. "We might be here a long time."

Joel thought with comfort that the Blades wouldn't find him for a while. But what if the police traced him here? Sooner or later, they would connect him to the attempted robbery, realize he had moved out of his apartment, and start checking at every shelter in the area. It wouldn't take them long to find him, but at least he was safe for now.

He said, "Well, I guess we'll be okay here for a while." Then a hopeful question came to him. "Mom, what about Dad? Can't he help us out?"

Catherine pursed her lips and shook her head. "No. That will never happen."

"Why not?"

She sat on the cot and took Joel's hands in hers. "I never told you the whole story about your father, but you deserve to know." She sucked in a breath and then went on. "You were only about five or six years old when he left. Your father was… or at least I thought he was… a good man. He wanted to provide for us, but he never seemed to be able to keep a steady job. He always had some scheme or another to 'make it big,' as he used to say, but none of them ever amounted to anything. Sometimes there wasn't enough money to pay the bills, so he stole to make ends meet. I knew it was wrong, but… but we had to eat and have a place to live, so I just put it out of my mind." She paused, gazing at the floor, her head sagging a bit. "I should have seen it coming then. I should have done something before…"

"It wasn't your fault, Mom." Catherine let out a weak smile. "So, then what happened?" he said.

"Well, like I said, he started stealing money or merchandise from stores. Sometimes, he would get caught, sometimes not. Sometimes he had to spend a month or two in jail; those were the worst times, especially when you were just a baby. I don't know how I made it from one day to the next back then." Her voice trailed off dreamily and she stared down at nothing.

"But where is he now?"

"I don't know," she said with a shrug. "His jail sentences were getting longer and longer. And when he was home, it seemed like he could never stay out of trouble. I think he had made friends with some bad people while he was in prison. He started to drink heavily every day and I'm pretty sure he was involved in selling drugs. 'That's where the *real* money was,' he'd say. Anyway, one day, he was convicted of assault and battery and armed robbery. He had hit a man in the face with a pistol while stealing a car. He was sent to federal prison for five years." She paused for a moment, as if remembering the rest of her story. "And that's the last I heard of him."

"So if that was around eight or nine years ago, he's been out for at least three years. That right?"

"Uh huh. That's about right."

"So why didn't he ever come back?"

"I don't know, Joel. I guess he felt he was better off without us. But, now that I think of it, maybe we're better off without him, even in this place. Maybe his leaving was a good thing in the long run."

Joel wasn't sure what to think. He tried to remember what his father was like, back when he was just starting kindergarten. But he just couldn't bring to mind a solid vision of his father spending time with him. Most of the distant, incomplete memories were of heated arguments between his parents, doors slamming, and his mom crying. He remembered he was scared sometimes and had hid under an end table in a corner of the living room, away from his angry parents while they shouted at each other in another room. It was the way things were. It never dawned on him that family life could be anything different.

---

The long days at the shelter melted into weeks. Life among people who were going through tough times was not as bad as Joel had imagined. There was always someone with an interesting story of how they came to be in that place. Some women had lost their jobs and then their homes. Without a family to take them in, they had no other place to live. Others were recovering from alcohol or drug abuse and were required to stay there by court order until they had completed a rehab program. Joel never realized that there were people in situations worse than his. But what surprised him most was that these people seemed to accept their situations, or else they were too numb to care.

He looked forward to days when Miranda was able to spend some time with him after she had looked in on the other residents. One mid-afternoon, he sat in the spacious cafeteria across from her at the end of a long row of tables. Lunch had already been served and the room was nearly empty.

He said, "Miranda, why do you work here? Aren't there other things you would rather be doing than hanging out with us...you know...homeless people?"

Miranda smiled. "Oh, there are plenty of things I could be doing, but I am here because it is part of what I know God wants me to do. And it gives me great pleasure to be able to do what He asks."

"But how do you know what God wants you to do? Does He talk to you?"

Miranda giggled. Joel thought she was as happy and carefree as a young child, but that she was also very wise. He listened intently to her answer.

"God talks to each of us in many ways. The Bible, other people, but lots of times, He talks to us through this." She pointed to her chest. "Your heart. We, all of us, are capable of great things for the Lord, but only if we allow His Spirit to work with ours. Only if we allow ourselves to shed our selfish desires and follow God's plan for us. It's only then that we can begin to accomplish His purpose for us. It's kind of like going on a military mission. You won't be able to accomplish it unless you've received your orders and have gone through the training required for whatever it is that you are being asked to do."

Joel cocked his head. "You mean God put you on a mission?"

Miranda beamed. "Yes, he did. All of us have a life-long mission, and it entails many tasks and experiences. It involves your God-given personality and abilities, where you live or can go, the people you interact with. And, when you come to know Jesus as your personal Savior, you are given special gifts that you didn't have before. They are called spiritual gifts and they are always used to glorify Him. I don't know the gifts God has blessed you with or the specifics of your particular mission, but if you will just allow Him to show them to you, He most certainly will."

Joel remembered how he had looked forward to moving up in the Blades and eventually being the leader of his own gang. He winced at the image of his own participation in vandalism, robberies, and other crimes. For the first time, he wondered what God must have thought of his life up to now and it gave him a horrible feeling, worse than getting caught with your hand in a cash register drawer.

Miranda went on. "Reading the Bible is also an excellent way for God to speak to us. In the book of Hebrews, it says, "For the word of God is living and active. Sharper than any double-edged sword."

The image of Derrick's double-edged blade, dripping Eddie's blood, burst into Joel's mind. If only he could have stopped the fight before it started…

He said, "Miranda, I don't think God can use somebody like me. I've done some pretty bad things in my life. It's like I've been working against Him all this time. Why would He want me to be on His side?"

Miranda got up and sat next to Joel. "Oh Joel, God loves for someone like you to be on His side. You know, there's a story about a man called Moses who did a terrible thing; he murdered an Egyptian because he was treating a fellow Hebrew badly; but God used him in a mighty way and he freed over a million Israelites from slavery in Egypt. And he's just one of the many people in the Bible who were dirty rotten scoundrels, and yet, God was able to use them to do great things. The only thing they had to do was to trust God and allow Him to work through them. God accepts you the way you are, but loves you too much to allow you to stay that way."

Joel said, "Wow. Maybe there's hope for me yet."

Miranda hugged him. "You bet there is!"

---

The ever watchful Abner smiled at Joel's remark. *Yes,* he thought, *there is true hope now that you are on the right path.* He marveled at the Father's perfect wisdom and timing to intertwine Miranda and Joel's paths at this critical point in his life.

# CHAPTER 13

Because the shelter was in a different neighborhood than his old apartment, Joel went to a different high school. It was hard at first, finding his way around the school and getting used to the teachers, but he soon learned the new routines. From the first day, he could tell this school was different. The rooms were cleaner, the halls brighter and wider, and there was no sign of the graffiti that was a regular occurrence at his old school.

Even his classes were more enjoyable. Although he still struggled in algebra, instead of ignoring his difficulties like Mrs. Avery had, his new math teacher, Miss Clay, actually spent extra time with him in class. She even encouraged him to come back after school for some remedial lessons, which he often did.

Joel had been attending his new school for just over a month, but still he hadn't made any real friends. In a way, he felt good about no one knowing him or his reputation. He didn't have to be the vicious person everyone at his old school expected him to be as a member of the Blades, which earned him a certain amount of respect—or fear, depending how you felt about the gang. Either way, he was seldom ignored. But here, it was hard for him to socialize with people who didn't know about him. He couldn't use his reputation or gang activities to strike up a conversation and he realized he didn't have much else to talk about.

Eating alone during lunch period one day, Joel heard a crash at the table near him. A girl had nearly tripped and slammed her lunch tray on the table. Her sandwich, milk carton, and slice of cherry pie had miraculously remained right side up. A boy standing nearby chided her.

"Gee, Beth, did that chair just jump out and grab you?"

Beth scrunched her nose at her tormentor. "Very funny, Nate. Did you think that up all by yourself, or did you read that in a comic book? Oh, I forgot. You're allergic to reading." She pulled a long lock of bright red hair behind her ear and adjusted her wire-rimmed glasses.

"Ha ha. Okay, truce," said Nate. He had darker red hair, the same light freckled complexion, a muscular build, and was a bit taller than her. He turned to Joel. "Is it okay if we sit here? She seems to have staked a claim already."

Beth tilted her head to the side and stuck her tongue out at Nate and then smiled at Joel.

She said, "Don't mind him. They don't have manners on the planet he's from."

Joel instantly liked these two. He said, "Sure, have a seat."

"My name's Beth. This is my so-called brother, Nate."

Joel told them his name and shook Beth's hand and then Nate's. Beth sat across from Joel, and Nate sat next to him.

Joel said, "You two sure look alike. Are you twins?"

Beth said, "Yep, we are." She leaned over the table, cupped her mouth, and almost whispered, "But we're not identical. I got the brains."

Nate laughed. "Yeah and she also got the two left feet!" Beth laughed too.

"Thank you *big* brother," said Beth. Then, responding to Joel's puzzled look, she added, "I was born ninety seconds after Nate;

so technically that makes him my older brother." Then she half whispered, "*But not smarter.*"

Nate smiled. "Clumsy ox." Beth took a playful swing at Nate, who easily avoided her touch. "*Feisty* clumsy ox."

After everyone started eating, Beth said, "Hey Joel, I haven't seen you around before. Did your family just move here?"

Joel wasn't sure how much he wanted Beth to know about his past, but it couldn't hurt to tell her about his current situation. "Well, actually, we did just move in. We live in the…ah…the family shelter down on Nineteenth Street." Joel felt a twinge of embarrassment. It was the first time he had told anyone in school where he was staying. "What happened was our apartment burned down and…"

"Oh, I'm so sorry," said Beth. "Is everyone alright?"

"Yeah. It was just me and my mom. We're okay, but we pretty much lost everything in the fire."

Nate said, "Wow. That is way uncool. Sorry, man. Hey Beth, don't we have a…what is it called at our church?"

"You mean the Care Closet? That's right. They have all kinds of clothes and other stuff for, you know, homeless folks or when you lose everything in a fire. Anything you need. And it's free."

"Well, I don't know," said Joel.

"Tell you what. Nate and I are going to stop by our church for a little while on the way home from school. It's only a couple of blocks away. Why don't you come with us and check it out? It can't hurt, and besides, you just might find something that you or your mom could really use. What do you say?"

Joel could hardly believe his ears. Just the other day his mom had told him she wished she had a sweater, since the shelter wasn't always as warm as she would like. Now, here were two complete strangers offering him clothes from their church! Joel had a weird but happy feeling that everything was going to turn out all right after all. He felt his mouth turn into a grin. "Why not," he said. "That would be great."

The bell rang. Lunch period was over. Nate jumped up still chewing on the last bite of his sandwich. "Oh man, I forgot to finish the book report before next class. Beth, lemme see yours."

Beth and Joel got up from the table. "No way in *this* life," she said. Then to Joel, "See you out front after school. Nice meeting you."

Joel raised a hand. "Me too. See you later." He shook his head in amused astonishment as he watched Nate continue to beg Beth for her book report while they walked out of the cafeteria.

---

After the last period, Joel met Beth and Nate in front of the school. As they started walking together, Beth said, "Oh, do you need to call your mom about coming home late so she won't worry about you?"

"Nah," said Joel. "She knows I stay after school sometimes." When he was at his old school, he would almost always come home late, if he came home at all. It was way better to hang out with the gang than to go straight home after school. But it had never occurred to him until now that his mother might be worried about him. He tried to push the guilty feeling away without much success.

Joel was amazed at how different the church was from the cold, dark churches he had seen before. And there was no padlocked, chain-link fence around it. Beth assumed the role of 'tour guide' as they entered and walked into the large brightly lit common area.

"Pastor Andy's office is off to the left. He's our youth pastor. The sanctuary is straight ahead through those double doors. Off to the right are the nursery and the Sunday school classrooms. Further down is the kitchen, the youth lounge, and then the Care Closet room at the end of the hall."

"Wait a minute," said Joel. "You guys have your own room?"

"Sure," said Nate. "C'mon, I'll show you."

Nate led the three down the long hallway then pointed toward the youth lounge door.

"Here it is. Check it out."

Joel looked through the window in the door while Nate continued. "It's got a TV and stereo, comfy couches, chairs, tables, books, magazines … the works!"

"Wow," said Joel. "You guys've got it made."

The dirty and cold abandoned apartment that was the Blades' headquarters flashed through Joel's mind. It contrasted sharply with this comfortable, inviting place.

"Can you come here any time you want?"

"Well," said Beth. "It's usually locked when no one's around. But we always meet here for Sunday school and on Wednesday evenings, and sometimes on special occasions, like when we work on service projects and stuff like that. Mostly we sit around talking about God and what He says in the Bible, and what it all means to us." She looked at her brother, who made a slight nodding motion at her, then said, "So Joel, what do you think about joining us sometime?"

"Me?"

"Uh huh. We don't have a really big group, mostly girls and a few boys our age, but I think you'd fit right in. And it would be great having you. What do you say?"

Nate broke in, "Yeah, we're kind of outnumbered. We could really use another *male* point of view." Beth shot Nate a disapproving look.

Joel could feel a battle going on deep inside of him. He liked the idea of talking with other kids his age about this 'Christian' stuff, because he still had a lot of questions. But at the same time, he wasn't sure he was ready to join this group just yet. Experience told him he needed to be cautious about joining other groups. He fingered the scar on his hand that reminded him of the Blades' initiation. Was there some kind of an initiation ritual that he would have to go through? Would they still accept him if they found out about his past life as a gang member?

He said, "Well, let me think about it, okay?"

Beth said, "Sure. Not a problem. You'll always be welcome whenever you're ready."

"C'mon Joel," said Nate. "Let's hit that Care Closet and see what we can find. It's right next door."

---

Joel beamed as he walked back to the shelter with a colorful sweater for his mom and a pair of jeans for himself. He still couldn't believe how kind Beth and Nate were. Even though they had just met, they treated him as if he had known them all his life. If the other kids in the youth group were like them, maybe it would be cool to join in with them. They would be like...a Christian gang!

The thought made Joel smile even more, but then it dissipated as visions of the last gang he had joined swirled around in his mind like poisonous gas. He knew sooner or later he would meet someone from the Blades—maybe even Derrick himself—and they would want him to do something that he knew was wrong. What would he say? Would he break down and go along with them, knowing God was watching? Would he make a stand and refuse to rejoin the gang? He didn't want to think about what they would do to him if he tried to leave the gang. Sooner or later, he knew there would be a confrontation.

# CHAPTER 14

Ever since the night before the fire, Joel kept playing variations of the conversation he wanted to have with his mother over and over in his mind. It started off something like this:

*"Mom, something happened to me a while ago in the sports arena. It was the coolest thing ever! Let me tell you about it..."*

But the right moment never seemed to come up. Either his mom was too tired, or sad, or his own doubts kept getting in the way. Every time an opportunity to tell her about his becoming a Christian passed by, for whatever reason, Joel would go through a period of frustration. Why was it so hard to talk about the greatest thing that had ever happened to him? How would she react if he did manage to tell her?

That evening after supper, Catherine stared blankly at the TV in the entertainment room. Joel presented the sweater to her.

"Here mom, this is for you."

He had hoped she would ask him where he had gotten it, and he could begin to tell her about his recent experiences.

She looked at the sweater and frowned. "Now Joel, you take that right back to where you found it. They don't take too kindly to stealing around here."

"But Mom, I didn't steal it. It was donated. I wanted you to have it. Didn't you say the other day you wished it was warmer around here?"

Joel's mother smiled weakly and put her hand on his. "Thank you, Joel. That's very kind of you to think of me, but I can't accept it."

"*What?* Why not?"

"I can't be wearing a fine sweater like this when there are people here who have none at all. And besides, I don't want to take any more charity than I absolutely need, and my old coat is just fine. It'll keep me warm enough."

"Well, it's yours anyway. You can do what you want with it." Joel threw the sweater on the couch next to his mom and stormed out of the room.

He tossed himself on his cot as angry thoughts burned in his mind. *Why can't mom see the good I'm trying to do for her? Why bother giving her a gift if she won't accept it? How can I ever make her happy again?*

Suddenly, he had a brainstorm. If he went back to the burned out apartment, he might find something that would cheer his mom up, at least for a little while. Maybe he could find her jewelry box or a photo album that had somehow escaped the fire. Then, once he brightened up her spirits, he could talk to her about how God had changed his life—and maybe even convince her that He could change hers too.

The next day Joel took a bus to his old neighborhood. As he approached his building, he realized it blended in with the many others that were abandoned for one reason or another. Some had caught fire, but others were just too badly in need of repair and were left to rot. Plywood sheets covered most doorways and windows.

Joel stared at his building for several minutes. The furniture that had been tossed on the sidewalk by the firemen was gone.

The wall above his mom's bedroom window was marred by dark smoke stains, its paint blistered from the intense heat. The black gaping doorway looked like the opening to a cave. Then Joel noticed something strange about the entrance. A plywood sheet lay flat on the sidewalk near the building. It had been nailed to the opening to prevent intruders, but, apparently, it had not served its purpose well enough.

He cautiously started up the dark staircase, ready for anything. Pausing in the last swatch of sunlight, Joel found his key and held it tightly in his hand. He sniffed and took in a strange mixture of mildew and burnt wood as he ascended the gloomy stairway. At the landing at the top of the stairs, Joel slid his hand along the wall and found the light switch. He flipped it up and down twice, but the darkness remained. Either the firemen or the fire itself had cut the electricity to the building.

As his eyes became accustomed to the dim landing, he realized the door was ajar, kicked in, by the looks of the splintered doorjamb. Had the firemen done that or...someone else? He hesitated for a moment and listened for any sounds within the apartment. Nothing.

Joel pushed the door open just enough to fit his head through the opening. It was much lighter in the apartment since the sun shown fully through the barren windows, only slightly shaded by soot-stained glass. Joel looked behind the door then quickly withdrew. If anyone was behind ready to take a swing at him, he would have missed and given Joel a chance to smash him against the wall as he made a hasty retreat. But the room was empty.

Joel let the door creak open the rest of the way and the tension dropped a bit. Maybe he was just being over cautious. He walked into the almost unrecognizable living room. The TV, couch, coffee table, and two sofa chairs were gone. The walls were stained with a thin coating of soot, but not burned. A strong odor of burned wood and paper attacked his nostrils. Glass cracked under his feet as he nimbly walked down the hallway to his mother's bedroom where the fire had started.

The bedroom was an eerie charcoal cave. The exposed beams in the walls and ceiling looked like cracked, charred bones. Joel shuttered when he thought about what might have happened if he hadn't gotten his mother out in time. He realized he must have been crazy to think there was anything left to bring back to his mom. Everything was either burned to an unrecognizable crisp or had been dragged out with the smoldering furniture.

Shaking his head, Joel turned to leave—and ran right into Derrick.

Instinctively, Joel bent back, fist clenched, ready to strike a blow, but he quickly recognized Derrick and paused.

In that same instant, Derrick put up his left hand to block the anticipated punch, then swung his right fist around and struck Joel on the side. Joel stumbled sideways, crashing into the nearby wall. Pain exploded inside him. He gasped, but showed no other sign that he was hurt.

Holding his bruised ribs, Joel said, "*Derrick*...what are you doing here? And what's the idea of sneaking up on me like that?"

"Listen, kid," said Derrick menacingly. "I was just going to ask you the same thing. I live here now."

Joel felt the old anger bubble up inside. He didn't care what he said to Derrick anymore. He said, "How'd you get in here? This is still my place, you know?"

"This ain't your place no more. It went up for grabs the day you moved out and I grabbed it. You got any objections?"

The cut that Derrick had gotten in the accident had become a jagged purple scar above his eye. His long matted hair partially covered a dark bruise on one cheek. He wore dirty, torn jeans and a red plaid shirt that hung off his body. Joel realized he'd been living and hiding on the street, probably stealing food and clothes from wherever he could find them.

"Listen," said Joel, his anger subsiding. "I don't mind you staying here for a little while. I mean, we won't be coming back anytime soon. But when we get the place fixed up, we're gonna live here again. Okay? So just don't get too comfortable."

Joel couldn't believe he was telling the leader of the Blades what to do! Not long ago, he would have been thrown up against the wall by one of the older Blades for even hinting that they were on equal footing. But this was not the same Derrick he had last seen. No longer the commanding general full of confidence, this Derrick looked bone weary, the fight beaten out of him.

Derrick shuffled out of the room saying, "Yeah, whatever."

Joel followed him down the hall into his own bedroom, which had hardly been touched by the fire. Derrick had made a place for himself there. A thin mattress and a plastic milk crate were the only pieces of furniture. Empty soda cans, plastic bottles, and food wrappings littered the floor. Derrick threw himself down on the mattress, and Joel sat on the crate. It still bothered him that Derrick had taken over his bedroom without even asking, but there wasn't anything left except the four walls anyway. Because of the fire, the whole apartment had become no more than a shell. For the first time in his life, Joel felt sorry for Derrick.

For long moments, they sat in silence. Joel was desperate to open up a conversation with Derrick, so he said, "So, what happened to the gang?"

Derrick stared at the wall behind Joel, propped up on one elbow. "There ain't no gang." After a pause, he continued, his voice raising a notch, "They all scattered. Wimped out! Every last one of 'em!" He hit the wall behind him with the side of his hand. It seemed to calm him down a bit. "It's just as well. Who needs gang members that cut and run at the first sign of trouble anyway."

Joel pressed for more information. "What about Jack and Randy? Are the cops still looking for us? What happened to Eddie?" Joel knew that last question was a risky one to ask. Eddie had become Derrick's enemy because of the fight. And if you cared about Derrick's enemy, you became his enemy too.

Derrick just shrugged his shoulders and stared up at the ceiling.

Then, as if suddenly remembering he had a visitor, he sat up and said, "Hey… what've you been doing? Where've you been?"

Joel mentally ran through the changes he had been through during the last two months—the fire, living in the shelter, going to a new school, and meeting new friends. But most of all, he thought of the incredible night at the arena and how he gave his life to Jesus. He was sure Derrick wouldn't understand what that meant and how that had changed him. Before he could answer, Derrick cut into his thoughts.

"You look like you're living pretty good. I'll bet you can get all kinds of stuff." Derrick moved closer to Joel. The old fire was back in his eyes. "Yeah. And that's just what you're gonna do."

He stood up. Joel stood too, uncertainly. Derrick went on. "Listen. Go steal some food and money for me. Lots of it. Enough so I can get out of town for a while, at least until things cool down here. I'm gonna go someplace where the cops will never find me *and you're gonna help me.*"

That last statement sent a shiver up Joel's back. He knew what his answer had to be. Calmly, he said, "No, I'm not doing that. That would be wrong."

"*What?* What are you... turning chicken on me?" Derrick reached into his pocket and with a blur of motion produced the switchblade. At the touch of a button, the six-inch blade shot out of its handle.

"You do what I say, or I'll cut you. You remember what happened to Eddie."

Without a thought, Joel darted through the door, bounced off the opposite wall, and then ran down the hall. The unexpected move startled Derrick for an instant, but he soon gave chase.

"Come back here you worthless piece of...!"

Joel slammed the apartment door against the wall and then ran down the stairs sideways, skipping every other step. Derrick bounded after him and quickly closed in. Joel jumped over the badly cracked fourth step from the bottom, burst out the doorway, and into the street.

He knew Derrick would quickly catch up to him if he kept on a straight run, so he searched frantically for some obstacle that would add a second or two to his dwindling lead.

Two seconds later, Derrick hit the fourth step with full force, and it collapsed under him. Momentarily trapped within the staircase, he shouted, "You're dead when I see you again. You hear me? *Dead!*"

---

Twenty years before Joel was born, two men had carried an old refrigerator down those same steps. The heavy appliance had been dropped on the fourth step from the bottom, cracking it. Over the years since then, human traffic, the constant pull of gravity and, more recently, a colony of carpenter ants had weakened the step just enough so that the heavy force of Derrick's foot was guaranteed to break it. Abner, watching the chase with growing concern, gasped in awe as he realized that the Father had instigated all of those events with perfect timing so that Joel could escape from Derrick's deadly onslaught this very day!

## CHAPTER 15

Joel showed the cashier his free lunch meal card then sat at an empty table in the school cafeteria. For days, vivid images of Derrick's violent attack played through his mind. The flash of the deadly knife. Derrick's explosive anger. Running wildly and looking desperately for a place to hide. But then he remembered looking back over his shoulder and seeing that Derrick had fallen through the steps. What a lucky break! If that hadn't happened, Derrick surely would have caught him. Would he really have killed him if he had gotten the chance? In his mind, he saw Eddie lying in a pool of blood, and Joel shuddered.

Joel's opinion of Derrick plummeted to a new low, and he winced at the thought that he once wanted to be just like him. All he wanted now was to never meet up with him again. He wished he could finally forget about his past and start enjoying his new life. But somehow, he knew his past would catch up to him again, and he might not be so lucky next time.

Beth, tray in hand, swooped down opposite him. "Hey Joel, you look like you could use some cheering up. Anything wrong?"

Joel looked up and smiled. "Nah. Just thinking, that's all." He was grateful the disturbing thoughts quickly dissipated.

Nate plopped down next to Beth. "Can you believe they ran out of chocolate cake? Man, what's this world coming to, anyway?"

Joel chuckled. It was amazing how close he had become to Beth and Nate in such a short time.

"Hey Joel," said Nate. "What's going on?"

"Nothing."

Beth said, "I know something going on. Nate and I were just talking about the weekend retreat coming up next month."

"What's that?"

Nat chimed in. "It's gonna be way cool. We're going upstate with our youth pastor and a bunch of kids in our youth group at church."

"What do you do there?"

"Well," said Nate. "We'll be playing all kinds of games, sitting around a big fire, sleeping in cabins, that kind of stuff."

"And," Beth continued. "We were wondering if you'd like to go with us. I'm sure it would be all right with Pastor Andy. What do you say?"

"Me? Well, I don't know. I mean, it sounds like fun and all, but…"

Nate cut him off. "And you know what else? Since you lost your home and all, well, maybe the church will pay for the trip for you. Besides, I need somebody to help me keep her out of trouble." He jabbed a thumb in Beth's direction. Beth promptly slapped Nate's arm.

"Listen, I'd really like to go but, well, my mom kinda needs me right now. She's not doing too well."

"Oh," said Beth. "I'm so sorry. Is there anything we can do to help? Is she sick?"

"Oh no, nothing like that. It's just that she's still pretty torn up about the fire and everything. She…um…lost her job and …uh…she had been drinking that night. I guess she was smoking when she went to bed and they say that's what could have started the fire. So she feels really bad about the whole thing."

Memories of that terrible night swirled around in Joel's mind, guilt stabbed at his heart. If only he had put her cigarette out…

After an awkward silence, Beth said, "Oh Joel, I'm really sorry."

"It's okay. I can't really blame her. She's had it rough."

Beth smiled. "You have a good heart, Joel."

Joel smiled, but he didn't think that was true. He said, "Tell you what; maybe I'll talk to my mom about the retreat. Okay?"

"Super!" said Beth.

---

That evening, Joel and his mom stood in line in the shelter cafeteria. Volunteers had prepared the meal in the tiny kitchen—spaghetti, meatballs, salad, and garlic bread—and were serving it on three-section Styrofoam plates. Joel noticed that the servers, a group from a different church every day, always seemed to enjoy what they were doing, whether it was cooking in sweat-drenched aprons and hats, washing grimy pots and pans, or mopping the floor. Not long ago, he would have looked down on them. He would have written them off as pathetic people who obviously had nothing better to do than to serve homeless folks, without even getting paid for their work. Now he realized that the warm and filling meals he gratefully devoured each day were made possible only by their generosity. He wondered if he could ever become as good as they were.

Joel sat across from his mom and started swirling the steamy pasta.

"Guess what, Joel," his mom said. Joel looked up and was surprised by her wide grin. "I finally got another job. I start in a couple of weeks."

"That's great, Mom! What are you going to be doing?"

"I'll be working as a cashier at the supermarket near where we used to live."

Joel stopped chewing. "Are we going to be moving back into our old apartment?"

"Oh heavens no." She paused for a moment, and then said, "You miss that place?"

"Nah." Inside, Joel felt relief wash over him. Derrick could keep that old burnt up apartment, for all he cared. "I never did like that place anyway," he said. "Too hot."

They both laughed for the first time in a long time.

After the laughter subsided, Catherine said, "But you know, we could get an apartment near there. And you could go back to your old school and see your friends again. Wouldn't that be nice?"

Joel paused while slurping a strand of spaghetti into his mouth. The old neighborhood was the last place on earth he wanted to live. Still chewing, he said, "Ya know, Mom, I kind of like the friends I'm making now at my new school. Couldn't we live around here someplace?"

"Well, apartments are more expensive around here. Besides," she tilted her head and gave Joel a questioning look. "Since when did you start caring about making new friends? You never even talked about your friends before."

She was right. He was bound by unwritten gang rules never to speak to anyone— especially adults—about any gang member or the gang's activities. Squealers were sure to be kicked out or beat up, or both. He said, "Well, I have a couple of new friends now. Beth and Nate. They go to church."

"Oh?" said Catherine, raising an eyebrow.

Church was never discussed at home. Never even mentioned. It would have been as unnatural as talking about the latest scientific discovery or politics in some faraway country. It had no bearing on everyday life. Until now.

Joel felt like he was about to walk out on a very thin limb. "Yeah, they do. They're really cool, and I like hanging out with them, but…"

"But what?"

Joel took a deep breath. "Well, they invited me to go with them to something called a weekend retreat. A bunch of kids from their church are going and the pastor and other adults too. And it sounds like a lot of fun and all, and it won't cost us anything. But, well, I didn't think you would let me go."

Joel's mom gave a concerned look. "Well, I don't know. What kind of people are they? They're not in a … a *cult* or anything like that, are they?"

Joel didn't know exactly what she meant, but he could tell she was skeptical. "No, Mom. They're just really good people, like Miranda."

"You mean Mrs. Benton, who works here at the shelter?"

"Yeah. She's real nice. She's been talking with me about God and the Bible and stuff."

"I see."

"So can I go to the retreat?"

After a long hesitation, she said, "Well, I guess so. Just don't come back with your head shaved or wearing strange tattoos or anything."

Joel laughed. "Aw Mom, you don't have to worry about that!"

---

On Thursday afternoons, Joel had gotten in the habit of meeting Miranda in the little library at the shelter. He thought she was the kindest, friendliest, and wisest adult he had ever known. And he enjoyed their times together.

Fresh from her Wednesday night church service, Miranda always talked about the Scripture the pastor had preached on. Joel thought most of the Bible was hard to understand. But Miranda had a way of making the stories come alive by putting them in her own words. Then she would explain the deeper meaning of the story and how it applied directly to real life and sometimes, without knowing it, to a situation in Joel's life as well.

On this particular Thursday, Joel waited patiently for her. Sometimes she came a little later than usual if she had to work with a new shelter family or help another volunteer. But after thirty minutes had gone by, Joel sensed something was wrong.

He walked to the admissions office down the hall near the shelter entrance, where his mom first signed them in over two months ago. By now, he knew just about everyone who worked there.

Poking his head through the open door, he said, "Hey, has anyone seen Miranda? She was supposed to meet me in the library but…"

Mrs. Sutherland, a large older woman who always talked with a big grin, looked up at Joel from her desk. Her expression was unusually serious.

"I'm sorry, Joel. She was taken to St. Mary's hospital late yesterday."

Joel felt a sudden weight in his chest. "What? What happened? Is she going to be all right?"

Mrs. Sutherland stood and sat on the corner of her desk. "We're not sure. All we know is a neighbor of hers called in early this morning and said she was taken away in an ambulance. She had collapsed in her home and … well, we don't really know more that. I'm sorry."

"Can … can you take me to see her?"

"No, I can't leave the office right now; I'm the only one here to answer the phones. But there's a shuttle bus that runs out to St. Mary's every afternoon. In fact, it should be out front soon."

Joel had already started toward the door. "Thanks Mrs. S."

# CHAPTER 16

Within a half hour, Joel was on his way to the hospital on the shuttle bus. A few residents from the shelter rode with him. A thin man with a scraggly beard and long, uncombed gray hair coughed uncontrollably. An elderly woman had a patch over one eye. Another woman, her arm in a sling, stared straight ahead. A very old bald man with a cane and a bad limp seemed to be already asleep by the time the bus stopped at the first intersection. All of them seemed desperately in need of the services at St. Mary's free clinic.

Joel let his arms droop over the back of the seat in front of him, lost in thought. How could Miranda have gotten so sick so quickly? Just a week ago she seemed fine. He struggled to bring up every detail of their last meeting. Did she seem a little tired? Was her smile not as full as usual? He couldn't think of anything that might have given a clue about her illness.

As the small and aging bus slowly bounced and creaked its way across town, Joel's thoughts turned to helpless dismay. In the past, when he was a Blade, you always knew your enemy. If someone got hurt, you always knew just who did it, and revenge was simple and quick. But how could he fight this? Who would pay if Miranda—he choked at the thought—if Miranda died? He shook his head to try to dissipate the sickening thought.

Joel tried to imagine what Miranda might look like based on countless TV shows he'd seen. An image came to mind of a person lying on a hospital bed that was bruised and bandaged. After a while, the person limped out on crutches. People always got better in a hospital. That's usually how it went, didn't it?

The bus finally screeched to a stop at the clinic entrance. Joel had to work his way through the maze of corridors until he found the information desk at the main entrance on the other side of the hospital. He quietly approached a woman busily typing into a computer. She wore blue scrubs under a flowery lab coat. Joel thought she looked tired and would probably be grumpy. But her wide smile caught him off guard.

"Can I help you?"

"Uh yeah," he stammered. "I wondered if you could tell me what room my, uh, grandmother is in." Joel hoped his lie would give him a better chance of seeing her.

She began typing. "Name?"

"Miranda."

"Last name?"

"Benton."

The nurse read in silence for an uncomfortable period of time. Finally, she said, "Hmmm … she's in Intensive Care. Immediate family members only." She looked over her glasses at Joel. "You're her grandson?"

Joel felt his face flush. "Yes."

"Okay then. Second floor. Room two-eighteen." The nurse pointed a pencil down the hall. "Elevator's on the right." Joel started to trot down the hall. The nurse continued. "You can only visit for a few minutes. When you get to the ICU area, just press the intercom button and tell them who you are. They'll buzz you in."

"Okay," called Joel over his shoulder. "Thanks."

Joel entered the empty elevator, fingered the "two" button, and watched the single elevator door close with a low swish. As he felt the small room rumble upward, he suddenly had a sickening feeling that he didn't want to be there.

The elevator door opened to a small waiting area. On the left, he saw large double doors with the letters "ICU" over them. An intercom was positioned just to the right of the doors. Joel pushed the button. "I'm here to see Miranda Benton."

A mechanical lock unlatched and the doors swung silently open. Joel spotted a sign showing the direction of rooms 200–220. Miranda's room would be near the end of the hall. Immediately, he was aware of intense activity. Nurses in green scrubs darted back and forth, barely noticing Joel. A doctor was being paged over the speaker system, and a soft but persistent tone chimed from somewhere. As he made his way down the hall, he glanced past partially opened doors of the patient's rooms. Some were filled with visitors; others were filled with frenzied doctors and nurses, while still others were dark and empty.

At room 218, Joel paused before going in. What if she wanted to be left alone? What if she was too sick to see anyone? Pushing his hesitation aside, Joel strode in.

He was not prepared for what he saw.

Miranda lay slightly propped up in bed. Her eyes were closed. A small tube crossed her face with two inlets going into her nostrils. An intravenous needle was taped to the back of her hand. A tube from the needle led up to a pouch of clear liquid, its contents slowly dripping through one section of the tube. She had patches attached to her head and upper chest. Wires connected the patches to a machine nearby that slowly beeped, its screen drawing several wavering and pulsing lines that Joel could only guess had something to do with her bodily functions.

Miranda's shoulder-length hair, usually smoothly brushed, lay in a tangled mess under her head. Her skin was pale and Joel thought her face looked thinner than usual. He gently touched her bare arm and her eyes slowly fluttered open. She turned her

head toward Joel and gave a little grin, not nearly as big as the smile he was used to.

"My precious Joel," she said in a sleepy voice that was not her own. "How nice of you to visit me."

"Hey Miranda, how are you doing?" Joel mentally scolded himself for asking such a stupid question.

"Oh, I've seen better days, that's for sure." She tried to chuckle, but only managed a little cough.

"I just wanted to see how you were doing. So…uh…what happened? Mrs. S. at the shelter said you fell or something and…"

"Well, the doctors say my heart's not working very well. It's a type of heart disease."

"They're gonna fix you up, right? I mean, don't they have medicine for that?"

Miranda's weak smile told Joel all he needed to know even before she spoke. "No. Unless they can find me a new heart pretty soon, they won't be able to fix me."

Joel felt a shiver wash over him. He swallowed hard. "What do you mean? Why can't they fix what's wrong with you?"

Miranda strained to lift her head a bit. "Don't worry, Joel. It's in God's hands now. And you know, He'll make everything just right. Just the way He wants it. No matter what happens, just remember the best is yet to come!"

Just then, a nurse came in with a metal clipboard and addressed Joel. "Can I ask you to step outside for a few minutes, please?"

Joel looked at the nurse then back at Miranda. "Maybe I should be going now, anyway." He squeezed Miranda's hand. "You hang in there. God'll get you though. You'll see."

Miranda managed a weak smile. "I know He will."

"Well, see you later. Okay?"

"Good-bye, Joel."

Back in the elevator, Joel closed his eyes and prayed silently. *Please, God. Don't let anything happen to her. Not her.*

Joel ambled through the large hospital entrance area barely aware of his surroundings. He glanced to the side and froze.

Sitting on one of the couches in the waiting area was someone he thought he'd never see again: Eddie Moran!

For a few seconds, he thought about how he could avoid being seen by him. The last thing he wanted right now was a confrontation. As he swiveled his head looking for an escape route, he heard Eddie's unmistakable voice.

"Hey Joel!"

Joel hoped his uneasiness didn't show. "Hey Eddie."

Eddie motioned him over. "C'mere, I wanna talk to you."

Joel swallowed hard. Eddie wouldn't try anything in a hospital, would he?

As he approached the couch, he said, "What are you doing here, man? Last time I saw you, you were hurt real bad when Derrick…you know…"

Joel stopped outside of striking distance, just to be on the safe side.

"Yeah. You guys dumped me. Left me for the cops. Not cool at all."

"Hey, I was on your side, man. I didn't want to go along with Derrick's stupid plan either. What was I supposed to do? Fight Derrick, maybe get cut, or worse? He was way out of control. You know that."

"Forget about it. There's nothing you could have done, anyway." Eddie sat up, anger crossing his face. "But Derrick's gonna *pay* for what he did to me," he said while stabbing the air with his finger. "I would have died for sure if the cops didn't call an ambulance as soon as they found me." He paused and leaned back into the couch. "The doctor said I was real lucky. One inch higher and my spleen would have ruptured. He said I would've bled to death on the spot. Makes you think about death and all, you know?"

After another pause, Eddie continued. "Anyway, they had to sew me up inside. I had to stay in the hospital for like a week." He rubbed his side. "Still hurts, too. That's why I'm here. They want to do another examination. They say it might be infected."

Joel relaxed a bit "So what happened, with the cops, I mean?"

"They talked to me...a lot. Every day they would come into my hospital room and ask me questions about the Blades, Derrick, the video store job. Stuff like that.

"What'd you tell them?"

"I didn't tell them nothing. They tried to scare me. Kept saying I'd be locked up for a long time unless I cooperated. But they got nothing on me, nothing they can prove, anyway. Besides, when I take my revenge on Derrick, it'll be on my terms. I'll hit him when he least expects it, and he's gonna know it was me who brought him down. I don't need the cops to help me do that."

"What are you going to do?"

"Start another gang. Kids that have a grudge against Derrick will be happy to join up." His eyes locked on Joel's. "You oughta be first in line. He's treated you like dirt most of the time. Just think. You would have a chance to get back at him for all the trouble he's caused you; *plus* you can start off pretty high up as my first recruit. Maybe even second-in-command. What do you say?"

Joel could hardly believe his ears! This was what he had been waiting for ever since joining the Blades: to be the second-in-command of a gang. He was both honored and ashamed at the same time. Was this some kind of a test God was putting him through?

He said, "Let me get this straight. You want me to be second-in-command?"

"Sure, why not?"

"And our main goal would be to find Derrick and make him pay for what he had done to us?"

"Uh huh. Then we'd do what the Blades never could, because of Derrick. We'd build up until we took over this town. We'd be the top gang in Brooklyn. Maybe even the whole city. So are you with me, or what?"

Joel fell silent. There was a time when he would have jumped at the chance to do exactly what Eddie was talking about. It had been his dream for a long time. But now...now he was surprised at how little that meant to him.

He shook his head. "No way, man. I'm through with gangs. They are nothing but trouble." Eddie cocked back his head and squinted as if Joel was speaking Latin. Joel continued. "Besides. I found something better."

"Yeah? What?"

"God."

"*God?* Are you kidding me? He's not real, man. He's just a fairytale moms tell their kids to keep them in line. Besides, if He was real, don't you think He would have fixed all the problems of the world by now? Look around you. You see that happening? I don't think so!"

Eddie's fiery response was not what Joel expected. His protective defenses immediately kicked in. "You don't know anything about God. I've seen what He can do. And I know people who know a lot about Him. He *is* real, whether you believe in Him or not."

"Wow. You really have been brainwashed, haven't you. I feel sorry for you."

"Maybe *you're* the one who's been brainwashed. Ever think about that?"

Eddie fell silent for a moment and then chuckled. "Yeah, maybe so. Anyway, it sounds like your mind is made up. You'd be no good to me anyway, with all that God-talk coming out of you all the time. I can't have you turning my gang members into choirboys, now can I?"

A vision flashed across Joel's mind. In it, he was telling gang members about God and Jesus, and they eagerly accepted his message. Eddie's idea might not be so far-fetched. Maybe someday…

Joel said, "Well listen, I've got a bus to catch. See ya 'round."

They butted fists. "Okay dude. Later," said Eddie.

## CHAPTER 17

Light-sensing streetlights nearby flickered on when Joel stepped onto the shuttle bus back to the shelter. He was the only passenger and was grateful to be alone with his thoughts. As the bus rumbled through the city streets, Joel replayed the times he had spent with Miranda in his mind. In each vision, he saw her either smiling or telling a story, or laughing, or hugging him. She was always friendly, always understanding, and always helpful. She was the best friend he ever had. And now... he could hardly bring the words to mind; he might never see her again.

A heavy sadness took hold of Joel. Sadness morphed into simmering anger. Anger pushed poisonous questions into his mind. "Why should this happen to Miranda? What did she ever do to anyone to deserve this? *God*, why did You let this happen? You could have kept her from getting sick. Why are You taking her away from me? Can't You see I need her?"

Joel buried his head in his upper arm and wiped moist eyes on his shirtsleeve.

God whispered to a place in Joel's mind where dreams are formed. "I will never leave you nor forsake you." Then he said, "Put your hope in me. You can trust me. You are troubled now, but one day you will understand that there is a purpose for all things, and that my blessings far outweigh all the troubles of the world. For now, be at peace and let my Spirit rest upon you and I will show you that the best is yet to come."

---

The best is yet to come.

Joel lifted his head and remembered what Miranda had told him less than an hour ago. Somehow, it echoed in his mind like when you hear a little song and you just can't shake it off.

*The best is yet to come.*

What did she mean by that? How could she be in the hospital with a bad heart and still say, "The best is yet to come"? Did she know something he didn't? Was she trying to tell him something? It didn't seem like the best was yet to come, in fact, it seemed like things couldn't get much worse. But Miranda wouldn't tell him something that wasn't true, just to make him feel better, would she? Somehow he knew that she would fully recover, and that she would be able to live a long and normal life. He smiled at the thought.

---

Joel and his mom were driving back to the shelter from the mall. Now that she would be starting a new job soon, she needed some new clothes. On the way, they passed a large cemetery. Joel gazed out across the rows of low granite markers.

"Hey Mom," said Joel. "What happens when you die?"

"What are you talking about? What kind of a question is that?"

"I just want to know, that's all."

"We don't talk about such things. It's morbid."

"But why?"

"Don't we have enough to worry in life about without adding … that?" She glanced at her son's still questioning face. "Joel, no one knows what happens when you die. As far as I know, you're gone. That's it. There is nothing after that."

Joel needed to know why this was such a sensitive subject for his mother. He said, "Did you ever know anyone who died?"

Catherine drove in silence for a long time. Joel looked out the window thinking the conversation was over. Finally, she spoke.

"When I was a little girl, eight or nine years old, I lived with my parents in an apartment building near the downtown area. It was much nicer back then. Cleaner and safer, too. We were always happy. We'd go to the shore during the summer and concerts and plays all year round. We were always going on trips to one place or another, sometimes halfway across the country. Usually, I went with them, but one day, they went somewhere without me. I think they were looking for a new home in the suburbs while I stayed with my aunt."

She paused and bit her lip. "They never came home. There was a terrible accident. They … they were both killed instantly. After the funeral, everything just sort of fell apart. I cried and cried for a long time. I stayed with my aunt and uncle, but they were nothing like my parents. She worked two jobs to make ends meet. He had to stay home because of some kind of disability. He hated me and made me feel like I was a burden to him. It was like I was being punished for doing something wrong, but I didn't know what I had done. All I knew was I hated living there.

"Just after the accident, I asked my uncle the very same question you just asked me. I still remember his answer to this very day. He said, 'Catherine, death is to be feared. You take your shot in life and when it's over, you better hope you've done more good than bad. You might make it out okay. But if you've been bad, well, there's a fiery pit waiting for you.' I never forgot that, after all this time. Every time I did something I wasn't supposed to, even if I accidentally did something wrong, he'd remind me about the 'fiery pit.'

"I prayed at first... I really did. But God or an angel never came to rescue me. It never got any better, in fact, it got worse. Sometimes, my uncle would hit me while he was on one of his drunken binges. I just had to stay out of his way. I did that for ten long years. Until I met your father. Then I got out of there as soon as I could."

Joel was stunned. He had never heard anything about his mother's life before she married his dad. He never even thought to ask. A growing sadness flowed over him as he watched his mother wipe away teardrops. He put his arm across her shoulder.

"I'm sorry that had to happen to you, Mom," he said.

She smiled and patted his hand. "That's all right. It was a long time ago. But let's not talk about death anymore. Okay?"

"Sure," said Joel.

He was sure he would talk with his mom about what happens after you die someday, but it wouldn't be for a very long time.

---

Joel had invited Beth and Nate to meet him at the shelter. He figured it wasn't so bad to let them know where he lived. After all, everybody lives somewhere. They walked out behind the shelter where there was a small picnic area and a playground. At the far end of the playground was a basketball court. A ball sat near one of the poles. Nate gestured toward the court. "You play B-ball?"

"Nah. Never had the time."

"No time like the present. C'mon. I'll show you a few moves."

Nate and Joel played one-on-one basketball while Beth watched. Joel wasn't very good, not having played much, but Nate talked him through the basics and he caught on quickly.

After a while, the three sat at a picnic table nearby. Miranda was still very much on Joel's mind. In the two weeks since she had been taken to the hospital, he had felt guilty about not visiting after that first time. He had constantly asked the volunteers at the shelter if they had heard any news about her, but there never was.

Nate broke his line of thought. "Hey, you were getting pretty good at those lay-ups. You've got the speed and coordination. A little more practice and you could try out for the team at school."

"No thanks," said Joel. "I mean, this is fun and all, but I'm not cut out to be a team player. Besides, look at me. I'm too short for basketball."

Nate tapped his temple. "You're only as short as you think."

Beth said to Nate, "What's that supposed to mean?" Then she turned to Joel. "Joel, you can try out for any team or sport you want. But don't let Joe Jock here push you into something you don't really want to do."

Joel laughed. "Hey, he could be my agent. Of course, I wouldn't sign on for less than ten million dollars, plus advertising rights!"

"Yeah," chimed Nate, "then we could get them to name some shoes after you!"

"We could call them 'Joel Jumpers'!" said Joel, still laughing.

Beth grinned, but shook her head in mock disgust. "Jocks."

While they were still laughing, Mrs. Sutherland walked over to the picnic table.

"Joel, I've got some very bad news."

Joel quickly stopped chuckling. Mrs. Sutherland had a pained expression that he had never seen before. He wanted to say something to cheer her up, but nothing came to mind. She hesitated, her hands tightly clasped together. He said, "What is it, Mrs. S.?"

"Mrs. Benton … Miranda … she passed away early this morning. I'm so sorry."

---

Black pants. Black jacket. White shirt. Black tie. Joel stared at someone he barely recognized in the men's room mirror at the shelter. He couldn't believe he was going to Miranda's funeral. Just three days ago, they had gotten the news about Miranda and since then thoughts seemed to drift around in his head without meaning or purpose. He never said he wanted to go to the funeral, but, then again, he never said he didn't want to either. It was like he was running on automatic. Just letting things happen as they came.

Joel had never been to a funeral before, and he wasn't sure how he felt about it. In all the street fights he'd been in or seen, he had never seen a dead person, at least not that he knew of and not up close. A tap on the door fizzled his thoughts. It was his mother.

"Joel, we've got to go soon. Are you almost ready?"

"Yeah," said Joel, as he straightened his tie. "In a minute."

*A minute. A day. A year. What difference would it make? Time would keep going, on and on,* thought Joel. But not for Miranda. Time had run out for her. And he would never spend another second with her again. Ever.

---

Joel walked into the chapel at the funeral home and quickly sat in the back. Miranda lay in her casket at the front of the room. She looked so peaceful, like she was sleeping. With her makeup on, hair neatly combed, and wearing a fine dress, she didn't look like the Miranda he knew.

Every pew in the little room was packed. Joel certainly expected to see volunteers from the shelter, and they were all there, but he had no idea Miranda had so many other friends and family. Most were older, but many were young adults, teenagers, and a few younger children. A thin girl, younger than Joel, sat next to him. Joel caught himself staring at her when she looked at him. He averted his gaze, but the girl's tiny voice made him look back.

"How did you know Mrs. Benton?" she asked.

"Oh, uh," stammered Joel. "She was a volunteer at the family shelter where I live." Joel no longer felt any shame in saying where he lived. Miranda had made him feel like the shelter was just as much a home as any place else.

"She taught me a lot about God and Jesus and the Bible. How about you?" he said.

"She was my Sunday school teacher," she said with a sniffle. "She always made us laugh. Always made Bible stories fun. She…" The girl let out little sobs between the words. "She… was… she was the best teacher I ever… ever had." With her head bowed, the girl wiped her nose with her sleeve.

The girl made Joel feel even more miserable. He began to realize that Miranda must have brought happiness to everyone she met. And now, only a deep wound and memories were all that remained of her. His thoughts took an ugly turn. Why did God take her away? What was the point of getting close to someone if they were just going to die anyway?

The pastor of her church got up to speak. He paused at the podium, cleared his throat, smoothed his notes, and then began the eulogy.

"Dear family members and friends of Miranda Benton, it is with great sadness and yet great joy that we meet on this occasion of her change of address from earth to heaven. Jesus said, 'I am the resurrection and the life. He who believes in me will live; even though he dies; and whoever lives and believes in me will never die.'"

The pastor's speech helped Joel see Miranda's death as a necessary part of life. He still missed her, but he realized she was in heaven now, a much better place to live than here. And he felt a twinge of hope when the pastor reminded him that, as a believer, he would see her again someday.

## CHAPTER 18

Early on a warm Saturday morning in May, Joel, Nate, and Beth boarded a school bus along with twenty other teenagers for a two-hour trip to the retreat camp. While most everyone else engaged in excited conversation, Joel stared out the window in silence. *This would be a good time to get away,* he mused, *especially because of all the places at the shelter that reminded him of Miranda.*

Soon after the trip began, the tall buildings of the city gave way to one- and two-story homes spread further apart, then to sprawling farms and green rolling pastures. The city was the only place Joel had ever lived or seen, so each scene that rushed past the window was a new and absorbing experience. As the bus neared the camp, he marveled at the high rocky hills that rose steeply from both sides of the road. His ears popped as the bus ascended the mountain highway.

Finally, after carefully negotiating a narrow, twisting gravel road through dense forest, the bus squeaked to a stop at a large log cabin. The "Lodge," Nate told him, housed the counselors' sleeping quarters, a large dining room for all camp attendees, and smaller rooms with large comfortable sofas and chairs for hanging out. Everyone jumped out of the bus squealing in anticipation, but Joel took his time soaking in his new surroundings. He was out of his element, uneasy at the wide-open spaces. But at the same time, he was strangely attracted to the place and especially wondered what was beyond the thick row of trees at the edge of the camp.

The last one off the bus, Joel surveyed the camp. Surrounding the Lodge was a large open field going off in all directions. Along one edge of the field, near a thick wall of trees, were about twenty small log cabins where they would be sleeping. Closer to the Lodge and to the left, the field sloped down to a lake with a dock where several row boats and canoes were tied. Further along the lakeshore was a small sandy beach and a roped-off swimming area. Behind the Lodge were three smaller buildings and a paved basketball court.

After registering at the Lodge, Joel followed Nate to one of the log cabins that they would be sharing with two other boys. Nate called out, "top bunk" and threw his sleeping bag and small suitcase onto the upper bunk. Joel was happy to take the bottom bunk. It would be easier to negotiate in the dark from there.

Having some free time before lunch, the four boys sat on their bunks getting to know each other. The two other boys, brothers named Ben and Chuck, were from another church. Joel told about his life now—even talking about living in the shelter—with surprising ease, without mentioning his former exploits with the Blades. It still embarrassed him to think about the life he had led not so long ago. Ben asked him, "So, Joel, what church do you go to?"

The question had taken Joel by surprise. "Well, I, um…"

Nate cut in. "He goes to my church. That right, Joel?"

Joel glanced at Nate and grinned. "That's right. Just what I was going to say."

The large bell outside the Lodge rang out to signal that lunch was ready. Everyone ran to the Lodge and stood in line at the double screen door entrance. The line moved smoothly and soon Beth, Nate, and Joel were happily eating hotdogs and potato chips, and drinking fruit punch that Nate called "bug juice."

Joel was curious. "Why do you call it 'bug juice'?"

Nate smiled. "Leave a half-cup outside in the summertime. Come back an hour later and you'll know what I mean. They love it!"

That afternoon was spent playing a game called "Soul Survivor." The group was divided into two "tribes" and competed in a series of physical challenges, including an obstacle course in which the smallest team member was carried by the rest of the team over, under, and through various obstacles. Joel was the one carried on his team, and although he hated being the center of attention, his team won easily.

After a supper of meatloaf, mashed potatoes, beans, and bug juice, everyone went to a wooded corner of the camp where a mound of ashes lay inside a circle of large stones. A U-shaped string of split-log seats surrounded the fire pit. A large wooden beam cross stood at the top of the U. As the sun dipped below the treetops, camp counselors brought dry branches and logs from the surrounding forest and placed them upright in the fire pit. Soon a blazing fire became the center of attention.

Pastor Andy gave a talk about the beauty of God's creation and read some verses from the Bible. Next, one of the counselors produced a guitar and led the group in singing several songs. Joel was a little embarrassed that everyone knew all the songs except him, although he had remembered some of them from the youth conference at the sports arena.

Some of the campers held marshmallow-laden sticks near glowing logs while others carried on animated conversations with old and new friends. Nate showed Joel how to make s'mores with toasted marshmallows, Graham crackers, and a Hershey's bar.

The immense flames crackled and flickered. Hot embers occasionally escaped the inferno and floated up toward the pink streaked sky. Joel briefly flashed back to that terrible night of the apartment fire. But suddenly he realized if his apartment hadn't burned up, he never would have met Beth and Nate at his new school, and he never would have gone on this retreat. Bathed in the warmth of the fire and new friends, it occurred to Joel that he had never been happier and wished this time would never end. All his problems—Derrick, the Blades, living in the shelter, even the pain of losing Miranda—were no more than faint images in a distant fog.

Finally, though the flames and conversations hardly dwindled, Pastor Andy gave a final prayer and then sent everyone to their cabins for the night. Joel and Nate found their way to the cabin by the light of their flashlights. Halfway there, Nate stopped and shut off his light. Joel did likewise. In the near-total darkness, Joel gazed at the starry canopy overhead. He had no idea there were so many stars in the sky! Nate told him you could see more stars in the country than in the city because it was so much darker here.

"You know what else is cool?" Nate continued. "Pastor Andy says God made every one of the billions and billions of stars and put them exactly where He wanted them."

Joel had thought that God's power must be pretty amazing to have created everything on earth and to know even the number of hairs on his head, as he remembered Miranda had said. But now, realizing his power extended out into outer space and was multiplied billions of times, it was far beyond his wildest imagination.

Awestruck, he could only whisper a low, "Wow."

---

Hour after endless hour slipped by, but still Joel lay wide awake in his bunk. In the city, he would be lulled to sleep by the familiar sounds of cars and trucks rumbling by on a nearby street, people's shouts and arguments, and even an occasional gunshot. But listening to the constant rapid clicking of crickets, a hooting owl, and the intermittent bullfrog's bellow, he wondered if he had been transported to some alien planet.

He gently kicked the upper bunk. "Hey, Nate, you asleep?"

After a moment, Nate's head appeared over the edge of the bed. "Nah, just listening to the night. Awesome, huh?"

"You kidding? I can't stand it! How can anybody get any sleep around here?"

Nate let out a hearty laugh. Groggy complaints from Ben and Chuck made him whisper.

"This your first time? In the woods, I mean?"

"Yeah. Kinda spooky."

"You'll get used to it."

"Hey Nate..."

"Yeah?"

"I've been thinking about what Pastor Andy said last night."

"He's great isn't he? What about?"

"Well, the part about how Christians are supposed to confess their sins. There is something I want to get off my chest. It's really bugging me, and I don't know what to do about it."

"Hey man, you can trust me," said Nate as he swung his legs around to the edge of the bed. Cat-like, he jumped down and sat on Joel's bed. "What is it?"

Joel took a deep breath then told Nate about the life he had led in the past, even the staged accident, and the attempted video store robbery. He talked about Derrick and how he was the one who masterminded the whole thing and that the police had not been able to find him.

"And as far as I know," he said, "I'm the only one who knows where Derrick is hiding."

"Wow," said Nate. "That's some story. You gotta go to the police and tell them where Derrick is. You know that, right?"

"Me? I don't know. I mean, what if Derrick finds out? He'll kill me. I'm not kidding. He would. Besides, I'm sure the police would want to arrest me too. I... I've done some bad things too." The confession didn't seem to bother Nate. Maybe that's why he had become such a good friend.

Nate said, "Well, that's a decision you have to make. You might have to take what's coming to you in order to make sure Derrick gets what's coming to him. You know what I mean?"

"Yeah. Maybe. I don't know."

"Listen. Maybe you need to sleep on it. And then we can talk more about it tomorrow, if that's okay with you."

"Sure. See you tomorrow."

---

Early the next morning, Joel awoke to a new disturbance—the constant chirping and squeaking of a countless variety of birds that made their home in the nearby forest. He missed the city sounds he was more comfortable with and couldn't wait to get a good night's sleep back home.

The boys were already dressed and had brushed their teeth in the common bathhouse by the time the bell rang for breakfast. Nate and Joel sat down at one of the long bench seats saving a spot for Beth. As she walked down the aisle, her toe seemed to grab the wooden floor, and she almost flipped her tray full of scrambled eggs and bacon onto a group of campers. After profuse apologies, she sat between the Joel and Nate, her face beet red.

Nate shook his head solemnly. "You know, Beth, you really need to practice that walking thing some more."

Beth frowned and gave her brother a punch on the arm.

After they had started eating, Nate leaned behind Beth and tugged on Joel's shirtsleeve.

"Hey Joel, is it okay if I tell Beth what you told me last night?" Joel shrugged his shoulders.

Nate whispered the gist of Joel's story to Beth. After a moment, she stopped eating while Nate finished up the story.

"Joel," she said. "I had no idea. You know you have to tell the police where Derrick is, right?"

"I don't know. What if Derrick finds out? You don't know what he'd do to me if that happened. I'm sure it would not be a pretty sight."

"It's the right thing to do," said Beth.

"That's easy for you to say. You don't have to deal with him."

"That's true, but I really believe God will protect you in some way. You know, God is stronger than any problems we might have."

Joel thought for a moment. "I guess you're right."

Nate chimed in. "Hey listen, I could go with you, if you want. You know, for moral support."

"No," said Joel quickly. The last thing he wanted was to mix his good friends up with the bad side of his life. "I think it would be better if I did this myself."

"If that's what you want," said Nate. "But anytime you need me, you just say the word, and I'll be there. Really."

Joel smiled. "Thanks, Nate. I appreciate it."

Beth touched Joel's arm. "But the first thing you have to do is pray for God's protection."

Joel shook his head. "Yeah, I guess so."

"There's one other thing," she said.

"What's that?"

"You have to forgive Derrick for the way he's treated you."

"*What?* No way!"

"But Joel," Beth pleaded. "Weren't you forgiven for all your sins when you gave your life to Jesus?"

Joel bit his lower lip. "Yeah, I was. So what?"

"Well, since you know God is willing to forgive you even though you don't deserve it, don't you think He would also forgive Derrick?"

"I never thought of it that way. I guess so."

"So, if you don't forgive Derrick, it's like you disagree with God, and like it or not, that's the beginning of sin."

Joel thought for a long time. Some of the campers were already starting to leave the dining room. Finally, he said, "So do I still have to forgive him while he's bashing my head in?"

Beth laughed. "That's where the Lord comes in. No matter what happens, He's going to be on your side. You can count on Him."

Joel managed a little grin. "Well, I just hope he brings his boxing gloves!"

# CHAPTER 19

Muffled snoring, grunts, and an occasional cough were all that could be heard in the large darkened gymnasium full of homeless people. Joel lay in his cot at the shelter and stared at the back-lit clock on the wall. It was 3:30 a.m., but he was nowhere near sleep. For the past week, a single thought kept cutting through his mind: *Derrick wanted to kill him*. One thing he knew about Derrick was that he usually got what he wanted. If enough time went by, maybe Derrick wouldn't be so angry about his refusal to help him. But if he turned him in to the police, it would only make things worse. It would make him angrier and more determined to get his revenge. Somehow, some way, Derrick would find him and punish him. And he would make sure it was as painful as possible. Joel shook his head. *No. There's no way I can do this.*

Joel rolled on his side and tried to think about how he could get out of the city, at least for a few months. Minutes later, he fell into a deep sleep.

Joel's thoughts troubled God. He could clearly see the end result of the path he was contemplating. Although He would allow Joel to go his own way, He knew it would lead to unbearable hunger, emotional and physical pain, and an intensity of fear that he had never felt before. Even before Joel was born, God had lovingly laid out the path for his life with perfect foresight.

He caused Joel to enter a deep sleep and whispered to his subconscious mind, "Joel, I know the plans I have for you. Plans to prosper you and not to harm you, plans to give you hope and a future. Go to the police station tomorrow and do what you must do. It's the right thing to do. It's what I want you to do. Do not worry. I am faithful, and I will strengthen you and protect you from the Evil One."

---

The next day Joel found himself in a large, noisy room filled with police officers busily involved in the work of apprehending criminals and beginning the process of bringing them to justice. He had spoken to a policeman earlier and was now sitting next to his desk waiting for him to return. It was amazing how, when he had awoken this morning, he had no fear at all about what might happen to him if Derrick found out what he was doing. Not only that, he felt a strange calmness as he got dressed, ate, and then took a bus to the police station. Somehow, he knew—just *knew* deep down—that God wanted him to be there.

A little sign on the desk read, "Officer William DePaul." The officer returned from the file room and sat down examining the contents of a folder without saying a word. He was younger than most policemen, but had a tired face and never smiled. Finally, he read the list of charges against Derrick. "Vehicle theft, attempted robbery, aggravated assault…"

Joel shivered inside as he realized the seriousness and extent of Derrick's crimes. Officer DePaul went on, "...and Vehicular Homicide."

"What? What does that mean?"

DePaul gave Joel that "stupid question" look.

"It means he used a vehicle to kill someone."

"But...nobody was killed in the accident," Joel exploded. *"Were they?"*

"There was an elderly woman who apparently hit the car in front of hers, then another car hit her from behind. She had a heart attack on the spot and was pronounced dead at the hospital a few hours later."

Joel stared at the floor for a moment then said, "When you catch him, he'll go to jail for sure?"

"With your testimony and other witnesses' stories, there is very little chance that he will get off. It will be up to the court to decide what happens to him, of course. But my guess is he'll be tried as an adult and sent to prison for a very long time."

Joel looked into the officer's eyes. "Then I want to do whatever I can to make that happen."

"There's one more thing. You were in on the plan, right?"

"Yeah. So?"

"So, that makes you an accessory to the same crimes. You could be convicted as well."

Joel swallowed hard. He hadn't thought of that. Officer DePaul went on.

"Now, because you're willing to testify against Derrick, the judge will likely be more lenient in your case. And it would be even better if you could somehow help us apprehend him."

"What if I told you when and where to pick him up? Would the judge, maybe, go easier on me then?"

DePaul managed a little smile. "Yes, I believe that would be a distinct possibility."

Joel put out his hand. "It's a deal then."

After they shook hands, DePaul asked, "Let me ask you something."

"Sure."

"Why are you doing this? I mean, you know it's the right thing to do, but usually kids in a gang stick with it till the very end. They would rather go to juvy than rat out their friends. But you had a choice. You didn't have to come in here and help catch your leader, and possibly risk incriminating yourself. Why'd you do it?"

Joel didn't have to think about it. He said, "You know, God's watching everything I do. And I'm on His side now. He went to bat for me. He's my leader now. I wanna do what He wants. You know what I mean?"

Officer DePaul smiled broader this time. "Yeah. Believe it or not, I think I do."

---

Joel stared out of the bus window on the ride back to the shelter. Going back to his apartment where Derrick was staying was out of the question. He would have to contact him indirectly. But how was he going to get an unsuspecting Derrick to a pre-arranged place so the police could grab him? What would Derrick want? Then it came to him. In the burned out apartment, Derrick had said he needed food and money so he could get out of the city. He also had a hunger for drugs. Joel nodded to himself. That would definitely lure him out.

---

Joel approached the video arcade where most of the Blades hung out. Although he hated going back to his old neighborhood and talking with Blade members, it was the only way he could contact Derrick to set up a meeting. He said a short prayer for protection and hoped God would hear it.

It was Saturday night, and the arcade was packed and noisy. Just outside the video arcade was the last person Joel expected to see: Tonya. She was hanging out with a small group of girls. All of them had a red italicized "*A*" painted on their cheeks. Across the back of their black leather jackets was the word *Amazons*.

Joel wasn't ready for the conversation he needed to have with Tonya; but he had no choice. It was now or never. He tapped her on the shoulder and she turned dreamily.

"Hey Joel," she purred. "Where you been?" Her eyes were glassy and red around the edges, and Joel immediately noticed the scent of alcohol.

"Tonya, what are you doing here?"

Tonya started swaying to the music. "I'm havin' fun, that's what. So, like I said, where have you been? What are the Blades doing these days? You won't believe the great gang I'm in now. We do lots of stuff together. We're like sisters. It's just like you said it would be."

"Tonya," he said, "I need to tell you something."

Tonya tried to put her arms around Joel's neck, but he gently took them off. He noticed she was wearing heavy makeup masking the pretty face that had attracted him months ago. In that moment, Joel realized the relationship was over but that he still cared about her and worried that her life was headed in the wrong direction. He was especially determined to try to change her mind about joining a gang, because he was the one who had encouraged her to do so. He thought the direct approach would work best.

"Tonya, I need to tell you that I was wrong about gangs. They're no good. That's not the way to go. Listen, there's something better…"

Tonya pushed him away, squinting in anger. "What are you talking about? Things couldn't be better."

"Tonya, you don't understand. They'll take advantage of you. Then, when you really need them, they'll let you down. Every time. Believe me, I know."

Tonya shook her head. "Man, what happened to you? You're not the same Joel I used to know."

*That's truer than you know*, Joel mused. He opened his mouth to answer, but Tonya continued.

"You don't know what you're talking about. We Amazons, we're tight, you know? Maybe they won't make my life any better, but I feel better about my life hanging out with them."

"You're wrong, Tonya. I'm telling you the truth."

"Then why did you tell me maybe I should join a gang? Huh? You said it was better than family. Wasn't that the truth?"

"I thought it was, at the time. But I was wrong."

"So how do you know you're not wrong now?"

"I just know. That's all. Listen…"

Tonya put her hand up cutting him off. "You're so full of it, you know that? For once in my life, I feel like I'm part of something. I'm with people who care about me, and you're not going to take that away from me."

Joel knew Tonya would not listen to him. His words were like rubber bands hitting a brick wall, incapable of making the slightest impression.

He shook his head and said, "Then I guess this is good-bye, Tonya." She opened her mouth to speak, but Joel walked past her and into the arcade.

Nick, the thin and bearded night manager of the arcade, wore his usual Superman T-shirt and rumpled blue jeans. He was much older than most of the players and had deeply set bloodshot eyes and long, scruffy hair. His job was to simply stand guard over a glass counter filled with boxes of assorted toys and trinkets. Little numbered signs were attached to each box. Occasionally, a player gave him a long string of tickets, and he lazily passed it through a counting machine and then handed over an appropriate prize.

With a couple of dozen conversations going on at once and music blaring over the din, it was too loud to speak in a normal tone of voice. Joel stopped at the counter and half shouted, "Hey Nick, you seen Derrick?"

Nick gave an uneasy expression, stroked his short goatee, and then spoke louder than necessary. "I don't want no trouble.

Derrick comes in here, you take your business with him outside. Okay?"

Four months ago, Joel would have relished the fear incited by the Blades' reputation. But now, it hurt to see a grown man cower at the mere presence of a gang member. He tried to console Nick.

"Listen, I don't want to cause trouble. I just need to see Derrick. I need to talk to him for a minute. That's all."

A shrill voice sounded behind him. "I seen him the other day." It was Mickey.

Joel turned around. If there was anyone who made it his business to know everything that was going on, it was Mickey.

In his mind, Joel replayed Mickey's last words to him after their run-in at his old school: *You better watch your back.*

Words like those could never be ignored, especially when someone's reputation was at stake.

Brian Evans, the Blade member who pulled on Tonya's hair in the school cafeteria, came up beside Mickey. Joel remembered how he humiliated Brian that day. Arms folded, the larger boy wore the smirk of someone about to get his revenge.

Joel didn't want to give away the fact that he knew where Derrick was hiding. He glanced at Brian and then said to Mickey, "Do you know where Derrick's hiding out? I need to talk to him."

Mickey gave a devilish grin. "Maybe. Maybe not. Why do you want to know and what's in it for me?"

"Listen, you don't need to know my business, 'cause it doesn't concern you. If you know where he is, you better tell me."

"Hey," said Brian, menacingly. "Don't be threatening Mickey. You got a beef with him, you gotta go through me first. You got that?" He emphasized his last words by poking Joel's chest.

The old Joel would have mocked Mickey for needing a bodyguard because he's too weak to fight his own battles. Then he would have swiftly attacked Brian to put him in his place. He knew now it was the wrong thing to do, but he didn't know how to handle the situation any other way. The crowd surrounding them had taken an interest in the heated conversation, no doubt hoping to see a fight.

Joel said, "Look, I'm not looking for a fight. I just need to…"

"Well you found one!" said Mickey as he pushed him through the crowd backward with a force multiplied by anger.

Someone caught him and shoved him back by the shoulders. Joel flew helplessly toward Brian, but he stepped aside and let him stumble past, glancing off an old pinball machine. By now, everyone in the arcade knew a fight was going on. They surrounded them, yelling and chanting, cheering them on.

Brian flipped open his blade and trudged toward Joel. Joel instinctively felt for his switchblade, even as he realized he never carried it anymore. Although Brian was a new Blade member and probably wouldn't fight well, he could still cut Joel with a lucky stab.

He took off his jacket and wrapped it around his arm to use as a shield. The two boys circled each other amid the charged spectators. Brian's uncertain expression and obvious lack of experience in handling a knife told Joel he had the upper hand, even without a weapon.

Knowing it was the unexpected thing to do, Joel lunged at Brian with his head low, sending him sprawling. Before Brian could recover, Joel rolled and threw his foot into Brian's chest, knocking the wind and the fight out of him.

Joel got up and rushed at Mickey, pinning both his wrists to a slopping video game. He could feel the old anger boil up inside him. It took every bit of strength to hold his voice steady.

"Listen up, Matchstick, you see Derrick, you give him this message: You tell him I've got what he wants. Tell him to meet me at the clock tower at ten o'clock Friday night, and I'll give it to him then. If you *don't* tell him and he finds out you were holding back—and he *will* find out—there won't be much left of you when he gets through with you. *Got it?*"

Mickey's demeanor quickly changed to obedient servant. "Yeah, I got it. I'll tell him for sure. Don't you worry."

The squeal of approaching sirens cleared the arcade. Joel was glad Nick had the guts to call the cops. He rushed out with the others into the warm night. Even though Joel knew he would probably pay dearly for what he was about to do, he felt good inside. Way better than the best day he ever had hanging out with the Blades. It didn't matter what Derrick might do to him. There was no fear anymore. None. As if riding on the shoulders of a mighty, fully armed giant going into battle, Joel could already sense the coming victory.

He felt badly that he wasn't able to talk Tonya into leaving the gang, but he hoped that maybe someday she'd learn the truth on her own like he had. As he rounded a corner, Joel suddenly had the horrible thought that Tonya might tell someone in the Blades that he wasn't who he used to be, and that he was actually opposed to the gang life. If word got around to Derrick, the whole plan could fall apart. And Derrick would have yet another reason to take his special revenge out on him!

# CHAPTER 20

Joel sat on his bed at the shelter amid a hundred other beds; most were occupied or soon would be. It was Friday night, the night Joel would meet Derrick at the clock tower.

Joel had remembered when Pastor Andy said how important it was to pray, to let God know about the things you were thankful for, and also to tell Him the things that were troubling you. He had watched as the young pastor led the campers in prayer and was struck at how natural it seemed to them. Prayer had felt pointless to him at the time, but now it seemed like a good idea, especially when he realized how dangerous his meeting with Derrick could be. He bowed his head and folded his hands.

"God, I know You care about me. And You know what I'm about to do. Please protect me and make everything go all right tonight. Thank you, In Jesus' name…"

…Amen.

God breathed in Joel's prayer with pure delight. The simple but pure and deeply meaningful words were to Him far sweeter than the most fragrant perfume on earth. In an instant of time, immeasurable by human standards, the Infinitely Powerful One carefully considered how He would answer Joel's heart-felt plea.

---

At 9:50 p.m., Officers DePaul and Matthews were heading toward the clock tower where Joel had told them Derrick would be. Their plan was to hide the patrol car in an alley a block away, then discreetly make their way to the tower. Wearing their street clothes, Derrick would not suspect they were police officers until it was too late.

As they turned on the road that would lead to the downtown area, they came upon a row of stopped cars. Before either could speak, the first engine of a mile-long freight train leisurely rumbled along the gated tracks.

DePaul smacked the steering wheel. "That's the nine-thirty cross-country freight. Why's it so late? Maybe we should turn back and take the expressway. It's only five minutes out of our way."

"The train might be past in five minutes," said Mathews. He glanced out the rear window as a car pulled up behind them, blocking their retreat. "Besides," he said, "we're stuck here for now."

DePaul thought briefly about turning on the siren, but in the same instant, realized it would do no good. He shook his head and raked a worried hand through his thin hair.

"Every second counts, I just hope Joel can hold out until we get there."

---

Just before 10:00 p.m., Joel arrived at the clock tower. A three-legged triangular structure higher than a two-story building, it stood on a stepped granite base. Below the clock face, near the top, was a mechanical man holding a hammer that struck a large bell once for each hour of the time.

Joel swung the book bag off his shoulder and hid it among some low bushes at the edge of the square fifty feet away. Street-sense said you always protect something of value before you give it away, just in case the deal goes bad. Derrick was expecting enough food and money to get him out of the city, and maybe some cigarettes and drugs to feed his habit. But Joel had no intention of helping him get away if he somehow evaded the police. He had stuffed the bag with newspapers and a rolled up towel he hoped would feel like a loaf of bread. He also put in an old Bible he had found in the library at the shelter. He hoped it would do Derrick some good.

A light drizzle began and Joel moved under the tower for its partial protection. He heard a whirling sound, and an instant later, the mechanical man hammered the bell, signaling the arrival of the tenth hour.

*Bong… bong… bong… bong*

Covering his ears at the thunderous reverberation, Joel wondered why the police hadn't let him know that they were there, waiting for the right moment to arrest Derrick.

*Bong… bong… bong…*

He scanned the surrounding streets and spotted two figures walking toward the square. Was it the police or…

*Bong… bong… bong…*

As the last chime dissipated into the night, Joel could see that Derrick was approaching. And with him was someone he thought he'd never see again: Karl, the leader of the Skulls. Although he was afraid of Derrick, Joel was pretty sure he would be able to hold his own with him, at least until the police took over. But joined by Karl, he felt the familiar scary sickness build up in his stomach that comes when you realize you've made a really bad mistake, and you're about to pay for it big time.

Joel wondered if Karl would remember him, and whether that would be a good thing or not. As Derrick and Karl drew near, he tried to think through how he should handle this new situation. He briefly hoped that Derrick would side with him if he told him that Karl was one of the boys who almost killed him the night he wandered into Skull territory. But experience told him Derrick would fight against even a fellow Blade if it suited his purpose. If he was with Karl, there was probably a truce between the two gangs. No doubt Derrick was consolidating his power, maybe trying to be the leader of both gangs.

Derrick stopped within arm's length of Joel. He gestured with his head and said, "I heard some interesting news about you."

---

Abner could feel the paralyzing dread that consumed Joel as the increasingly tense situation unfolded. Momentarily taking his gaze off the three boys at the clock tower, he reverently addressed the Father, "Surely Joel is in mortal danger, Father. Will You send a warrior angel to fight for him?"

God presided over all of human activity simultaneously, lovingly investing His attention to each individual. "That will not be necessary," He said. "But before he can claim victory over the evil ones, he must first deny himself. As I have said through my Son, 'Whoever loses his life for my sake, will find it.'"

---

Joel's heart slipped into his throat. "What do you mean?"

"Somebody said you don't like being a Blade no more. That true?"

A sudden pang attacked his stomach. This was it. The confrontation he had dreaded and hoped would never come had finally arrived. For a fleeting moment, he was glad. The sickening anticipation and worry was finally over. But it was quickly replaced by an intense fear of punishment as images of the beating Karl and the other Skulls had given him assaulted his mind.

Through parched lips, Joel blurted, "Look, it's not working out for me. I just don't think I'm cut out for the gang life anymore, you know? I mean, I'm doing okay now. With... without the Blades... but you don't have to worry. I would never tell anyone about..."

Derrick spat out, "Do you know what happens to *deserters?* They get taught a lesson, then tossed aside like a useless rag doll. There's no such thing as not being a Blade once you're in. You're either a Blade for life, or you're dead. Simple as that."

Joel swallowed hard. Derrick went on, feigned kindness entering his voice. "But I'll tell you what. I'll cut you some slack, seeing as how you're willing to help me get out of the city and all. If I like what you brought me, I might let you off the hook. That sound like a fair deal?"

Joel could only nod wordlessly. The drizzle had strengthened to a light but steady rain. Thunder echoed somewhere in the distance. He desperately needed more time. If the police didn't come in the next few seconds, it would be way too late. He looked at Karl, then back at Derrick. The knot in his stomach had tightened, twisting up his insides.

"Well, there's not enough for both of you," he said, hoping to buy a few precious seconds.

"Don't worry about that. It just better be what I need. Where is it?" Joel pointed in the direction of the bushes. Derrick said to Karl, "Go get it."

In a few seconds, the bag's contents would be discovered, but there was nothing he could say or do to stop the inevitable. Fear invaded every part of his body, paralyzing his arms and legs, choking the very breath out of him. The only thought that bubbled up was: *Run. Run for your life before ...*

Out of the corner of his eye, Joel noticed a shadow meandering in their general direction. The man plodded along, shoulders slouched, without purpose or definite direction. Lightning flashed nearby, and Joel could see it was Abner, the homeless man he had met in the church. A second later, a crack of thunder exploded, shaking the earth.

Abner almost passed them by, but then he seemed to recognize Joel and headed toward him with a wide grin.

"Well, hey there young man," he said. "What's going on?"

Derrick growled, "Hey, you drunken old fool, you got no business here. Keep moving."

Ignoring Derrick's command, Abner came between the two boys and greeted a stunned Joel with a vigorous handshake. He then turned and held out a hand to Derrick.

"Abner's the name. And you are…?"

"Hey Derrick," Karl called out. "The little twerp duped you, man. There ain't nothing in here but a buncha newspapers, a towel, and an old Bible."

Derrick clicked his switchblade. "Man, you're gonna pay for all the trouble you caused me. And you can forget about getting off the hook for wanting to leave the Blades. You're dead for sure!"

"Now hold on there," said Abner. "That's no way to settle an argument."

Derrick let out a sinister laugh, then shot a hateful gaze at Abner. He waved the blade in front of Abner's face. "What are you, some kinda bodyguard? So is that why you don't want to stay in the Blades, huh?"

Derrick walked around Abner, sizing him up. "You think this bum is going to protect you?" He slapped the back of Abner's head from behind. "Huh? What do you say, old man? You willing to take me on?"

"Derrick," said Joel, "quit picking on him. He's got nothing to do with this."

"Oh, but that's where you're wrong, little man. Your friend has stumbled onto something here. I can't let him talk about it to the police, now can I? He's a witness to what I'm about to do to you. And we can't have *that!*" Derrick suddenly thrust the blade into Abner's midsection. Abner let out a short anguished scream, then doubled over and fell hard on the wet stone steps.

Joel was shocked into action. He set his stance in front of Abner's still form, fists clenched. The scary sickness was gone. Fear had transformed into anger, enough anger to right a terrible wrong, or die trying.

"You shouldn't have done that, Derrick. You and Karl are nothing but cowards: two men picking on a kid and an old man. You come near him again and *you're* gonna pay. I swear!"

Joel's threatening tone of voice caused Derrick and Karl to step back, surprise crossing their faces. But after a moment's hesitation, Derrick's sinister smile returned, and he set himself to lunge at Joel. "Whatever you say, punk!"

Behind Joel, Abner slowly stood up. Before they could take a step toward him, Derrick and Karl's mouths fell open, mesmerized by the risen Abner. No longer the frail homeless man, Abner stood tall and straight, a fierce and powerful adversary. He spread his arms wide as thunderous lightning exploded overhead and a fierce downward wind rooted Derrick and Karl where they stood. Abner projected into their minds a glimpse of their own putrid black souls and showed them a vivid image of the eternal torturous wrath that awaits all enemies of God.

It was more than they could bear. Screaming, they turned to run and stumbled over each other. Derrick shot a quick fearful glance back, and then both boys dashed away into the night as Abner returned to his slouched stature.

Joel couldn't believe it! Two of the most feared gang leaders in the neighborhood scampering away from him like scared rats. How could they have been so terrified of him? Joel turned to help Abner up, but was surprised to see him already standing.

"Abner!" he said. "Are you all right? I thought you were hurt real bad. Lemme see where he stabbed you."

Abner removed his hand from the place the blade had entered. There was no blood, no wound. Even his shirt showed no sign of being penetrated. "I guess I got lucky," he said with a grin.

They looked in the direction Derrick and Karl had fled, just as the police officers intercepted them. Joel smiled as he watched them handcuff the hysterical boys.

"Guess they won't be causing trouble for a while," said Joel. He took a long, deep breath. The ordeal was finally over.

---

Abner and Joel walked together in silence. Officer DePaul had offered to drive him home, but Joel had refused, preferring instead to walk off his troubling thoughts. The rain had stopped and the street glistened with distorted reflections of the surrounding lights. Joel sniffed the dank air and looked up at Abner. There was something strange about him that Joel couldn't quite figure out, something that didn't add up. He wanted to know more about this mysterious homeless man who seemed to come out of nowhere right when he needed him most. But it seemed like a silly question to ask who he really was, and so the silence continued.

At the next intersection, Joel had to turn right to go back to the shelter, but Abner started to go straight. Joel hoped he could spend more time with him, so he said, "Hey, Abner, why don't you come to the shelter with me. I'll bet you could use a hot meal and a comfortable bed."

Abner grinned. Joel thought he looked happy but kind of sad at the same time.

"No," he said. "It's not time for me to go there. You go on. Your mom's wondering where you are."

"Will I ever see you again?" he said, a lump growing in his throat. He didn't really want to hear the answer.

Abner put his arm around Joel's shoulder and gave him tight squeeze. "Sure," he said with a chuckle. "I can guarantee you will see me again someday!"

# CHAPTER 21

Three weeks after the incident at the clock tower, Joel walked into the courtroom where Derrick's trial was being held. All the walls in the brightly lit room were covered floor to ceiling in dark walnut panels. A group of men and women sat behind a low wooden wall on the right side of the courtroom, near the front. In the back of the room, dozens of people watched the proceedings, including his mom, Beth, and Nate.

"All rise," said the bailiff. Everyone in the room rose in unison. "Hear ye, hear ye, the Criminal Court for the City of New York is now in session. The Honorable Judge James Keeling the Third presiding. All having business before this honorable court draw near, give attention, and you shall be heard. You may be seated." The judge, a white-haired man wearing a black robe, sat at a high desk that resembled a fortress.

"State of New York versus Derrick Wicker," called the Bailiff.

Another man stood. "The State calls Joel Somers," he said.

As he was led to the witness stand next to the judge, Joel noticed Derrick sitting at a table across the room and a flutter of panic gripped him. He imagined the anger that must be burning inside him. He was a trapped animal and would stop at nothing to take his revenge. Derrick's angry sneer sent a clear message that meant: *When this is over I'm going to kill you!*

The lawyer for the state, Mr. Welton, flashed a friendly smile at Joel. He asked him questions to clarify the facts of the case.

"Please state your name for the record."

"Joel Somers."

"Please speak into the microphone, Joel. Was Derrick the leader of the gang called The Blades?"

"Yes."

"Was he involved in stealing Jack's brother's Jeep?"

"Yes."

"Did you see Derrick grab the steering wheel and purposely swerve into oncoming traffic?"

"Yes."

"Did he use the accident as a distraction so other gang members could rob the video store?"

"Yes."

"When the police arrived, did he run away to avoid capture and without helping Jack, who had been injured in the crash?"

"Yes."

Mr. Welton turned toward the judge. "No further questions, your Honor."

Judge Keeling said, "Your witness, Mr. Ferguson."

Derrick's attorney, who was appointed by the sate, stood up and approached Joel. He was young and well dressed in expensive-looking clothes. He had a devious grin, as if he knew some secret that would change everything. If it was enough to cause the jury to decide that Derrick was not guilty, he was as good as dead.

The defense attorney leaned on the rail that surrounded Joel. "Joel," he said, in a friendly tone. "You are a member of the Blades. Is that correct?"

"Not any more."

"But you were a member in good standing at the time of the...um...incident in question? Is that right?"

"Yeah, I guess so."

"Yes?"

"Yes. I was."

"And you and Derrick are best friends. Isn't that right?"

"No, I wouldn't say that." Joel was getting nervous. Where was he going with these questions?

"Did you ever have an altercation with Derrick?"

"A what?"

"A fight. Did you ever have a fight with him or maybe a heated argument? Anything like that?"

"Yes. We had a few."

"Tell us about them."

Joel talked about the time Derrick threw him out of the Jeep after the accident and when he had chased him out of his own apartment at knifepoint. He also told how Derrick threatened him the night he was captured by the police.

"So, you really don't like Derrick very much, do you?"

"No, I don't." Joel glanced at Derrick, who flashed an odd grin. "I don't like him at all."

"Could it be that you're trying to get back at him? To take revenge on him for all the grief he's caused you?"

"No."

The attorney ignored Joel's response. He moved closer and raised his voice a bit. "And that maybe you never really saw all the things you said he did earlier?"

Mr. Welton jumped up. "Objection, your Honor. Leading the witness."

"Sustained," said the judge.

Ferguson ignored the warning. Raising his voice another notch, he said, "You are making this story up just to get back at Derrick, aren't you? Answer me, Joel. *Aren't you?*"

A loud commotion raced across the courtroom as the judge slammed the gavel several times. "Order! Mr. Ferguson you will refrain from this line of questioning or find yourself in contempt! Order in this courtroom!"

As the courtroom quieted down, Mr. Ferguson addressed the judge. "Your Honor, I am attempting to establish that Joel Somers is a hostile witness and that his testimony may unfairly influence the outcome of this trial. If the fate of my client hangs on the story of one disgruntled boy, I do not see the basis for continuing…"

While Mr. Ferguson was speaking, Joel started to get that sickening feeling that meant this was going very badly and something had to be done quickly to make it right again. He clearly remembered the way Derrick had almost gleefully taken control of the Jeep to force a head-on collision and could almost feel the bone-bruising impact of the collision seconds later. He remembered he almost killed Eddie and then Abner. Derrick was way out of control and had to be stopped.

Joel leaned close to the microphone and shouted, "Can I say something?" The courtroom froze. Mr. Ferguson stopped in mid-sentence, his mouth stuck open. All eyes were on Joel at the sudden outburst. Then to the judge he said, softly, "Can I?"

The judge said, "This is highly irregular, son, but I would like to hear what you have to say."

"Your Honor," Mr. Ferguson stammered. "I must protest. This is a *hostile* witness and my client…"

"Clamp it, Charlie," said Judge Keeling. Then to Joel, "Go on, son."

Joel took a deep breath, then continued. "What Derrick did was worse than anything he had ever done to me. I used to look up to him. I used to think he was cool. But now I know how bad he really is. And I know if I tell the truth, he will get what he deserves." He glared at Derrick then at Mr. Ferguson. "And you can't change the truth no matter how hard you try."

Beth and Nate sat with Joel and his mother on a long bench in the hallway outside the courtroom. Two hours after Joel's testimony, Mr. Welton sat down with them. "The jury is ready to give their verdict to the judge," he said. They shuffled into the court room.

Murmurings in the courtroom suddenly stopped as Judge Keeling walked in from a side door and sat at the bench. The bailiff ordered, "All rise."

Judge Keeling banged his gavel once. "This court is now in session," he announced. "Pleased be seated." Silently, the bailiff handed him a paper from the lead juror. The courtroom collectively held its breath. "Will the defendant please stand," said the judge. Derrick and his attorney stood.

"For the charge of vehicle theft: *guilty*!" barked the judge. "For the charge of attempted robbery: *guilty*. For the charge of aggravated assault: *guilty*. For the charge of vehicular homicide." He paused before pronouncing the most serious charge. "*Guilty*!"

Keeling pounded his gavel to quiet the excited buzz in the room and then addressed the accused. "Derrick Wicker, do you understand the severity of this verdict?"

"Yeah, whatever." His lawyer elbowed him. "I mean, yes sir. Yes, your Honor."

"Mr. Wicker," said the judge. "You have been convicted of some very serious charges against society, for which you will pay by spending some length of time confined to a correctional institution. It is the hope of this court that during that time, you will realize the error of your ways and emerge as a law-abiding citizen. Do you have any final statement you would like to make?"

"No, not really. Yeah, on second thought, I want to say this whole thing is a farce. And when I catch the runt who set me up, I'm gonna…"

The judge hammered the gavel several times. "That's enough, young man. Bailiff, take the prisoner back to his cell. The sentencing hearing will commence in four weeks. This case is closed." He slammed the gavel once as he spoke his final word.

The court clerk, sitting nearby at a lower desk, handed the judge a file, the next case on the docket. After sifting through the papers for a few moments, he called out across the courtroom, "Joel Somers. Approach the bench."

Joel walked up to the large fortress-like desk alongside Mr. Welton. He was shivering inside. Even though the attorney said the judge would probably be lenient, he knew that he could rule any way he saw fit, for any reason, and there was no arguing with his final decision.

The judge spoke to him in a low, kind tone, but still deep and full of authority. "Joel Somers, you have got some very bad marks against you, young man."

"Yes, your Honor, I know."

"You are what we call an accessory to the crimes committed by Derrick Wicker. That means you were there during the planning and the commission of those crimes and you went along with them. In the eyes of the law, it's as if you committed them yourself and therefore deserve the same punishment for them. Do you understand that?"

Joel swallowed hard. "Yes sir, I understand."

"You have also cooperated with the police to capture Derrick, at significant risk of personal injury or possible loss of life."

Memories of that terrible night flashed across Joel's mind. Derrick would have stabbed him for sure if he hadn't been spooked. He never did figure out why Derrick had suddenly bolted away screaming, right into the arms of the police. The judge's penetrating voice brought him back to the present.

"Your testimony helped convict Derrick, and I am convinced that you now see the error of your ways. But I cannot simply ignore your past behavior."

*Here it is.* Joel knew the next words the judge spoke would determine how he spent his immediate future and probably affect the rest of his life.

"Therefore, this court charges you of being an accessory to vehicle theft and attempted robbery." The courtroom gasped. The judge ignored the response. "You will be placed under probation for a period of six months. During that time, you will have no involvement with any gang or group bent on breaking the law. You must not break any law or disturb the peace in any way. You will meet with your probation officer once each week, who will report your activity back to the court. Six months from now, a hearing will be held, at which time a final decision will be made. If at that time it has been determined that you have met all of these conditions, these charges will be dropped. Do you have any questions, Joel?"

Joel had slowly absorbed the verdict. When he heard the part about being charged with vehicle theft and attempted robbery his mind took a fuzzy, downward spiral. What had he said? Probation? Six months? Aloud, he said, "Charges dropped?"

"After six months of good behavior. Are you clear on these conditions, son?"

Finally, the full meaning of judge's speech came flooding to him. He was free! "No questions at all, sir. Thank you, your Honor!"

---

Mr. Welton rejoined Joel, his mother, Nate, and Beth on the steps leading up to the courthouse. "Since Derrick was found guilty on all counts and was tried as an adult, chances are he'll get the maximum time in the state penitentiary."

"How long is that?" asked Beth.

"At least ten to fifteen years."

Nate chuckled, "Wow, by that time we'll be..uh..lemme see…"

Joel finished the stuttering thought, "We'll be *really old* when he gets out. And that's just fine with me."

Beth hugged Joel while Nate patted him on the back. "All right!" he said. "Case closed!"

Catherine leaned over, took his head in both hands, and kissed him on the forehead. She said, "Now maybe we can get on with our life, hmm? Someday we'll be on our own again and…"

Beth turned to Catherine. "Mrs. Somers, I've wanted to tell you something for a while now and this is as good a time as any."

"What is it Beth?"

"My parents have talked it over and, well, we have an empty apartment in our basement and we wanted to invite you and Joel to live there. They said you wouldn't have to pay any rent until you got back on your feet, and then just enough to cover the extra expenses. So, will you stay with us? Please?"

Joel's mother put a hand to her mouth. "Oh my, I don't know. That would be such a burden on your family. We couldn't possibly accept…"

"Mom, don't you see?" said Joel. "This is our chance to get on with our life, just like you said. We could start all over again. Be a real family again."

Catherine looked at her son with moist eyes and nodded. "Yes, maybe you're right. Okay Beth. We'll take you up on your very generous offer. Thank you."

## CHAPTER 22

While waiting for his sentencing hearing, Derrick was temporarily incarcerated at the Staten Island Correctional Facility, since the local jail was full. He had just turned eighteen, so he was placed in the general prison population. Sitting alone on the lower level of one of two bunk beds in his cell, his thoughts were a swirling storm of anger and revenge. "*Joel*," he said to the concrete floor. "When I get out of here, he's dead. No way he's gonna live after what he's done to me. No way."

The vanilla-colored cinderblock jail cell was bare except for the beds on both sides and a small metal sink and toilet unit at the back wall. The beds took up nearly all of the space from the back wall to the iron bars in front. A three-foot aisle the length of the cell was the only open space. The cell was illuminated by a single flickering fluorescent light in the ceiling. The two top bunks held bare, rolled-up mattresses. The other lower bunk was being used by another prisoner, its sheets and blanket tossed aside as if its owner had just gotten out of bed.

Derrick paced back and forth, a caged animal building contempt for its captors. He was clad in the orange jumpsuit and Velcro-strapped sneakers issued to all inmates. Although this cell block was reserved for temporary prisoners, he was told there was no separation of first-time offenders and hardened criminals. He stretched out on his bunk and idly wondered what his cell-mate was like. As if to answer his question, the electronically-controlled cell door unlocked and slid open with a loud *clank-clank*.

A uniformed prison guard appeared at the doorway, scanned the cell, and then stepped aside. Derrick's cellmate shuffled in. The guard said, "Hey Skunk, looks like you got a little roommate. You two play nice, ya here?" Skunk was a tall, thin man, with long tangled dreadlocks that draped over his shoulders. His face was sickly white and he wore a short goatee and moustache. A swirling multi-colored tattoo ran the length of one arm. He snarled at Derrick, and then threw himself on the lower bunk.

"Close A-five," shouted the guard and the heavy cell door slammed shut with electronic swiftness. The guard gave a sinister little laugh, then walked away, letting his night stick drag across the bars.

Derrick eyed his cellmate. He looked harmless enough. After all, he had fought boys just as tall and heavier. He grinned at the thought that he had never lost a fight in his life.

Suddenly, Skunk was on top of him. He grabbed his wrists with such power Derrick felt his hands weaken for lack of blood. He couldn't move, but no words of protest escaped from his shocked mind. Skunk's face was just inches from his own, his dreadlocks forming a tent surrounding them. He slowly opened his mouth to reveal stained, crooked, but sharp teeth. His breath smelled like rotting garbage and for a terrifying moment, Derrick thought he was about to be bitten by a vampire. Skunk spoke in a deep, raspy voice. "You got a problem with me, little boy?"

"Get off me, you freak!"

Skunk reared up his head and let out a horrifying laugh. Then he got so close their noses almost touched. "Boy, you got a lot to learn if you're gonna make it in here. From now on, you see me comin', you look away. If I see your eyeballs, I'm gonna rip 'em outta your head and stuff 'em down your throat. You got that, little boy?"

Derrick had known intense fear only once before in his life. After a terrifying vision of hell itself, he had run right into the police and gladly went with them. But this time, there was no place to run. He heard himself say, "Yeah, okay. Whatever you say, Skunk."

"*Mister* Skunk."

"Mr. Skunk."

Skunk chuckled. "Now you're gettin' the picture." He briefly pressed down hard on Derrick's wrists, then got up and returned to his bunk.

The daily routine at the prison was simple. Wake up at 5:00 a.m. Shower every other day. By 5:45 a.m., you were on the breakfast line with some five hundred other men. Twenty minutes to eat, then you were lined up and sent back to your cell. Lunch was the same. Between meals, if there wasn't a lockdown for some minor infraction of a single prisoner, you had access to the yard to exercise, walk, or just stare off into space. The ever-present armed guards didn't care what you did, as long as you didn't start a fight or try to escape. Then, at 5:45 p.m., you were on the supper line. After supper, you were marched back into your cell for the night. Every day was the same as the next day and the next day and the next day…

For weeks, Derrick spoke to no one, keeping a slow burning anger just below the surface. Nothing fazed him. Not Skunk's constant harassment, the endless monotony, or the tasteless food. But he watched everyone and everything that happened. And he learned and plotted.

It was during supper that the idea came to him. Silently staring out the window, oblivious to the hundreds surrounding him in the noise-filled cafeteria, Derrick realized how easy it would be to escape. As he watched, a garbage truck pulled up to the back of the kitchen. The truck inched to within a foot of a large dumpster; its long appendages smoothly glided into square handles on each side of the bin. The driver revved up the engine, threw a lever, and powerful hydraulic arms lifted the bin effortlessly over the cab. It tossed the contents of the dumpster into the rear of the truck, tapping it noisily on the edge just to make sure everything fell out.

Derrick knew if he were one of the men working in the kitchen, it would be a simple thing to just hop in the dumpster, hide in the garbage, and wait for the garbage truck. Once it had collected its cargo, he'd be a free man within minutes.

But how was he going to get on the kitchen crew?

Across from him sat an older man, hunched over his soup. He was bald, wore thick glasses, and seemed pathetically harmless. Derrick said, "Hey you."

The man looked up from his bowl in slow motion and stared at Derrick without expression. Derrick immediately hated him for his lethargic demeanor, but he needed some information. He leaned across the table. "You look like a smart guy. How do I get on the kitchen crew?"

"You can't get in there. That's for long termers. You're not going be here that long."

"How do you know…?" Derrick stopped short of asking the obvious question. One thing he had learned was that ignorance was a sign of weakness. Another thing was that somehow, everybody knew everything about everybody else. Part of prison culture was that nobody liked secrets. Keeping secrets led to suspicion, and suspicion could get you hurt or killed if someone thought you were a snitch or a mole.

"Name's Albert," said the little bald man. "Some call me Albie. Most call me Einstein."

"You don't look like the criminal type. What are you in here for, stealing computers or something?"

"You're thinking of escaping through the garbage truck."

"How did…? Never mind. So what if I was? You got a better plan?"

"Like I said, you're not going to be here that long. You're a transient. In a couple of weeks, you'll go to minimum security for first-time offenders. You're what, seventeen, eighteen?" Derrick understood why they called him Einstein. Everybody in prison had an edge. Einstein's was his brains. He nodded his answer to Einstein's question. Einstein leaned across the table. "Well, don't even try it. You'll get caught. It's been tried before, but no one has ever gotten out that way. Then they'll lock us down while they sweep for contraband and weapons. And they'll likely find most of it." He leaned in a little closer and widened his eyes, magnified by his thick glasses. "And everyone will know you caused the lockdown. Are you catching on yet, *Newby*?" Einstein went back to eating his soup as if the conversation had never taken place.

Derrick was not about to let some four-eyed con-man tell him what to do. Day after day, he watched the kitchen crew. After two weeks, he had the schedule down. Every Tuesday and Thursday at 6:00 p.m., the garbage truck eased up to the dumpster at the rear of the kitchen. The large covered bin filled with half-eaten food and an assortment of dirty food containers was emptied into the gaping back of the truck. Derrick was sure his plan would work. Either he took the trash to the dumpster himself and then suddenly jumped in it, or he would somehow hide in a trash can and have himself dumped into the bin. Either way, he would be carted away to freedom, and one step closer to taking his revenge.

Einstein was right about one thing, there was no way he was going to get on the kitchen crew. Even if he was a "long-termer," he found out it would cost several cartons of cigarettes or several hundred dollars to be put on the waiting list. Even then, he would have to wait until somebody was transferred, made parole, or died before being allowed to work in the kitchen. Derrick didn't have time for such nonsense.

As was the standard procedure this Tuesday morning, inmates were lined up and sent through the serving area to collect their breakfast. The line ran along the cafeteria wall and past the kitchen entrance. Guards were spaced along the line and eyed each prisoner briefly, but they couldn't see everyone at all times. Just before Derrick passed the kitchen entrance, the nearest guard looked away. Seizing the moment, he ducked low and hid behind the end of the serving station.

Those in line with him immediately knew what Derrick was up to, but said nothing. One of the most important unwritten laws in prison was that you never turned in a fellow inmate, even if that inmate might cause trouble for the rest.

Derrick swiftly slid into the kitchen area and spotted a large trash bin at the end of a long steel table, its hinged cover hanging down the back. A few of the kitchen crew nearby saw him and then casually went about their chores. In one smooth motion, Derrick mounted the table and dropped into the trash bin. Trash from the preparation of breakfast—eggshells, coffee grinds, and bacon grease-laden paper towels—layered the bottom of the bin. Suddenly, as if on cue, someone slammed its cover shut, pulled it outside, and pitched its contents—and Derrick—into the dumpster.

Four days of kitchen trash nearly filled the dumpster. In the stench-filled darkness, Derrick slipped halfway down into the food and cardboard waste. He managed to sit on a relatively stiff portion of garbage with his back against the slimy steel wall of the container. As the day wore on, the full heat of the sun began to bake the small prison, steaming its contents. Sweat dripped off of Derrick's face and body and the ache in his stomach intensified, a constant reminder that he hadn't eaten since the night before.

Finally, twelve hours after he had entered the dumpster, he felt it being tilted and rolled to the waiting garbage truck. He was dumped into the top of the truck and then quickly buried himself among the trash that had been collected earlier. Peering through the garbage, he spotted the hydraulic compactor at the rear of the truck and wondered if he would survive its trash-squeezing pressure.

After five minutes, the truck still remained where it had parked. Derrick wondered what they were waiting for, just as he heard the dogs barking. They had found him! After all he had been through, it was all for nothing.

A voice called out, "C'mon out. We know you're in there. It'll go easier on you if you give yourself up." Derrick consoled himself with the thought that there would be another chance to make his escape someday. He started to dig his way out when he felt movement from within the garbage itself. Another inmate was making his way out of the trash! He slowly got out of a side door of the truck and stood with his hands up before his captors. They quickly rushed off with him and the dogs while the truck driver got into the cab and drove off.

An hour later, the garbage truck arrived at the waste management docks on the other side of the island just across the Narrows from Brooklyn. At the edge of a partially filled barge, it tilted up and vomited its contents. Derrick rolled out unnoticed, then quickly scrambled behind a mound of garbage near the side of the barge. He was tired, hungry, and oozed a putrid stench. But he was free. Free to find Joel and make him pay for the trouble he had caused.

## CHAPTER 23

"We thank you for this meal that you have provided for us, Lord, that it may nourish our bodies for your service. Thank you also for allowing Joel and his mom, Catherine, to visit with us this evening. We ask blessings of your comfort, and that you multiply their faith, hope, and love through Jesus Christ, in whose name we pray. Amen."

A faint shiver rushed through Joel's body as Nate and Beth's father ended the blessing. He always enjoyed eating with the Thompson's on Sunday evenings. They had graciously put them up in their basement apartment rent-free and had become fast friends with him and his mom. Mr. Thompson was what Joel considered to be the perfect father: tall, strong, soft-spoken, but stern when he had to be. He was always concerned about whatever was going on in each family member's life. That extended to Joel and his mom too. In a genuinely interested voice, he said, "So, Catherine, how's the new job going?"

"Oh," said Catherine, as she quickly swallowed. "It's all right. My supervisor says I'm coming along nicely in my training. She said I should be up for a raise in a few months."

"That's great! They must know a good employee when they see one." Catherine managed a weak smile. "And what about you, Joel? How's school? You keeping Nate out of trouble?"

Both Nate and Joel laughed. "No sir!" said Joel. "That's a bigger job than *I* can handle. Besides, I thought that was Beth's job."

"It would be a full-time job for the entire faculty to keep *those* two in line!" said Beth.

"Now Beth," said Mrs. Thompson, smiling. "Let's not exaggerate. Surely the boys must have *some* redeeming value." Nate and Beth's mother was obviously the source of the twins' red hair and fair, freckled skin. But her neatly braided auburn hair and tanned skin gave her a stately, almost royal look.

Beth looked at Nate. Nate looked at Joel. Joel looked at Beth. In unison they said, "Naaah!" Everyone laughed at the comical conclusion.

Joel felt very much a part of this loving, happy family. As he watched them during the meal, he couldn't help wondering what his own family might have been like if his father had stayed with his mother. Mr. Thompson was telling an animated story about something funny that had happened at work that day. Joel tried to imagine his own father's face and in his mind overlaid it onto Mr. Thompson's. But after nearly ten years of absence, he couldn't be sure whose face he had conjured up, his father's or some TV personality from long ago that had stuck in his mind. Without substance, the visual image quickly faded.

Everyone was suddenly laughing at the conclusion to Mr. Thompson's story. Joel had not been paying attention, but he smiled as if he had. Still lost in thoughts of what might have been, he remembered the story his mother told him about his father, how he had begun stealing to make ends meet, and how his crimes had gotten more serious and the jail sentences became longer and longer. If he could forgive Derrick, he could certainly forgive his dad for his life of crime and for leaving them. The thought made him wish for his dad even more.

Suddenly, Mrs. Thompson appeared with a blazing birthday cake. Someone had turned off the lights and everyone started singing "Happy Birthday to you." Joel sat in stunned silence. He didn't think anyone knew about his sixteenth birthday and had no idea this was coming. He looked around at the happy faces—even his mom seemed cheerful—and he cracked a smile.

"Happy birthday, dear *Jo-el*, happy birthday to you!"

Everyone clapped, and the cake was placed in front of Joel. "Make a wish, man," said Nate. Although it had been years since he had had a real birthday party, he knew the routine. He thought, *I wish my dad would come back.* Then took a deep breath and extinguished the flickering candles.

Nate gave Joel a pat on the back. "Way to go, dude. Now you're older than me 'n Beth."

Seemingly from nowhere, colorfully wrapped gifts appeared on the table, while Mrs. Thompson cut the ice cream sheet cake. "Open 'em up, man!" said an impatient Nate. Joel picked up the nearest box. It was heavy for its size. He shook it. It was solid. He tore open the wrapping and opened the box. It was a soft-cover Bible with his name inscribed in gold lettering along the bottom edge.

Joel had never owned a Bible before; never even seen one until he lived in the shelter.

"That's from both of us," said Mr. Thompson. "It's God's Word. I hope you'll read it often."

"Thanks, Mr. Thompson. I will."

Nate handed Joel a thin gift. "And this is from me 'n Beth"

"What is it?"

"Open it up and see."

Joel quickly ripped through the paper as Beth and Nate eagerly look on. "What's this? A video game?"

"Not just any game," said Beth. "It's based on all sorts of heroes in the Bible like Abraham, Samson, and David in the Old Testament and the apostles Paul, Peter, and John in the New

Testament. They are all fighting evil in one way or another. You pick who you want to be and let the fun begin."

Joel looked over the sample graphics on the cover. "Cool!"

A few other wrapped boxes were stacked on one side of the table. They contained an assortment of blue jeans, shirts, socks, and T-shirts from his mom. Joel knew they didn't have much money, and he did need each item, but as he opened each gift, it became harder and harder to keep up the outward appearance of joy. All he could think of was the wish he made when he blew out the birthday candles. Who was he kidding? Nothing in these boxes matched up to what he really wanted.

After the last gift was opened, Joel started to thank everyone, but his mom cut him short. "Wait. There's still one more gift for you," she said as she abruptly left the dining room.

Joel tensed up. Could it be that his wish would come through after all? He had been talking about his dad with his mom a lot lately. Maybe she realized how much he missed him and found him. God would want him to have a complete family, wouldn't He?

Joel's mom appeared a moment later holding a black and tan puppy clinging to her shoulder like a baby. "Happy birthday, Joel," she said and handed it to Joel.

"What's this?"

"Well, I thought you could use a friend. They said at the pound that he was abandoned by his owner. He's already house trained and has had all his shots. He's a Beagle, you know, like Charlie Brown's dog, Snoopy?"

Joel examined the dog at arm's length. He had never held a dog before, much less owned one. "I don't know how to take care of a dog! What does it eat? Do I have to train it?"

Beth gently took the puppy and cradled it, scratching its nose. "He's so cute! What are you going to name him?"

A name was the furthest thing from Joel's mind. He wasn't sure he even wanted it. Beth let the puppy scamper around on the carpeted floor. Nate got down on all fours and followed it around to the amusement of everyone.

Mr. Thompson said, "Certainly is a spirited little guy, isn't he?"

"That's it!" declared Beth. "Why don't we name him *Spirit*? He is kind of shadowy and he gets around really fast."

"*Spirit*," said a frowning Nate. "Isn't that like a ghost or something? He doesn't look like a ghost to me."

Beth's enthusiasm was undaunted. "What do you think, Joel?"

Joel was no where near the conversation. He knew he should accept the pet, especially since his mom went through the trouble of getting it and everyone else seemed to have fallen in love with it. But he just couldn't get out of his mind the fact that he had asked for his father and got a dog instead. Was this God's answer to his wish? Was this God's way of saying, "Well, I know you wanted a father, but I can't give that to you, so here's your consolation prize."?

Only half realizing what had been said, he blurted out, "Sure, whatever."

---

Later that evening, Nate and Joel sat in the Thompson's den studying for a final exam in history while Spirit slept on one end of the couch. Textbooks, notebooks, and papers were spread out on the coffee table. Nate stared at the mountain of information, clutching his hair. "I just can't remember all this stuff. All the dates and people and places and what it all means and..."

Joel was at a loss too. In the past, on the rare occasions that he bothered to prepare for a test, most of the time was taken up creating cheat sheets that he would hide in a slit in his cuff. He knew now, though, that he had to do the honest thing. God was watching him, even if the teacher wasn't.

"Look," he said out of desperation, "maybe your sister can help us out. You know, maybe she can quiz us or something, or show us how she does it. She's a straight-A student, isn't she?"

Nate rubbed his forehead. "I don't know. Yeah, she's smart. Real smart. Makes up for her two left feet. But I don't think any amount of tutoring is going to cram this stuff into this thick head of mine. The history final's in two days. Then math the day after. Science next Monday. Man, I'm doomed!"

Just then, Beth bounded into the room carrying a piece of Joel's birthday cake. She started to say "Hey guys," but never finished the words. Her toe caught on the deep carpet and she tumbled to the floor. The birthday cake flew across the room and spattered on the sliding glass door leading to the backyard. It began to slowly drift down the glass leaving a chocolate and vanilla ice cream streak.

Nate was the first to recover from the shocking incident. He bounded over the table and ran into the adjoining kitchen. "Quick!" he said. "Get something to catch that cake before it hits the floor. I'll get some paper towels!"

Beth had gotten to her knees and put a hand to her face. Joel ran to her. "You okay?"

"I'm such a klutz," she said with a little pout. "But I'm all right." They both looked at the piece of cake on the glass. It was just inches away from the carpet. Joel grabbed his notebook and caught the oozing mass just before it started to infiltrate the rug. Nate returned with a wad of paper towels and the kitchen trash can.

"Flip it in here," he said, nodding to the can.

In one motion, Joel scooped it up and flung it into the trash can while Beth began wiping the glass.

"Man, that was close!" said Nate. The three looked at each other and laughed.

Nate said, "Okay Beth, you owe us big time."

"What do you mean?" she said.

"Well, we just saved your life. The least you could do is to help us study for the history final."

"Hmmm, I guess you've got me there. What's the problem?"

"I just can't remember this stuff. It's like my brain is made of concrete."

Beth smiled. "I always knew that about you!"

"Hey!"

"Listen," said Beth, "it sounds like you just need a break. Don't you ever have to rest after a couple of laps around the track? Then after a few minutes, you can start up again, right?"

"Yeah, so?"

"So, it's the same way with your brain. You just need to give it a rest, or at least completely change what you're thinking about for a little while. I do that all the time."

"So what do you suggest?" said Joel, intrigued.

"Believe it or not, I watch TV for a little while. Not something that's real interesting, but something I can focus on for ten or fifteen minutes. After that, I turn it off and can concentrate on whatever I'm studying. It works pretty well."

Nate raised his eyebrows. "Wow. That's pretty cool. Does Mom know about this?"

Beth got up and grabbed the TV remote. "Mom doesn't care, as long as I get good grades." She flipped through a couple of channels. "Let's see, something not too boring…"

Joel said, "Wait! Go back." Beth went back to the previous channel. "There! What is that guy saying?" A news announcer was speaking outside of a large building. A high chain-linked fence topped with a coil of razor wire surrounded the building. He was caught in mid-sentence.

"…escapee from the Staten Island Correctional Facility last evening."

Front and side booking photos of the escaped prisoner displayed on the screen. It was Derrick Wicker. He had an expression of smug defiance, just like the last time he had seen him in the courtroom.

Joel gasped. "Oh no! It can't be!"

Beth sat on the couch next to Joel and put an arm around his shoulders. "Don't worry," she said. "He'll be captured soon."

Joel wasn't convinced.

Suddenly, Spirit jumped off the couch and stared at the sliding glass door, wagging his tail expectantly. Nate got up and turned on the backyard floodlight. The beam lit up lawn chairs and a table, a basketball on the grass, and the small shed in the far corner of the yard. He studied the scene, then bent low to Spirit. "Nobody's there, boy."

"Maybe he's waiting for the next 'snack' to hit the glass," said Joel giggling.

"*Ha ha.*" Not amused, Beth catapulted a pillow at him.

---

Abner smiled fondly at Joel, Beth, and Nate. They were forming a strong bond beyond mere friendship. Good. There would probably come a day that they will need to depend on each other's strengths. He bent low to regard the excited dog staring at him just on the other side of the glass door. Most animals and a few humans had the ability to sense a nearby spiritual presence.

Losing his smile, he gazed somberly at Joel. He didn't have to see the news report to know that he would soon be in grave danger. A new threat had been unleashed that was ultimately the work of the Evil One, or the black soul of a man, or both. It didn't really matter. What did matter was whether he would have the strength to overcome whatever sinister weapons would be brought to the inevitable battle to come.

Abner's only comfort was that he was on the side of the Creator, Father God Himself.

"Father in heaven," Abner prayed. "Shield these children from evil's onslaught. Amen."

## CHAPTER 24

The sun had just dipped below the horizon when Derrick scrambled to the top of the tallest trash heap. His first order of business was to shed the filthy and unmistakable orange prison jumpsuit. He rummaged around in several huge trash piles until he found a pair of blue jeans with holes in the knees, an oil-stained shirt, and a large winter coat with a broken zipper.

Derrick looked across the bay toward Brooklyn some two miles away. There was no way he could swim across. Stowing away on a ship was risky, and there was no guarantee he would be taken straight across. He scanned the horizon, and his eyes soon rested on the distant Verrazano Bridge, the only bridge from Staten Island to Brooklyn. *That's my ticket across,* he mused.

The next necessity was food. It had been more than twenty-four hours since his last meal, and the ordeal of his escape was beginning to sap his strength and concentration. It was obvious he would find nothing edible on the barge. Derrick knew he didn't need to travel all the way back to home turf to find a meal.

All he needed was the trash bin of a fast food place or a convenience store to find nourishment. And then he could get on with his ultimate goal.

---

Derrick blinked open his eyes. He had been sleeping on a pile of plastic trash bags in a narrow alley near Brooklyn's downtown area. Although the sky was a cloudless bright blue, the alley was still deep in shadow. Images of the torturous night before oozed across his mind. Unwilling to risk hitchhiking and possibly being reported, he had walked all the way from Staten Island, a distance of nearly ten miles. The few fast food places he passed were not open, their trash bins empty. He didn't have the strength to break into the restaurants, so he pressed on, hoping for easier access to food. But it never happened.

Now in his second day without food or water, it felt as if his whole body were wasting away. The pain in his stomach was unbearable. All pretense of stealth vanished as he envisioned himself robbing the next person unlucky enough to walk across the alley entrance.

Derrick stumbled weakly out of the alley with one hand on the brick wall to steady himself. He squinted in the glare of the sun's reflection off a window. Turning his head to avoid the light, he spotted a street vender half a block away. Hot vapor rose from steaming biscuits on the surface of the vender's aluminum stand. Without a thought, Derrick ran toward the vender, grabbed a sweet roll, and kept on going. The vender yelled "*Hey*," but there was no chance of pursuit as the experienced thief quickly weaved through morning pedestrians and was gone.

Derrick turned into an alley and sat against the wall to wolf down his prize. "This isn't going to be so bad," he said aloud. His thoughts drifted to when Joel had refused to help him, showing his true colors. The scene in his mind shifted to the courtroom and of Joel testifying against him.

Derrick bolted up and out of the alley, his thoughts raging. Anger drove him on. It would keep him focused on the task, keep him fed when hungry, warm when cold, and moving when tired. Nothing else mattered until Joel was hurting or dead, and it didn't matter which.

---

"Yes," Pus whispered to the place in Derrick's mind where intense emotion overpowers reason. "Look at what Joel has done to you. You have been swept aside by that little boy for far too long. Sweet revenge is your right. You must claim it. Think of the pure ecstasy you will feel when you finally have Joel in your hands!"

---

Derrick roamed the city for hours. His anger, although honed sharper than any blade, could not keep the hunger away. As lengthening shadows began to creep across the cityscape, Derrick found himself in yet another alley. A small dumpster with an open side door squatted near the back door of one of the buildings.

Derrick leaned into the dumpster and saw what looked like a half-eaten hamburger, but he soon realized he could only reach it if he were inside. He swung one leg into the dumpster opening, then his head and upper body. Just as he was about to bring his other foot in, a strong hand clamped it.

"Hey! What the...?"

The voice attached to the hand was deep and hoarse. "Whatta think you're doin', *boy?*

Before Derrick could even think of a response, the hand had dragged him out of the dumpster and onto the pavement. He looked up and saw a large and wide man in a tight T-shirt. His arms bulged with veined muscles. The man grabbed Derrick's jacket and easily lifted him up. Before he could mouth a protest, the man dragged him through the doorway of the building. Finally, the first shock of being tossed around subsided and Derrick managed to shout, "Hey, let go of me! Where're you taking me?"

The man said nothing. Effortlessly, he yanked Derrick through a kitchen area, through double swinging doors, and finally deposited him hard on a barstool.

The room was dimly lit and smoky. T-shirt walked over to a man sitting in a nearby booth with his back turned to Derrick and whispered something to him. Derrick instinctively knew he would not get far if he tried to run. He surveyed his surroundings. Polished brass and wood was everywhere. A white-shirted, black-tied bartender calmly toweled a long stem glass. Through a wide arched doorway, he could see a restaurant with subdued lighting and dozens of tables covered in white tablecloths. Although it was still early afternoon, a few men were standing at the bar drinking or playing pool at the far end of the room. Most of the men were huge and looked like they were just itching for someone to pick a fight with them.

The man T-shirt spoke to slowly rose, walked over to Derrick, and sat down at a nearby table. He wore an expensive-looking, pin-striped suit, and was as wide and tall as a doorway. He had a broad, flat face with a scar that ran down one cheek. Derrick noticed that the other men at the bar and elsewhere in the room seemed to focus on his movement without stopping what they were doing. It was obvious the man was their leader.

The man motioned to Derrick. "C'mere."

When Derrick didn't move, someone lifted him off the barstool and dumped him onto the chair opposite the leader.

"Lay off me!" said Derrick as he jerked around to see who dared treat him so roughly. To his utter surprise, it was Skunk. The sight of scraggly dreadlocks and stained, sharp teeth froze him solid.

The man on the opposite side of the table spoke almost in a whisper. "I see you two have met."

Derrick felt his defiance quickly drain out of him as a sickening fear began to take hold. "Who do you think you are?" he said with more courage than he felt.

The man smiled briefly, showing a perfect set of white teeth. "I'll be asking the questions here, if you don't mind. What's your name?"

"Derrick."

"Does Derrick have a last name?"

Derrick looked around. Although fear crouched just below the surface, this new encounter gave him a rush of excitement. He was in the midst of big time criminals. If he could join this gang, it might be the next step toward fulfilling the Dream. Besides, with these guys to back him up, it would be a simple thing to find and crush Joel once and for all. "Wicker. Derrick Wicker," he said with confidence.

"Well, pleased to meet you, Derrick Wicker. Some call me Chameleon."

In Derrick's experience, whenever you met someone for the first time, there'd be a handshake of some kind. The man offered no such gesture. His eyes narrowed.

"That's my property you were rummaging through."

"Nobody owns the trash when it's out in the dumpster. It's up for grabs, man."

Someone slapped Derrick in the face so hard he almost flew off the chair. Only then did he realize Skunk was still standing behind him.

Chameleon chuckled. "As for the trash in the dumpster, you are mistaken. I own it. I own everything: the trash, the street, this building, and many others. Right now, I even own you."

"Listen." Derrick hoped he didn't sound as helpless and scared as he felt. "I didn't mean nothing. I didn't see anything in the dumpster. I was just looking for food, ya know?"

Chameleon put a finger to his lips as if contemplating a deep mystery.

"Hmmm, the way I see it, I have two choices." He stuck a thick forefinger up in the air. "One. I kill you now to keep you quiet about what you may have seen in that dumpster; or two," sticking up a second finger, "I keep you around for a while to see if you are of any use to me. If I like what I see, I won't kill you. If I don't, well then, we're back to option one."

Derrick swallowed. "I would like … I mean, how about letting me join in with you?"

Chameleon seemed amused. "Why do you want to become a member of our organization? Certainly the 'fringe' benefits are excellent." Brief muffled laughter surrounded them. "But there's no turning back. It's a lifetime membership. How ever long—or short—that life may be."

"I got a debt to pay. I got ratted out. Maybe you guys could help me and … "

Chameleon's voice raised up a notch. "We don't allow freelancing in our organization. You'll do only what I tell you to do and nothing else." He leaned in close. "Is that clear?"

"Yeah, sure. Well, besides, I'm, uh, pretty good with a switchblade. I even had my own gang once. The Blades. Maybe you heard of them?"

Chameleon raised an eyebrow. "Is that so? Well then, Derrick, you might be of use to me yet. All right then, we'll go with option two, for now. There are a few rules, though." He stood and nodded slightly. Skunk suddenly wrapped both Derrick's arms behind the chair. He felt as if he were encased in cement.

Terror quickly rose inside Derrick. "*Hey*, what the … "

Chameleon flicked out a switchblade and calmly brought it to Derrick's neck. The point of the knife poked his skin. As if calmly reading from a shopping list, he said. "You try to bring the law against me, I kill you. You steal from me, I kill you. You disobey me, I kill you. You run, I find you, let Skunk here take a bite out of you, and then I kill you. Do we have an understanding?"

Derrick said, "Yeah, I got it."

Chameleon held the knife at Derrick's throat a bit longer. A small bead of blood trickled from its point. Finally, he pressed a button and the blade quickly retracted into its handle.

"I believe you do."

The men around the room hung on his next words. "Show him around, boys."

Later that evening, Derrick was cleaning the latrine. It was one of several demeaning jobs he was forced to do as the new "lackey." Chameleon stepped in. Behind him were the T-shirted body builder who first discovered him in the dumpster and another man. "Derrick, I want you to go with these guys. They're going to do a little job for me, and you're going with them. Think of it as a training exercise."

Derrick had no choice but to obey. He didn't want to think of the consequences if he didn't.

## CHAPTER 25

"So, what are you guys into?" asked Derrick from the back seat of the car. "I mean where does the...uh...business get its money?"

Sal—T-shirt—was driving. Gus, larger than Sal, but not as muscular, sat in the passenger seat. He wore a short goatee, but was otherwise completely bald.

"We're in the...uh...insurance business," said Sal without turning his head. Gus let out a low chuckle.

"*Insurance*? What do you mean?"

"When people pay their fees, we keep the bad guys from visiting. When they don't, well, sometimes bad things happen to them." Gus chuckled again. Derrick wondered if Gus could speak at all.

"I got ya." After a pause, Derrick said, "So, where're we going tonight?" Sal continued to drive in silence while Gus stared lifelessly through the windshield. "Are you guys deaf? I said..."

"You know, you got a big mouth," said Gus, still staring straight ahead. "Someday I'm gonna do you a favor and fix that for ya."

"He's just a dumb kid, Gus. Don't let him get to ya. Hey kid…"

"Name's Derrick."

"Yeah, whatever. You wanna know where we're going? The boss wants us to expunge some charges against a friend of his. Kind of like a favor."

"I wouldn't think Chameleon had any friends."

"He's not really a friend. It's more like a business transaction. The boss just likes people owing him."

"Humpf," said an uninterested Derrick.

Sal went on. "Hey, you want us to look you up? Erase what they got on you?"

Derrick sat up. "You can do that?"

"Sure. But it'll cost you down the road."

"I don't care about that." Derrick's mind was in full gear now. "What about other court records? Can you look up addresses of people on probation? I need to find a … a friend."

"Piece of cake."

Sal, Gus, and Derrick waited at the rear of the Circuit Court building. It was 10:00 p.m. and the judges, clerks, attorneys, and sheriff's deputies had long since left for the day. Only a small team of cleaning contractors occupied the locked building. The door lock clicked and Derrick reached for the handle, but Sal held him back. "Hold on," he said, barely above a whisper. "The janitor don't need to know us and we don't need to know him." After a few minutes, the three silently entered the building.

Sal and Gus glided upstairs to the second floor, down a hallway past offices on both sides, and then stopped at a glass door at the end of the hall. " Circuit Court Clerk" was written in gold lettering on the door. Derrick wondered how many times they had done this before. The office door was unlocked. Obviously, the janitor had been there earlier.

Stealthily, Derrick, Gus, and Sal entered the dark office. The only illumination was one obligatory fluorescent light required by the fire code. Gus went straight for the file cabinets while Sal sat down at the nearest PC and began speed typing as if he worked there.

Derrick felt useless. "What do you want me to do?"

Sal had already logged into the case management system, and began searching for a certain offender. Without looking up from the screen, he said, "Why don't you keep a look out for unfriendly janitors."

"What about that friend I wanna look up?"

Sal furrowed his brows in disapproval. "First we finish what we came here for; then we do the side stuff. You got it?"

"Yeah. Whatever."

# CHAPTER 26

Finally, the absolutely best day of the year arrived: the first day of summer vacation! In the past, Joel had always looked at this day as the first day of freedom to wreck havoc, to steal hubcaps and gas caps, and to stay on the streets until the early morning with gang members smoking, drinking, and planning their next adventure in crime. On the one hand, he hated the person he used to be. But on the other, he wondered what his old friends were doing, what trouble they were getting themselves into, and having fun doing it. Joel knew it was wrong to do such things now, but why did he still have a yearning to do them? He had thought he was past that now, that he was a new person, only caring about the things that God thought were important and worthy of His approval. He wondered if he would ever become completely good, good enough for God.

A Thompson family tradition on the first day of summer vacation was to spend the day at Coney Island. Mr. Thompson was insistent. "Joel, we'd like you and your mom to go with us too. We wouldn't have it any other way."

On Saturday morning, the day of the planned trip to the shore, Joel walked up the basement stairs and into the kitchen. Beth and her mother were making sandwiches and packing them in a large cooler.

"Mrs. Thompson, can you talk to my mom?"

"What is it, dear?"

"Well, she doesn't feel like she can go with us."

"Is she ill?"

"No, not exactly. I don't know. She won't get out of bed."

Mrs. Thompson gave a tight smile. "I'll go down and talk with her."

---

The Thompson's aging Chevy van was loaded up with the cooler, a large umbrella, and four beach chairs, all of which were strapped on top. Everyone piled in—including Spirit, who found a nook under one of the bench seats—except for Joel's mom. Mrs. Thompson could not convince her to come with them. Joel overheard her talking to Mr. Thompson about it in the car.

"She said she's just tired, but I think she's suffering clinical depression. I just wish there was something we could do to help her. Maybe I could get her to talk to one of the doctors at the free clinic."

"Good idea," said Mr. Thompson. "We could see if she'll talk to the pastor about it too. She has been through a lot, you know. A single mom raising a teenager, losing her home, the trial, dim prospects for the future. All that would take a toll on anyone."

Mrs. Thompson nodded. "You're right. We'll certainly have to pray for her."

After a short drive, they pulled into a parking spot fairly close to the beach area. At this time of year, still a week away from the official start of summer, only the most devoted beach goers braved the cool breezes and cold ocean temperature.

As they unstrapped the gear, Nate asked Joel, almost as an afterthought, "Hey Joel, you ever been to the beach?"

"Nah. Never been."

Nate's eyebrows arched high. "Really? You're kidding me, right?"

"Uh-uh. Never."

"Wow, are you in for a treat!"

Nate and Beth took off their sneakers. Joel followed their lead and felt the hot, sandy pavement. They walked out of the parking lot and under a boardwalk. The fine sand, cooled by the boardwalk's shadow and pock-mocked by countless feet, squished between and around Joel's toes. Prickly grains of sand pelted his skin, driven by a stiff breeze coming off the ocean. They emerged from under the boardwalk and Joel drank in the scene with all of his senses.

The immense openness made Joel feel like a bird released from its cage. Directly ahead, the dark blue ocean stretched for as far as he could see until it met the sky in a straight line at the horizon. Looking left and right, the sparsely populated beach stretched on for miles until it faded into a fuzzy mix of gray and white. A nearby jetty made a straight rocky line from the dry beach to a point far out in the ocean. Occasional sprays marked where the undulating sea crashed into unyielding, black boulders. Closer to shore, white, curling breakers continually slammed the beach with the sound of distant, rolling thunder.

Spirit ran to the where the surf reached its furthest point, followed closely by Joel. The thin, foamy water looked like a soda spill on a kitchen floor. It rushed up the gently sloping, wet sand until, having lost all momentum, it receded swiftly back to the sea. He tested the water temperature with a toe. Ice cold!

"Hey Joel, c'mere, will ya?" It was Nate, struggling with three beach chairs and the cooler. Joel ran to unburden his friend.

Mr. Thompson picked out a spot halfway between the boardwalk and the constantly shifting edge of the water. He pitched the umbrella while Nate and Joel faced two of the chairs toward the ocean with the cooler between them. Everyone stripped down to bathing suits and went about enjoying the day. Nate's parents took a stroll down the beach, holding hands and pointing out sights to each other. Beth, having greased herself up with SPF 30 suntan lotion, stretched out on a blanket. Spirit chased after the receding water line then quickly turned and retreated when it rushed up toward him.

Joel plopped down on one of the beach chairs, while Nate grabbed two Cokes from the cooler, handed one to Joel, and threw himself into the other chair. He said, "Man, what a view. It doesn't get any better than this."

Joel stared at the horizon through dark sunglasses. "You got that right. I can't believe how wide open it is. This is great!" After a pause, he turned to Nate, lifting his sunglasses. "Hey, why don't we go for a swim?"

"You kidding? The water's gotta be sixty degrees."

"S'matter? Chicken?"

"You wish. Last one in has to buy the other an ice cream cone."

"You're on!" said Joel as both boys made a dead run for the frigid water.

Beth lifted her head and squinted toward them. She shook her head. "Boys."

---

Derrick circled the block twice. He mentally noted the location of every window and door of the Thompson house and mapped out every possible entrance and escape from every neighbor's yard. He had been waiting for this moment every day, ever since that night he was arrested in the park. Every thought and action had led him to this moment and place. Soon he would have his sweet revenge!

Once he had found the sealed orders at the circuit court clerk's office, carelessly stored in an unlocked cabinet, it was a simple task to discover that Joel's court-appointed attorney had applied for and been granted permission for him to live with Carl and Susan Thompson at 4780 East Nineteenth Street. He was a fifth grade science teacher, and she was a nurse. Since they were both working, he figured there should be times when Joel would be alone in the house.

Derrick fingered the switchblade in his jeans pocket as he eyed the front of the house from a safe distance. A Ford in the driveway told him someone could be home, but the empty oil-stained parking space next to it also told him at least one other car was missing on this Saturday morning.

Derrick entered the rear neighbor's yard and hopped over the fence. He kept low as he rushed from a small tool shed to a grill then to a bush next to the house. Peering in the window nearby, he saw no movement in a dark kitchen. He stealthily peeked in other ground floor windows and found the house empty. *Could they have all gone out?*

He nudged the sliding glass door and it moved. Pushing it just wide enough to fit through, he slipped inside the house.

---

Joel caught the Frisbee thrown by Beth just as a feeling of dread struck him. Standing at the third corner of the triangle, Nate said, "C'mon. Throw it, will ya? What's the matter?"

Joel stood motionless, trying to make sense of the feeling of horror that had come over him. Finally he said, "Something's wrong."

Beth ran to him. "What do you mean?"

"I … I don't know. All of a sudden I got the feeling something really bad is about to happen or maybe is happening right now."

"Like what? Do you think you left something on at the house? Your mom will take care of it." After a moment, she said, "Or are you worried about your mom?"

Nate ran over. "What's going on?"

"Did you ever get a feeling that something really bad is about to happen, and then it does?" asked Joel.

Beth said, "You mean like a premonition?"

"Yeah, I guess so. Does that really happen?"

"Sure," said Beth. "It happens all the time. I've read stories where angels give people special warnings to help them avoid danger."

Nate swished the air with his hand. "Aw, that's just fairytale stuff they use to sell more magazines or to make you watch TV. That's not real."

"It's in the Bible too, Nate, so don't tell me it's not real."

"Yeah, I knew that," he said sheepishly.

Beth turned to Joel. "Could you tell if there was anything specific, like where it's going to happen or to whom?"

Joel furrowed his brows. Suddenly he blurted out, "Mom. It has something to do with Mom. That's all I know."

Nate nodded. "Okay. I'm sold. I'll just tell dad Joel's not feeling well and we should go home right away."

"Tell him the truth, Nate. Dad'll believe you."

"Yeah, right. He already thinks I'm half-crazy as it is!"

---

Silently going from room to empty room on the first floor, Derrick's frustration grew by the minute. He padded up the stairs and then paused halfway listening intently for any sign of movement. Nothing. On the second floor there were four rooms, all with their doors closed. Derrick slowly creaked open each one, but the three bedrooms and a bathroom were empty.

Derrick went back downstairs, less careful of making noise, and went into the kitchen. As a consolation, he thought of looking for any money or other valuables he could find and then trashing the place just for spite. He turned to head back up to the bedrooms were money was more likely to be hidden when he noticed the open doorway and steps leading down to the basement. He clicked out the switchblade.

# CHAPTER 27

The car had barely stopped in the driveway when Joel jumped out and ran to the front door of the house. It was locked. Without waiting for Mr. Thompson to turn off the engine and unlock the door, he ran around to the backyard and tried the sliding glass door. Finding it open, he rushed inside just as a terrifying thought came to mind: *If I could get in, so could anyone else.*

He ran to the front door and opened it at the same time Mr. Thompson was about to put his key in the lock. "The sliding door was unlocked," he said.

Mrs. Thompson said, "I think I was the last one to leave the house. I don't remember checking it. It could have been unlocked when we left."

"Go check on your mother," said Mr. Thompson. "We'll see if anything was taken."

Joel ran into the kitchen and down the stairs, quieting his steps as he went down. The basement apartment had two bedrooms, a full bathroom, a kitchenette, and a small living room.

His mother's bedroom door was ajar. He peeked in and saw her lying on her bed with her back to him. He stared at her for a moment, then saw the slight rise of her back as she took a long breath. Relief flushed through him. He had hoped the premonition, or whatever it was that he felt at the shore, was just a false alarm. And now he knew she was safe.

Suddenly, a shock wave of terror exploded across his mind, shattering any thoughts of safety. On the table lay a broken six-inch knife blade.

Joel's hands trembled as he slowly picked up the blade and turned it around. It was razor sharp along both edges, and a needle at its point. There was no mistaking its owner. It was Derrick's switchblade, maybe even the same one that he used to stab Eddie. And there was only one way that it had gotten in his mother's bedroom. Derrick had been within inches of his mom. Joel shuddered to think that he might have hurt her. The next thought scared him. *Did he?*

Joel looked around the floor half expecting to see a pool of blood, but there was none. There was no sign of a struggle either. His mom rolled over and opened her eyes. "Mom, are you alright?" He was thankful that she was conscious. "What happened? Did you see Derrick?"

She stared at Joel as if trying to remember who he was. Then she blinked and said, "Who? Derrick? No, I didn't see him."

"I found this knife blade on your night table. I think it was part of Derrick's switchblade. He must have been here and..."

"Oh that. Yes, now I remember. I had gotten up earlier and went upstairs. I found that laying on the floor in the kitchen. I wanted to show it to you, so I brought it downstairs with me. I must have laid it on the night table and then fell asleep..."

Joel couldn't put together what she was saying. "In...in the kitchen?"

"Yes, right at the top of the stairs. Strangest thing. I'd never seen it before."

Joel tried to piece together what might have happened. There was no question that Derrick had been in the house—no one else he knew had a knife like that— but why was the broken blade in the kitchen?

"Hello?" It was Mr. Thompson coming down the stairs. "Anyone down here?"

"Over here, Mr. Thompson." Joel met him at the bottom of the steps.

"How's your mother?"

"She's fine. But she said she found this in the kitchen." He showed him the blade.

Mr. Thompson gingerly took it out of Joel's hand. "This is from a switchblade."

"Yeah. I think it was Derrick's. He's been here. Probably looking for me." He felt his throat tighten. "He wants to take revenge on me, and he doesn't care who he has to hurt to get to me. I gotta get out of here. He'll kill everyone…"

"Now just hold on, Joel. Nobody's going anywhere. You're safe here. Don't you worry, we'll get the police investigators on the case. We'll find him."

Mr. Thompson's words were not at all comforting to Joel.

---

Just before Derrick started down the basement stairs, a police cruiser pulled up in front of the house. Startled, he had dropped his switchblade and it hit the ceramic tile floor at just the right angle and force that the blade broke away from the handle. Cursing his misfortune and ruined weapon, he scooped up the switchblade handle, quickly left the house, and ran to where he had parked the car five blocks away.

Fuming all the way, he drove to the bar where he had first met Chameleon and his gang. Inside, he threw the keys across the table at Sal, taking out one pile of his solitaire game.

"Hey, what the hell are you doin'? You ruined my game, boy."

Derrick ignored him. "Man! What bum luck. First, nobody's home, then the cops show up, then I break my blade. What do I have to go through to get this guy?"

"You didn't go after that punk kid you were looking for, did you?"

"What if I did? What's it to you?"

"The boss don't like nobody *freelancing*, especially if it brings the law snooping around. You got that?"

Derrick felt a snide remark coming on, but Sal's wild eyes and bulging temple veins changed his mind. "All right. I'll check with the boss first next time. *Okay?*"

"See that you do, little man. See that you do."

Derrick sat down across from Sal, slouching in the chair. He looked around the room. "Hey, where is the boss anyway?"

Sal didn't look up while dealing himself a new hand. "He's got a special job to do. He said he needs to get something from somebody but he has to do it undercover-like. You know, blend in with the background."

"*Hmph.* Just like a Chameleon."

"*Ya think?*" Gus, sitting at the bar but facing the table, let out a chuckle. Sal went on. "You know, you're a very bright boy. Gus, you think he's a bright boy? Yessir, this boy is on the fast track to success. Pretty soon, he'll be the president of our little organization." Gus laughed louder. It was a deep, hearty laugh dripping with sarcasm.

Derrick pursed his lips. "Yeah, you wish." After a moment he said, "So who's in charge?"

Sal let a broad smile cross his face baring crooked, tobacco-stained teeth. "Me."

Derrick's mind scooted off in another direction. With Chameleon out of the picture, he wondered how many men there were between him and Sal and what it would take to rise up the ranks of the "organization."

---

Two uniformed police investigators combed the Thompson house and yard, looking for clues that might tell them who had entered just a few hours earlier. Clearly, burglary—breaking and entering a residence—had been committed. It didn't matter that the sliding glass door leading to the backyard had been unlocked. The charge was more severe because it was probable the intruder knew someone was home. If the suspect had a weapon or if theft or attempted theft could also be established, it would lengthen the eventual sentence handed down by the judge. But every charge had to be proven beyond a reasonable doubt, and the collection of evidence and facts had to be carried out with the utmost care and diligence.

One investigator, the older one whose name plate said 'MacDonald,' interviewed each family member, including Joel and his mom. When it was Joel's turn, he was ready to state his case.

Sitting across from Joel at the dining room table, MacDonald opened to a blank page in a thick, well used pad. This was his fifth interview, but it may as well have been the fiftieth. He wrote something at the top and then looked at Joel with tired but penetrating eyes.

"What's your name, son?"

"Joel Somers. I found—"

MacDonald cut him off. "First things first. You live here?"

"Yeah, but I wanna tell you about—"

The officer put up his hand. "Listen. We've got to take this one step at a time. I know you've probably got all these theories about who might have entered the house, but our job is to sort through the evidence and come up with a logical explanation that isn't filled with a lot of emotion and hearsay. You'll get your say in due time. Understand?"

"Yeah. Sure," said Joel, resigned to letting the interview run its course.

"Now, are you related in any way to the Thompson family?"

"Uh, no." The answer forced Joel to remember the incompleteness of his own family. "They're just good friends." He winced inside. The Thompsons had grown to be more than "just friends," but he didn't know of any other way to describe his relationship with them. MacDonald wrote something down and then continued.

"Do you know of anyone who might want to harm anyone in the household, including you or your mom?"

Joel perked up. Finally, he could get down to the important facts. "Yes. Derrick Wicker. He recently escaped from prison and because I turned him in and testified against him, I'm pretty sure he wants to hurt me."

MacDonald wrote for a while, but didn't seem alarmed at Joel's statement. "What is your relationship with this Derrick Wicker?"

A flurry of shame rushed over Joel. He hated bringing up the past. "I was…in his gang, the Blades."

MacDonald stopped writing and looked at Joel. "I see." After a pause, he continued. "Is there anything else you want to tell me?"

"Yes. I found part of a switchblade that I'm pretty sure is his. It proves he was here and…"

MacDonald reached into a folder on the table and produced a small plastic bag with the knife blade inside. "This it?"

"Yep. That's the one. I know that's his."

The officer's tired expression did not change. "And just how do you know that?"

Joel flashed back to the knife fight between Derrick and Eddie. Although it occurred months in the past, the scene was clearly stamped in his mind. "I've seen him use it."

"This blade or some other?"

"Uh, I don't know. I think it was this one. Can't you, like, dust for fingerprints or something?"

"Already have. It's smudged with several prints. Probably yours, your mom's, and Mr. Thompson's. If we could match it up with the owner of the handle, do a microscopic comparison, we might be able to say it was Derrick's. But without that handle, this is a nearly useless piece of evidence."

Joel's shoulders drooped. It had been so clear to him that Derrick was the one who was in the house. It had to be him. But now, he wasn't so sure. Was there someone else looking for him? Was it just a coincidence that someone else, some stranger, had broken into the house?

"Hey, Mac. C'mere. I think I've got something." It was the other officer who continued to search for clues during the interviews.

MacDonald joined his partner outside at the sliding glass door. The other officer had already lightly dusted the glass near the edge with a bi-chromatic powder showing a fingerprint. Mac said, "Go ahead and lift it. But don't forget to photograph it before you do."

Returning to the dining room, he sat down. "Now where were we?"

"You were saying the knife is a useless piece of evidence."

"Nearly useless. Yes, but you never know what will become important later. There may be other evidence we can find here. Taken together, we may be able to build a solid case." Joel looked down at the table. "Don't worry, son. We'll do our best to find the perpetrator, whether it was Derrick or not."

---

Glad the house was finally quiet again, Catherine sat on the couch in the basement apartment alone. The police officers left after two hours of interviews and scrutinizing every square inch of the house and yard. The only evidence found that might point to the intruder's identity was the thumbprint on the sliding glass door, a faint shoeprint in the kitchen, and the broken knife blade.

She let her eyes survey the room. The bare walls reminder her of the many family pictures she had hung throughout the apartment before the fire. She had had several photo albums too, filled with the memories of her youth and early adulthood. The small television produced a brief vision in her mind of the home movies her husband had made early in their marriage, while Joel was still a baby. A portable radio and speakers below the TV coaxed faint audible memories of the classical music she listened to during the many lonely months her husband spent in jail. Her eyes drifted toward the adjoining kitchen area, sparsely equipped with a toaster, microwave oven, and small refrigerator. She remembered the small appliances, dish and glass sets, towels, sheets, and other accouterments that she and her husband had received or bought during those first happy days after their marriage.

And now it was gone. All of it. Nothing survived the fire. Except…

Catherine went into her bedroom, pulled out the small metal box from under the bed and returned to the living room couch. She dialed the combination, then slowly opened the lid. Inside were the precious documents and keepsakes that defined an earlier, happier life. Her marriage license, birth certificates and life insurance policies were all there. She thumbed through the memories, grinning briefly at each card and letter that Jon had sent her while they were dating.

At the bottom of the box was something she hadn't remembered seeing before. She opened the thin, nondescript ledger book to the middle and read down the list of hand-written names, dates, and dollar amounts. She immediately recognized that Jonathan's hand had penned each entry. Flipping through the book, she found it was nearly full of the same information, noticing that some of the names repeated quite often. Jonathan was the only other person who knew the combination and must have placed it there years ago. But why? What was so important about it? As the unanswered question dissipated in her mind, she gingerly placed the book back in the box and clicked the lid closed.

Her mind returned to the night of the terrible fire. She compared her life to that charred apartment, burnt to a crisp from the inside out. Everything that was once an important part of her memories and a happier past was fused and blackened into an unrecognizable mass. What was left to live for?

Without forethought, she found herself in the kitchen and drew out the silver flask hidden in the back of the cabinet under the sink. She took a quick sip of the cheap bourbon, winced as it burned down her insides, and then took a longer swig.

She replaced the cap, wiped her mouth with the back of her hand, and bent to put the flask back in its hiding place. A twinge of guilt mixed with the slight dizziness of bending over was magnified by the first effects of the alcohol. She flopped back on the couch and again considered the lightly furnished apartment. There was a time when money was not a problem. They weren't wealthy by any stretch of the imagination, but there was always enough. Now, they were barely living, even with the low rent agreement with the Thompsons. At her current salary, it would take at least a year to save up enough money to move into an apartment of their own, and even then they would barely have enough money for food and other essentials. Was this her lot now? Was this the best it would ever be? If only Jonathan were still with them. Somehow, they'd make ends meet. Then again, wasn't he the cause of their current situation? If he hadn't left... *Why does life have to be so confusing?*

She thought about the flask again.

---

Teragon almost giggled as he spoke into Catherine's mind. "Yes. Go ahead. It will make you feel better. You've been through so much. You deserve a little something to keep you going. Don't worry. God will take care of you. You deserve good things because you've been *so* good."

He and Pus floated within a few feet of Catherine, both watching her reaction to Teragon's suggestion. To their immense delight, she walked unsteadily into the kitchen again.

"You see how easily one can manipulate this woman? In her state of mind, a mere suggestion has her rushing over the edge."

"Your Lowness," said Pus. "I certainly see how we might obtain this woman's eternal soul, but how does this help us acquire the greater prize, the soul of the human Joel? He has already given himself to the Enemy."

"Dolt! Must I explain everything to you? With his mother's deepening despair and tottering on the brink of sanity, young Joel is sure to let his guard down, perhaps even to the extent that he disregards the desires of our enemy in favor of his selfish desire to help his mother at any cost." Pus nodded in feigned understanding. Teragon went on. "To be sure, he is a new believer and easily swayed. Even if he has truly given himself to the Other Side, he can still be rendered ineffective by doubt and grief at recurring sin. And, even if he cannot be turned back to his evil ways completely, his lackluster, so-called faith will cause many others to turn from aspiring to the same path."

"Master, your wisdom and intelligence surpasses even that of Baal-Zebub himself."

"Watch and learn."

---

Spirit bounded down the stairs in front of Joel. "Mom, you down here?" As soon as he landed on the rug-covered landing at the bottom of the steps, Spirit began barking into the room excitedly. "What the … what's gotten into you, boy?" He continued to bark, but began backing up, his barking dissolved into whimpering as he hid behind Joel's legs. Finally, with one quick *yelp*, the frightened puppy ran back up the stairs.

Startled by the dog's behavior, Joel watched him scamper away and then walked into the room. As he approached his mother, an icy sensation of utter dread began to sweep over him and the hairs on his arms began to lift up and tingle. Then, just as suddenly as it appeared, the feeling was gone.

"Mom, are you okay?" Catherine stared blankly at empty space through bloodshot eyes and only after Joel's gentle shaking did she finally come out of a trance-like state. "Mom, what's wrong?"

Catherine slowly looked up at her son. She tilted her head, and tears filled her eyes. "Oh, my dear Joel," she said. "You have nothing to look forward to. There is nothing I can do to provide a future for you. Not only have I ruined my life, I've ruined yours too."

Joel sat down next to her. "Mom, I don't know what you're talking about. Our lives aren't ruined. We have lots of things. We have a place to live in. You have a job. We're doing okay."

"No, no we're not. Not really. We can't go on like this."

"Mom, listen, Mr. and Mrs. Thompson want to talk with you. They want to help you. They sent me down here to bring you upstairs. Will you come up with me?" She pursed her lips and shook her head. Joel stood and pulled her up by her hands. "C'mon, I won't take no for an answer."

Finally, Catherine allowed her son to pull her off the couch and stand her up. He wrapped her hand around her upper arm and walked her up the stairs. Joel got a whiff of the bourbon on her breath. Briefly embarrassed, he thought about what the Thompsons might think of her. But over the past several months of living with them, he had learned they honestly cared about everyone, regardless of who they were or what mistakes they had made.

By the time she reached the top of the stairs, Catherine was more responsive, as if coming up out of the basement had rejuvenated her. She walked unassisted into the living room and sat in a wing chair opposite the Thompsons. Joel, feeling uneasy about joining them, but having nowhere else to go, plopped down in a lounge chair perpendicular to the adults. Mrs. Thompson spoke first.

"Catherine, we know you've been through more trials and difficulties, especially in these last few months, than most people experience in a lifetime. We know how difficult single parenthood can be, even when things are going well."

"I'm fine. Really, I..."

"Catherine," said Mr. Thompson softly. "We want to help you. We know people in social services who are willing to provide assistance at no cost to you. They can work on getting grants and other types of financial support to help you get back on your feet. Susan can put you in touch with physicians, psychologists, and therapists at the free clinic where she works who can help with depression or any other medical issues you may have. And then there are several pastors at our church who would be more than willing to talk to you about spiritual matters, to help you see how God can be depended on to get us all through the hard times in life." Catherine was silent. Mr. Thompson went on. "But it's up to you. You have to want help. We—no one—can force it on you against your will."

*Ding dong.*

Joel happily jumped at the chance to leave the tense meeting. "I'll get it."

The conversation faded into the background as Joel walked down the short hall to the front door. He looked through the door's peep hole and sucked in breath. Stunned, he slowly turned the knob and allowed the door to creak open. He gaped up at the man he knew but didn't know. The man spoke in a voice that was both familiar and foreign.

"Hello, Joel. My, how you've grown!"

Joel finally closed his mouth, swallowed hard and said, "*Dad?*"

## CHAPTER 28

When Joel brought his father into the living room, the conversation abruptly halted. All eyes were on the tall, barrel-chested visitor, but it was Catherine's turn to gape. Carl stood and held out his right hand. "Carl Thompson. Welcome to our home. And you are—?"

"Jonathan. Jonathan Somers."

The two men shook hands. "*Somers*? Are you—"

Jonathan smiled broadly, showing a perfect set of white teeth. He seemed to enjoy being the center of attention. "Yes, I'm Catherine's husband and Joel's father."

Joel noticed a large diamond ring on his dad's right hand. It seemed to fit in with the expensive-looking pin-striped suit he was wearing, white silk tie, and pastel pink shirt. He wore two-tone wing tip shoes that looked brand new. Joel also detected a musky aroma about him.

Carl gestured toward the lounge chair. "This is a pleasant surprise. Please have a seat, Mr. Somers."

"Jonathan, if you don't mind. Thank you."

Susan rose from her seat and extended a hand. "I'm Susan Thompson."

Jonathan kissed her hand. "The pleasure is mine."

"Jonathan! What are you doing here?" Joel shot a startled look at his mother. Where he expected to see a smiling, joyful face, there was only an anger-filled stare. Immediately, a deeply buried memory of his parents fighting flashed through his mind. He was glad to see his dad reacted more positively this time.

Jonathan swung in his seat, facing Joel's mom with both hands extended. He looked sincerely sorry. "Catherine, I know you have every reason to be angry with me. I have ignored you for so many years. I can't blame you for being hurt. But please, hear me out."

Carl rose. "Perhaps we should give you two some time alone to…"

"Nonsense. I wouldn't hear of it," said Jonathan. "This is your home. I can't ask you to leave the room." He gestured toward the couch. "Please. Sit. Besides, I have nothing to hide, not anymore."

"All right, if you insist." Carl sat down, crossed his legs, and clasped his knee with both hands. Joel quickly grabbed a wooden chair from the adjacent dining room and sat down. This was one conversation he didn't want to miss.

Jonathan addressed his wife. "You remember when I went to prison, the last time? After I was released, it wasn't easy. I was convinced you didn't want to have anything to do with me. I figured you were better off without me. I couldn't get a job for a long time, so I did some things I'm not proud of just to survive. But then I was able to start a legitimate business. It grew rapidly and I did quite well financially."

"Um, Mr. uh, Jonathan, may I ask what business you are in?" asked Susan.

Jonathan turned to her and smiled. "I'm in personal and corporate insurance, actually."

"It must be a very profitable business."

"Susan, let him finish," injected Carl.

"No, that's all right. As I've said, I have nothing to hide." He turned back to Catherine. "Then, just recently, I realized that, now that I can easily provide for you, maybe you'd take me back. I… I've been looking for you two for over a year now. It was only after I hired a private investigator that I was able to locate you. And now that I've found you, I don't want to lose you again." He glanced at Joel. "Either of you. Can you ever forgive me?"

"You could have found us long before now if you wanted to, Jon." Catherine's voice grew more menacing by the second. "You left us all alone in the world without money, a house, nothing. We lost everything because of you. And now… *now*… you have the audacity to come back begging for *forgiveness*?"

Joel half expected his father to lash out at his mother, verbally or physically, if this was the same man from long ago. But this was not the father he had spent his early childhood trying to avoid. This was a different person, gentle and genuinely willing to make a fresh start. He could not understand or agree with his mother's harsh treatment of him.

"Catherine, you have to believe me when I say I've changed. I'm not who I used to be."

"Can a leopard change its spots? No, Jon, you're not getting off the hook that easy. You left me because you didn't care about me. Like you said, you were better off without me. And by the looks of things, you were right. So you can just take your fancy clothes and your puppy dog song and dance act and take a hike!" Face flushed, Catherine sobbed out the last words. "Go on, get out of here. I don't ever want to see you again!"

Joel was amazed that anyone could maintain his composure after his mom's brutal scolding. Jonathan simply put up one hand as if to ward off Catherine's verbal onslaught. "I can see you're not ready to have a serious conversation about this just yet." Standing, he continued, "Perhaps I need to give you time to think about us becoming a family again." He turned toward the Thompsons. "Thank you for inviting me into your home, and especially for taking such good care of Catherine and Joel."

"Our pleasure," said Carl, quickly standing. "Let me see you out."

"Good-bye, then. I'll be in touch."

Joel followed the two men down the hall. Mr. Thompson lowered his voice. "You know, when we came back from the beach earlier today, we found that the house had been broken into."

"Oh?"

"Yes. We were all pretty shaken up about it. Besides that, Catherine's been through quite a bit over the last several months. They lost everything in the fire, and then there was the trial, and now some financial and emotional difficulties. My wife and I...she's a nurse...we think she may have clinical depression. Her emotions seem to be quite frazzled right now. She could probably use some professional help. We thought we could..."

"I see," interrupted Jonathan. "Well, I can certainly help to change all that."

Joel felt like there was nothing his dad couldn't do to fix everything that was wrong with his and his mom's life. It excited him to think that all their troubles would soon be over. As he opened the door and stepped outside, he whispered, "I'll talk to mom."

His father grinned in a way that reminded him of the man he used to know. It made him feel uneasy then, as it did now, but for just a second. "You do that kid," he said as he briskly strode down the steps and walkway as if he had somewhere else to go. He climbed into the driver's seat of a gleaming silver Lexus parked in front of the house, put the luxury car in gear, and smoothly drove away.

Joel bounded into the living room. "Man, did you see those wheels? I'll bet Dad is loaded!" His mom quietly wept with her hand to her face. Susan bent next to her with one arm draped over her shoulder. Joel quickly realized no one was interested in luxury cars at the moment. "Mom, you shouldn't have yelled at him like that."

Catherine lifted her tear-soaked eyes. "Joel, he's ruined my life once. I'm not about to give him another chance to ruin it again."

"*What*? What do you mean? You heard him. He said he's changed. He wants to help us, and I believe him. Besides—," Joel paused when he realized everyone was staring at him. But he didn't care. If there was anything he was sure of, it was this. "Besides, this is what I've been praying about for a long time. Can't you see? This *has* to be what God wants. He answers prayers, doesn't He?"

"But Joel, you don't know what kind of a man your father was back before you were born and even when you were young, when we needed him the most. He never cared about us. Why did he wait until now before coming back? He wants something; that much is certain."

"Mom, I don't care about the past. Anybody can change. Why won't you give him a chance?"

"I … I can't. Some day I hope you'll understand."

Joel felt his face redden. He couldn't believe his mom's stubbornness. "No, I don't care what you say. If dad comes back and he still wants us, I'm going with him. Whether you come or not, I'm going!"

Joel didn't wait for a response as he stormed out of the room.

---

Catherine still couldn't believe what had just happened. When Jonathan walked into the room after all these years, she didn't know whether to throw something at him or rush into his arms. Or both. She and Joel had been without him for so long, his arrival was surreal, as if reality suddenly shifted.

Poor Joel! He needed a father even more than she needed a husband, but not that one. Not one who would come and go as if driven by shifting winds. "I just wish Joel could have known his father before … he'd understand then," said Catherine as she brought a hand to her face and wiped her moist eyes. "I … I must look awful … "

Susan pulled out a paper tissue from a box on the end table and gave it to her. "You look fine, Catherine, especially after a confrontation like the one you've just been through. If Jonathan was as bad as you say, you are right not to trust him."

"Then again," said Carl, leaning forward in his seat. "People can and do change. Sometimes drastically. I know I just met him, but he seemed genuine. How do you know he's not sincere?"

"But that's just how he is," said Catherine, her eyes wide. She extended one hand, palm up, for emphasis. "Whenever he wanted something from me, he would be all rosy and sweet talk. Then, as soon as he got what he wanted, it was like a switch turning off. He couldn't care less about me. He'd go back to his number one priority—himself—until he needed something else from me. That's how our whole marriage went. Like I said, a leopard can't change its spots."

"All I'm saying is everyone deserves a second chance," said Carl. "And what about Joel? If he's been praying for his father to come back and then he shows up at the door out of the blue, well, don't you think that might be an answer to prayer?"

Catherine stared at the floor, shaking her head. "I don't know. I just don't trust him. After all the trouble he's caused us…"

Susan gently rubbed Catherine across the shoulders. "Carl's got a point, Catherine. Even if he was the worst skunk alive years ago—even if he hasn't changed that much since then—if God brought him here, He must have had a reason to do so."

Carl continued. "Besides, if nothing else, God would want you to forgive Jonathan."

"What do you mean? Forget about the past and let him ruin my life again?"

"No, I'm talking about letting God have what is rightfully His. In the Bible, it says, 'Vengeance is mine, I will repay, says the Lord.' God's perfect justice will be meted out for every wrong committed over all of time. As Christians, our sins are paid for by Christ's death on the cross. When we forgive someone, we not only give the need to avenge ourselves to God, we also take the need for justice off of our own shoulders. We can live free from that burden."

"But what if I forgive him, as you say, take him back into our lives, and the same thing happens all over again? What then?"

"Well, God would want you to *forgive* him as many times as he wrongs you—after all, we would like Him to forgive *us* each time we wrong Him—but that doesn't mean we should necessarily *forget* past behavior. Unless the Lord intervenes, it can be very difficult for someone to change their ways, even if they know they're wrong, and nearly impossible if they don't. God does not want us to suffer needlessly. He would want us to protect ourselves from others' evil intentions."

"So, how do I know that Jonathan has truly changed?"

"You don't, not really, until he proves himself. But you have to give him that opportunity. You'll never know if you don't let him try."

Catherine was quiet for a while. Finally she said, "Maybe you're right. I'll have to think about it some more, though."

"I've got a better idea," said Carl, smiling. "Let's pray about it…"

---

Joel knew he didn't have much time. His dad might be back in a few days, maybe a week at the most. But whenever he returned, he had to be ready. What little he had left after the fire had to be packed and ready to move at a moment's notice. *But what about Mom?* The thought hung suspended in the thick of his mind, an unanswerable worry.

"Hey Joel, you down here?" Nate's voice cut into his gloomy thoughts. He turned to see his friend coming down the stairs. Beth was close behind.

"Hey, Nate. What's up?"

"We heard your dad came to visit. Wow! That's way cool!"

"Yeah! But how did you … ?"

"My brother's a snoop," said Beth. "He was eavesdropping at the top of the stairs."

"Hey Sis, you were right there with me."

"Not until you called me over."

Nate rolled his eyes. "Whatever. Anyway, it doesn't sound like your mom's too happy about getting back together with your dad."

"I know!" said Joel, venting his frustration. "I just don't get it. Here we are with nothing, no money, barely making it, no future; then my father shows up, obviously able to take care of us in a big way, and my mom says, 'Uh, thanks but no thanks.' What's up with that?"

"So what are you going to do?" said Beth.

"Well, I got kind of angry at my mom. I said I'd go with my dad whether she goes with him or not."

Nate let out a low whistle. "That's not good. Your mom's taken care of you all these years. You can't abandon her now."

"Yeah, maybe you're right. But I don't know what else to do. She says he was this criminal or something back in the day. But he says he's changed. And I believe him."

"Just because you *want* to believe him doesn't make it true," said Beth.

"What do you mean by that?"

"All I'm saying is maybe your mom has a point. Maybe she needs proof that he's changed; especially if he wasn't always truthful in the past."

"So what are you saying? I should stay with my mom?"

"Maybe just give it some time. I know you can't wait to have your dad back. I don't blame you—I don't know what it would be like without my dad around. But if you do go with your dad and your mom's still not with you guys, well, you're still down to one parent, right?"

Nate chimed in, "Yeah, but did you see the car he was driving?"

"Nate!" Beth's intense stare at her brother could have burned two holes in him.

"I don't know. I just wish everybody could agree with everybody else. I just want a real family, like you guys have."

"I know," said Beth as she put her arm around Joel's shoulders. Her warm touch stirred something in Joel he had never felt before.

## CHAPTER 29

Jonathan returned a week later with five tickets to Six Flags Great Adventure in New Jersey. Although little was said about it since his last visit, Joel hoped his mom would be more open to the possibility of accepting his dad into their lives. Joel, Beth, and Nate listened to their conversation from the top of the stairs.

"So, now you're trying to bribe us with this extravagant gift?" said Catherine.

"No, not at all. I just thought we could spend the day together, you know, to talk about … us … while Joel and his two friends had some fun."

"Well, I don't know…"

"C'mon, Catherine." Joel detected frustration in his dad's voice. But he was sure the father he once knew would have been screaming at the top of his lungs by now. "Won't you let me prove myself?"

Almost to herself, she said, "Carl said that." She paused for a moment and then said, "All right, we'll go."

Nate pulled his fist down and whispered, "Yes!"

Catherine continued. "Under one condition."

"Name it."

"Do not expect me to make a decision about us getting back together anytime soon… certainly not today. I still don't know if I can trust you not to run off again the first chance you get."

"All right. You've got a deal."

Joel had never been to an amusement park before, so he was able to hold his enthusiasm in check, not knowing what to expect. Beth and Nate, on the other hand, seemed to grow more and more excited as they drove down I-95 to central New Jersey. They talked about going to many local carnivals over the years, enjoying the rides, acts, music, and food, but they had never been to anything as grand as Six Flags.

After an hour-long ride, the silver Lexus came to a smooth stop in the largest parking lot Joel had ever seen. It was only half-filled, but it was still a long walk to the ticket booths. Joel, Beth, and Nate ran ahead and then had to wait for Joel's parents. Joel looked over a large map of the amusement park posted in the middle of the area outside the park entrance.

"Wow! Look at all these cool-looking rides—Dare Devil Dive, The Great American Scream Machine, The Twister…"

Nate fingered the map. "Ooo… Skull Mountain. Sounds scary. I definitely want to see that."

"There are at least three different concerts going on throughout the day," said Beth. "I'll bet they have lots of shows."

Nate eyed a sign posted between every other ticket booth. He let out a low whistle. "Sixty bucks a head just to get in. No wonder we've never been here before."

Joel's parents finally caught up with them. His dad led them around the row of ticket booths under a sign that read "Special Guests" and through a row of turn stocks, where tickets were checked and hands stamped with ink visible only under an ultra-violet light. He produced a single golden ticket, pointed to the group, and was ushered into the park with a flourish that might have been reserved for royalty.

Once inside the park, Joel's senses were overwhelmed by the constantly varying sights and the sounds and smells of the amusement park. On one side of the wide path, a group of acrobats tossed each other effortlessly into the air to the beat of a fast-paced tune. Across the way, three young women dressed in Bavarian costumes beckoned him to follow them. From somewhere deeper within the park, trumpets blared, and a tantalizing aroma of cotton candy caressed his nostrils. Every few steps, his attention was pulled to a different street act, souvenir shop, snack booth, attraction, or show. And then there were the rides.

One was called "Nitro." Its twisted yellow ribbon of steel tubing and girders looped and soared at impossible angles, like an exploding mass of spaghetti frozen in time. One part of the track bent low to the walkway at the bottom of a ridiculously steep section. Several attached cars whooshed by, filled with riders screaming in ecstasy or fear or both. It was as if the ride itself were taunting only the most reckless souls to dare approach its gut-twisting rails.

As they neared the ride entrance, Nate said. "Wow! Look at that line." Under a wooden canopy, a zigzagged mass of humanity stood waiting their turn to ride Nitro. Near the end of the line a sign read, "One hour wait from this point."

"Man!" said Joel. "At this rate, we'll be spending all day on lines."

His father said, "Not to worry," and led them to the front of the line. He showed the gold ticket to the attendant who promptly led Joel, Nate, and Beth to an empty car to the groans and complaints of those who had been waiting for the better part of an hour.

As the attendant pulled the restraint over their shoulders, Nate said, "Man, it's like your dad owns this place!"

Joel didn't respond. He wrestled with the special treatment they had gotten. Sure, it was great to get on the ride right away, but he didn't think they deserved to cut ahead of everyone else. Time and time again, long lines to rides and attractions were bypassed after Joel's father showed the golden ticket. Privilege turned to embarrassment whenever Joel felt the angered stares of hundreds of people. Finally, after getting in ahead of dozens waiting for ninety minutes at Skull Mountain, Joel told his dad, "Dad, I've had enough of this. I want to go home now."

He dad seemed genuinely hurt. "But why? We've only been to half the park. And there's a pretty good concert tonight, then a fireworks display to top it off. I just want to make sure you're happy."

"But Dad, it doesn't seem right, cutting ahead of the line every time and front row seats at all the shows."

"Son, you'll have to learn when you're with me, you'll be treated well. You're not just anybody, you're my boy. And that makes you special."

"But this... this special treatment isn't right. It feels like everyone is mad at us or something. It's like I'm above everybody else and I don't like it."

"Like it or not..."

Joel's mom pulled on his dad's elbow. "Jon, maybe Joel's right. Besides, we've been here most of the day. I'm sure everyone is exhausted."

Something like disgust crossed his face and then quickly vanished. Almost too quietly, he said, "All right then. I'll take you home."

The trip back home was spent in almost complete silence. Joel couldn't get over the way his father seemed so angry at him and his mom. Maybe he just wasn't used to being around family and needed time to adjust. Maybe they needed to adjust to him. But no matter what his father was like, it was still better than not having a father at all.

---

Lost in thought, Derrick drove toward the neighborhood where Joel lived. Over the past several weeks, he had spent most days riding with Sal and Gus collecting insurance "fees" or drumming up more "business" by intimidating small storeowners into making payments in exchange for "protection." During that time, he had made over $3,000 from his cut of the collections, enough for a small apartment above Chameleon's restaurant and bar, new clothes, food, and a down payment on a late model Camaro.

Last week's attempt to get to Joel failed so miserably; he vowed not to try it again until he was sure of success. He had to plan his move carefully in order to catch Joel at home alone. Now, on a Friday morning, he decided to watch the Thompson house, hoping to learn what everyone's regular schedule was.

He parked the car a half-block away from the house, close enough to watch anyone coming or going, but far enough away to not raise suspicion. It was nine-thirty in the morning when he arrived. The only car in the driveway was Joel's mom's beat-up Ford, which meant the others had gone to work. He had to assume Joel's mother was there, but where was Joel?

Late in the afternoon, Derrick began to doze after hours of waiting. He saw no one come or go for the six hours he'd been watching. It would be easy enough to just barge in and deal with whoever was there, but he didn't want to leave anything to chance. He wanted to make sure the next time he saw Joel, he could take out his revenge at his leisure. But he was beginning to realize, especially since the owners of the house would be coming home from work soon, that this was not his day of vengeance.

Derrick cursed the wasted day. Just as he reached for the ignition key to start the engine, a brand new silver Lexus drove up to the front of the Thompson house. After a few minutes, Joel, his mother, and a boy and a girl about the same age as Joel got out. He could not see driver's face, since the windows were heavily tinted.

*Hmm*... he mused. *Looks like he's got a pretty wealthy friend. It won't matter. No one will be able to protect you, Joel.*

Then something clicked in his mind. Maybe he could take advantage of this person who seemed to be so interested in Joel. A wild plan began to take shape. What if he kidnapped Joel and then demanded a ransom? How much could he get? $100,000? A million? Just having Joel in captivity would be enough revenge.

And if he could make that kind of money in the process, he would definitely be on track to finally seeing the Dream come true. This was getting better and better all the time!

The Lexus pulled away from the curb and Derrick instinctively ducked down just before it passed. Watching it in his rearview mirror, he started up the car, made a U-turn, and followed.

Derrick knew he would have to know everything about who this person was if he was going to be successful in his kidnapping scheme. Where did this person work? Where did he live? What did he do for a living? And more importantly, how much was he worth and how much was he willing to pay to get Joel back?

As he drove, he started to fill in the details of his plan. He would have to find a place to keep Joel while negotiations were going on. Would his apartment do? Probably. He'd have to feed him and make sure he couldn't escape until the deal was finished and money was transferred. And then, what would he do with him? Joel must never be willing or able to testify against him again. He would make sure of that.

But Sal's warning during the circuit clerk job haunted him. *The boss don't like nobody freelancing, especially if it brings the law snooping around.* Rather than giving reason for caution, it emboldened him. No one, not even the great and terrible Chameleon, had a right or the power to tell him what to do. In fact, Chameleon would probably congratulate him on a job well done after he pulled it off. Maybe even show his leadership potential enough to get him promoted to lieutenant or something. Derrick grinned to himself. Success would only make his life better in many ways.

Derrick's daydream almost caused him to lose the Lexus. Focusing on the task at hand, he sped up until he could see it stopped at a red light. He slowed down long before the approach to the intersection letting a few cars move into the lane in front of him. When the light turned green, the Lexus accelerated so quickly Derrick was afraid he would lose sight of it, especially if it turned down a side street. But it made no turns and soon entered the downtown area, with only one car between them.

The Lexus stopped in front of the Marriott Hotel in Brooklyn Heights. He parked the car across the street a safe distance from the hotel. The uniformed bellhop opened the driver's side door and took the keys from the driver. Derrick got a fleeting look at the car's occupant as he ran into the hotel, but it was enough to know exactly who he was.

*No way!*

The startling discovery caused Derrick's jaw to go slack. The man who seemed to be so interested in Joel and his mom was the same man he knew only as... *Chameleon!*

## CHAPTER 30

After supper, Joel sat alone at the picnic table in the Thompson's backyard. Spirit slept at his feet. Confusion clouded his mind and kept him teetering on the edge of depression. His thoughts spiraled downward. So his dad wasn't perfect. So what? No one is. Is that why his mom couldn't get back together with him? What about me? Doesn't anyone care about me anymore? What did I do to deserve this?

Spirit suddenly awoke and started clawing at Joel's leg. *Arf! Arf! Arf arf arf!*

"What's the matter, boy? You got problems too?" Joel gave the dog a good scratching behind the ears and then led him into the house.

Joel sat back down at the picnic table and buried his head in his folded arms. Like a cold heavy blanket, the icy dread of hopelessness began to seep into his bones.

Anxious to exploit Joel's depressed spirit, Pus cautiously drew near and whispered into his mind a deception he had learned from Teragon. "Everything will be all right. You know you can trust me. Didn't I say I would take care of you and your mom? You deserve good things because you're *so* good."

Suddenly, he was blinded by an intense beam of energy that could only mean an angel of the Enemy was about to present himself! He started to fly in the opposite direction, but was surrounded by a bluish sparkling light that held him in place as the heavenly being took shape directly in front of him. The being spoke with a thunderous voice matched only by Teragon himself.

"You will leave this place at once or risk annihilation."

Cowering and barely able to see through the intense light, Pus said, "Who... who are you and why do you threaten me so?"

"I am Abner, an Angel of the Lord. And this boy is under my protection. Go now before I strike you down and send your miserable body back to the stench-filled pit from which you've come."

Pus eyed his opponent. Although much larger than himself, this angel was not a warrior. A warrior angel, the likes of Gabriel or the Archangel Michael, would not have bothered speaking a warning to him before cutting him down. No, this weaponless angel was merely a guardian and probably much less powerful. He decided to test his theory.

"Surely an angel of the Lord would have mercy on such an inferior being as I. Why can't we reason together?"

The pause between Pus's statement and Abner's answer was enough time for him to thrust himself, talons first, at the intruder. Although they could not physically harm human flesh, the sharp appendages could shred a spiritual body in an instant.

Abner twisted and Pus flew by, missing his mark. But the demon's talons ripped through Abner's side causing the angel to cry out in pain. Pus landed a short distance away. Quickly recovering, he turned and lunged, but Abner was ready for him this time. Pointing the palms of his hands toward Pus, Abner focused the sparkling light of his aura into an intense dazzling beam striking Pus square in the face. The demon's scream quickly reduced to an echo as the elemental particles of his form were blasted into spiritual oblivion.

---

Joel lifted his head off his arms. As if the blanket had been lifted, the hopelessness was gone and was replaced with an idea. *Maybe mom can't trust Dad because she's not a Christian. If she would learn to trust God for everything in her life, she would certainly agree to let Dad back into her life. But how does she become a Christian? How did I?*

Visions of the day at the sports arena floated across his mind. Was there something like that for adults? Although he had tried and failed to tell his mom about his own faith many times before, now it would be different. Now he had help. It was time to talk to Beth and Nate about it. They'd know what to do. He got up and briskly walked into the house.

---

Abner was thankful for Joel's renewed hope. Nothing was as powerful as a faith-driven human spirit. And when aligned with Father's purpose, victory was assured.

Still aching from Pus's vicious onslaught, Abner focused on allowing his body to mend itself. He knew he would not be able to give Joel his full protection while he healed. But he also knew it was only a matter of time before he would again face a reconstituted Pus, or perhaps a stronger demon. And when that time came, he would have to be ready regardless of his injuries.

# CHAPTER 31

**B**eth and Joel sat on Nate's bed upstairs, while Nate straddled the wooden desk chair backward. Joel explained the problem to his friends and then said, "So, what do you think? How are we going to make my mom become a Christian?"

"You can't *make* anybody do anything they don't want to, especially something as personal as that," said Beth.

"You know what I mean. For me, it happened at the rally at the sports arena after listening to that guy talk about it. You know? It just suddenly made so much sense to me."

Nate chimed in, "But that wasn't the first time you'd heard about Jesus, was it?"

"No." Joel flipped through images in his mind. "There was a priest at the Catholic hospital, and then there was Abner..."

Beth tilted her head. "Who's Abner?"

Joel recalled every encounter he'd had with the mysterious homeless man. "I don't know, exactly. He's just a drifter who seemed to show up when you least expected it. He told me a lot about Jesus and the Bible back when I was still... um, you know, not a Christian. But he always seemed to have this... I don't know... this way about him like he was really a great man or something, but only pretended to be homeless..."

"Hmmm," said Nate rubbing his chin. "Doesn't the Bible say something like 'be kind to strangers because you never know who might be an angel in disguise?'"

"Something like that," said Beth. "It's certainly possible."

Joel chuckled. "Abner? An angel? No way. Besides, why would an angel visit me? I'm nobody."

Beth smiled. "You're not nobody. God loves you. Jesus died for you."

Joel thought a moment. "Yeah, I know. If only my mom could understand that Jesus died for her too."

"Maybe Dad or Mom can help explain it to her," said Beth. "I'll talk to them about it."

A tingling sensation swept over Joel's skin. "Thanks," he said, with a wide grin.

---

Catherine sat on the basement couch fingering the business card Jon had given her after coming home from Six Flags the day before. Torn between staying separated and renewing a relationship with him, she shook her head, unable to make a clear choice. He did seem to be a changed man, but still, could he be trusted?

Carl's words floated into her thoughts. *You'll never know if you don't let him try.* She wasn't sure about all that talk about forgiveness and what God wanted her to do. Who could know what God wants anyway? But Carl had a point. And besides, Joel needed a father. He deserved better than the little she could give him.

She lifted the receiver and slowly tapped in Jon's number.

Joel's jaw nearly hit the ground when the black limousine pulled up to the house. A black-suited chauffer stepped out of the driver's side and stood at the rear passenger door. Just two days ago, his mom had called his dad and agreed to talk about their future. And now they were on their way to what his dad had called one of the most unique restaurants in the city, The View.

Situated on the top floor of the Marriott Marquis Hotel in Midtown Manhattan, The View rotates once each hour, giving its patrons an unobstructed view of the entire metropolitan area including New Jersey on the west, the Empire State Building and Central Park to the south, and Queens and Brooklyn to the east.

Joel thought the dining room was by far the coolest one he had ever seen with its wall-high window running the length of the circular room and its fancy place settings. His eyes roamed the crowded table. Each setting was exactly the same as the next and included way more plates, glasses, and silverware than he would ever need. A waiter dressed in a black tuxedo handed out thick, leather-bound menus and spoke of special selections that were being offered that evening and then disappeared as quickly as he had arrived. Joel opened the menu. Most of the items were unpronounceable and no prices were listed.

"Dad," whispered Joel across the table. "Isn't this place just for rich people?"

His father smiled, "Well, not really, but I wanted to give you a taste of the 'good life.' After all, once we become a family again, you'll have to get used to eating in places like this."

"*If*, Jon," said Catherine. "If we become a family again. I'm still not convinced that we should—"

"Oh, come on, now Catherine, we've been over this already. You called me, remember?"

Joel saw a glimpse of frustration in his father's face, but he couldn't blame him. Not one bit.

"It's time to take the next step. You know it. I know it. Even Joel knows it. Isn't that right, Joel?"

Content to watch his parents discuss the issue, Joel felt uncomfortable having to state his opinion, to take sides, even though he knew deep down his father was right. "I guess so," he said sheepishly.

"There, you see?" said his father, as if he'd just won the argument. "So it's settled."

"No, Jon, it is not settled. How do I know you won't walk out on us again? What guarantee do I have?"

"Why would I do that, Catherine? The only reason I had to leave was because of being put in jail for mistakes I had made trying to support you and Joel. I needed money. Well, I don't need money anymore. Don't you see?"

Catherine scanned the room briefly. "Yes, that much is obvious."

Jon raised both eyebrows and stretched out his hands, face up. "That's what I've been trying to tell you."

The silence that hung between Joel's parents as they stared at each other was like a cinder block on a thin string. Joel looked at one parent, then the other, then back to the first. Finally, his mom spoke.

"I just don't ever again want to be in the position you put us in over the past five years, that's all. I need some kind of proof that it'll never happen again. Is that so much to ask?"

Both Joel and his mom stared at Jon. "I'll tell you what," he said. "I'll buy a house that the three of us will move into and I will sign ownership over to you, free and clear. That way, if I ever do leave again, which I won't, you'll at least have a place to live for as long as you want. How about that?"

This time, the stares were in Catherine's direction. The waiter suddenly reappeared. "Have you decided . . . ?"

"*No!*" said all three in unison. The waiter bowed quickly and ran off.

"Catherine, dear, pumpkin, I only want what's best for you and Joel. I know I've wronged you both and maybe I'll never be able to make it up to you; but just give me a chance and you'll see you've made the right decision."

Catherine blinked through moistened eyes. "You haven't called me that in a long time. All right then. You've got a deal."

"All right!" said Joel. Silently, he prayed, *Thank you, God, for giving me a real family again!*

---

Derrick sat at a small desk in his apartment, still amazed at his recent discovery. What was Chameleon's relationship with Joel and his mom? Was he a friend of the family? Joel never mentioned him. One thing he did know, Chameleon was worth a boatload of money. The question was how much was Joel worth?

He contemplated his next move. If he kidnapped Joel, then tried to get the ransom directly from Chameleon, he'd just get blown away. Chameleon was too powerful to confront directly. Somehow, he had to make it look like he's not the one doing the kidnapping. Someone else would have to do it for him. But who would be greedy yet dumb enough to...?

*Karl!* The Skulls' leader was perfect! He could even bring in a couple of gang members. They wouldn't have to be paid much—hungry, greedy boys will do anything for a little cash. But Karl's going to be as good as dead when Chameleon finds out. And what if he tells Chameleon who put him up to the kidnapping? Anyone will spill their guts when their life is in danger. Derrick nodded to himself. He'd have to make sure Karl never got the chance to talk to Chameleon, or any one else for that matter.

Derrick punched in Karl's home phone number.

"Yeaaaah?"

Derrick thought Karl sounded drunk, or on drugs, or both. Good. He'd be more agreeable that way. "Hey Karl, listen, I got a job for you and your boys. Big bucks. Like you've never seen before. Interested?"

"Sure. Whadda ya need, D-Man?"

Derrick hated it when Karl called him that. He suppressed the verbal attack he wanted to unleash on Karl. "I need you to kidnap somebody."

"Oh yeah? Who?"

"You know him. That boy, Joel. Used to be a Blade. Turned chicken. Ratted me out, 'member?"

"Oh yeah, I thought you were gonna stiff that pigeon?"

"Maybe later. Right now he's hooked in with a high-rolling benefactor." Derrick was careful not to disclose Chameleon's true worth and power. "He'll pay big to get Joel back. Guaranteed."

"How much we talkin'?"

"Fifty g's. Maybe more." Derrick knew fifty thousand dollars was pocket change for Chameleon, and that he was probably good for many times that amount, depending on how badly he wanted Joel back.

Karl gave a long whistle. "Man, that is some major green. So, what's my cut? Like, half, or what?"

Derrick would have normally negotiated a better deal, but he didn't want to risk Karl turning down the job. Besides, he would probably wind up getting at least ten times Karl's cut. "Okay, you do the job right, I'll cut you in for half." There was a long pause on the other end of the line. Too long. Derrick grew impatient. "So, what do you say? I ain't got all day. I got some other guys I can call if you can't handle it."

"I wus just wonderin'…Why're you askin me to do this? I do all the work and then you pick up half the paycheck. It don't sound right."

"Hey, I found the mark, I make the plans. All you got to do is follow 'em."

"I'll tell you what. Why don't you pick him up, bring him to my place, and I'll keep him nice and cozy until you get back to me with the money. That's the deal."

Derrick was fuming inside. It took all his inner strength to keep from exploding a barrage of insults at Karl.

His thoughts raced.

Then again, if Karl kept Joel under wraps, there would be no chance that someone working for Chameleon would see him bring Joel up to his apartment. The only problem was getting him to Karl's place without suspicion until it was too late. The only way to do it would be to pretend to be Joel's friend at least long enough to get him into his car. Then it would be just a short drive to the bank!

"Well?"

Derrick had forgotten Karl was waiting for him to answer. He was still annoyed at him, but made a point to sound angrier than he felt. "All right. It's a deal. But you better be ready at a moment's notice and be able to keep him for at least a couple of weeks with no problem. You got that?"

"Hey, you can count on m—"

Derrick hung up in the middle of Karl's sentence. Now came the hard part.

---

Joel thumbed through a magazine in the Thompson's living room. It was four o'clock on a Saturday and he was alone in the house. Apparently, everyone had someplace else to go, but Joel wondered whether it just worked out that way or was planned. After all, everyone knew his dad was going to take him to see a Yankee game that evening. Mr. Thompson had even said something about it being a good time for his dad to bond with him.

The doorbell rang and Joel looked up at the clock on the wall. He thought it was a little early to head to the stadium since the night game started at seven and the drive would take, he was told, less than an hour. *Well,* he mused, *maybe his dad wanted to get the 'bonding thing' over before the game.* He jumped off the couch and walked to the front door. As he opened the door he said, "Hey Dad, aren't you kind of early…"

His mouth popped open. The one person he never wanted to see again stood before him. *Derrick.*

He tried to slam the door closed, but Derrick easily held it open. "Easy little man, I don't want to hurt you."

"You get out of here right now. My dad'll be here any minute and he'll throw you out if you're still here." Joel felt good about having someone who could protect him.

"Listen, I know we've had our differences, but I want to start fresh, you know?"

"I don't believe you, Derrick. Last I heard, you wanted to kill me for testifying against you." Derrick's expressionless face told Joel nothing about whether he was sincere or not.

"Yeah, well, I finally realized that was the wrong thing to do. I was wrong. I've changed, Joel. How about letting me in and we can talk about it. I promise, I'm not going to hurt you. That's in the past."

Joel was startled. In his wildest dreams, he would never have guessed it, but here was Derrick, practically pleading him to forgive him. Could he have become a Christian too? He was torn between protecting himself and accepting Derrick's words at face value. Somewhere in the back of his mind, he remembered the story in the Bible where the Christian-hating Saul had become a Christian himself, but everyone was still afraid of him at first. He had to find out the truth. "Okay, come on in," he said as he opened the door wide.

## CHAPTER 32

Joel's mind raced as he led Derrick into the living room. He had to prove somehow whether Derrick had really changed into a better person. If he could get him to admit he had broken into the house, it would be a step in the right direction. Then he needed to know what had had happened to him since. If he had truly become a Christian, he should have no problem talking about it.

Joel turned and said, "Did you break into the house a couple of weeks ago?"

Derrick hesitated for just a second. It was enough to know he had. "What do you mean? Who told you that?"

"Derrick, we found your blade. You had to be here. It's the only explanation. Did you or didn't you?"

"Listen, I don't know anything about that. Maybe some guy broke in, had a blade like mine, dropped it, and it broke on the kitchen floor and then ran off. It could have been anybody. Why are you all up in my face about it?"

"I never told you where the blade was found."

Derrick's expression slowly transformed to one of anger. "All right, you got me there, smart guy. It was me."

"Why?" Joel already knew the answer, but he needed to hear Derrick say it.

In the ensuing silence, the doorbell rang. It had to be his dad. If Derrick tried anything, at least he would be protected now. Joel sprinted to the front door.

Jonathan walked into the living room. His confident demeanor quickly changed to shock when he saw Derrick. He said, "What are you doing here?"

Joel gestured toward Derrick. "Dad, this is Derrick. I knew him…um…back when we lived in the apartment."

Derrick's eyes couldn't get any wider. "This is your *dad*? Don't you know who this is?"

"What do you mean?" said Joel.

"Shut up, Derrick."

Derrick paid no attention to Jonathan's command. "You really don't have a clue do you."

"Derrick, I'm warning you…"

Joel looked at his dad, then at Derrick, then back at his dad. "You two know each other?"

Derek hesitated. "No, I…I don't know him. I seen his picture in the paper, that's all."

Joel's confusion grew. "Then how does he know your name, huh?"

Derrick glared at Jonathan, who looked at him through narrowed, menacing eyes. Finally, he said, "Okay. At least I get to burst your bubble. Yeah, I know your old man. I know he is the boss of a criminal organization that's spread all over the city. And I know he's got high ranking people and law enforcement officers in his pocket. If he doesn't own it or control it, he soon will."

"That's a lie. My dad is a good man. He's—"

"All right, Derrick," thundered Jonathan. "That's enough."

Joel could barely hold back the tears. "Dad…none of that is true, is it? Say it isn't true." Jonathan looked at his son with anger still in his face. His silence spoke volumes of truth. "*Say it*!

Why won't you tell him it's a lie?" Joel felt like his entire world was crumbling around him. A flood of confusing thoughts and emotions cascaded through him. Nothing made sense. Nothing felt right. Tears burst out, uncontrolled. He didn't care what he said anymore. "So, what…you just pretended to want to get back with Mom and me? Why? Why would you do that to us, after all we've been through?"

Jonathan exploded. "Your mother's got something I want. A book. It's evidence against me. And I *will* get it one way or the other."

Suddenly, from somewhere under his suit jacket, he pulled out a pistol and pointed it at Derrick. "We're moving to Plan B. Joel, I want you to find that book and bring it to me. It will be in a small metal box." Joel gasped at the large chrome-plated handgun, unable to speak or move. His dad thundered, "*Move it!*"

---

Abner decided it was time to act. Joel was in mounting danger and in dire need of protection. There was no telling what his deranged father would do in his present state of mind. He traversed the distance to earth in a matter of milliseconds, but when he arrived and prepared to materialize into the physical realm, he was met by a being from the Kingdom of Darkness. It was tall, taller than he, but he could see only the outline of it, since it did not naturally reflect light. And it had a stench like rotting meat.

The being spoke in a rasping, poisonous voice, as if its vocal chords hadn't been used in a thousand years. "And just where do you think you're going, Abner?"

If angels could fear, Abner would have crouched low in the agony of it, already defeated. But their only purpose is to serve the Father's Will, regardless of threats to their own existence. Abner spoke with the authority of the Father Himself. "Leave this place or I will strike you down where you stand."

The demon laughed derisively and then spoke in a condescending tone. "Come now, are you so stunted in mind to believe that you can threaten me with that barking the way you did my minion, Pus? I see no warriors at your side, ready to fight for you. And by the way, your destruction of Pus has furthered my anger toward you. Though a bumbling fool, he was at least marginally useful to me. But what has made me most furious is the fact that you are in the way of my objective, the destruction of the very one you seek to protect. And so I must destroy you first, before I kill the boy."

---

Joel dashed to the kitchen. He felt as if he were watching himself from outside of his body. His mind was still overloaded with conflicting, hurtful information. How could it be that his dad, the only father he had ever known, was holding him captive? There was no telling what he would do to Derrick for ratting him out. No telling what he would do to him either.

Joel knew the metal box was under his mom's bed, but he needed time to think about what to do. One thing was sure, there was no way he could fight his father directly, even if he could bring himself to do so. Surveying the countertop, his eyes stopped at the knife stand holding several large blades. Could he hide one up his sleeve and at an opportune moment stab his dad with it? He didn't think his courage or strength was up to the task, so he gave up the idea.

He went into the den off the kitchen, unlocked the sliding glass door, and nudged it open. A thought seized him, *Run, call for help*. But how far would he get before his father caught him? And what about Derrick? As much as he disliked Derrick, his life was in danger too. There must be something else he could do besides hightail it out of there.

Then he saw the phone on the end table and thought, *Call 911*.

The familiar voice boomed from the front living room. "Hey kid, what's taking you so long?"

*Kid.* There was a time, long ago, when Derrick had called him that and it made him feel special. Now the title felt hollow, impersonal. His dad could have been addressing any stranger on the street. "I'm still looking, Dad. I think it's downstairs."

Joel rushed down the stairs, not knowing how much time he would have. Already a plan was forming in his mind. He knew what he had to do.

On the table next to the couch was the extension phone. He dialed 911.

"This is the 911 operator. Is this an emergency?"

"Yes," Joel whispered. "There's a man with a gun in my house. And Derrick Wicker too. He escaped from prison. The address is 4780 East Nine—"

Joel stopped in mid-sentence. The hairs on the back of his neck tingled. Feeling someone behind him, he turned slowly and saw Derrick and his father at the bottom of the steps.

The 911 operator pleaded, "What's that? 4780 Ninth Street? Ninetieth Street? Hello? *Hello?*"

His dad held Derrick's collar in his hand while pointing the gun at the back of his head. He slowly pointed the gun at Joel. Almost in a whisper, he said, "Put the phone down."

---

"If you are so bent on my destruction, why not show yourself, so I can look at my executioner in the face." Abner knew demons burned with self-absorption and also had to use a fraction of their power to maintain a visible form. He hoped it would be enough of a difference to give him an advantage.

The demon shimmered and revealed its physical identity. Abner crouched, ready for battle. "Teragon. I should have known you were behind this pathetic plan. It's just like your kind to seek to overpower a weak, innocent child. Did your wretched master put you up to it or did you think of it all by yourself with that decrepit mind of yours?"

"Mind your tongue, you groveling worm. Prepare to be obliterated."

---

"Who'd you call?" said Jonathan. Anger frothed just below the surface.

Joel felt his hands moisten. "I was just calling Mom on her cell. I wanted to tell her not to come home because of…"

"It doesn't matter. This will be over in a few minutes anyway." He waved the gun. "Get the box."

Joel quickly went to his mom's bedroom, and a moment later handed the box to his father. Jonathan dialed the combination, opened the lid, and then flipped it upside down, cascading its contents onto the floor. He picked up the ledger book, flipped through it briefly, then snapped it shut.

"All right. Back upstairs, this time I won't let you out of my sight. Now find me an extension cord."

Joel led the way up the stairs, fished the cord out of the junk drawer in the kitchen, and held it up. Still pointing the gun at Derrick, Jonathan grumbled, "Now tie Derrick's hands behind his back. And make sure it's tight."

They went into the living room. Joel wrapped the cord around Derrick's wrists while his dad flipped a cell phone open. He punched a single number then after a few seconds said, "Sal. I want you and Gus to pick me up at the Thompson place. Bring the cargo van." He flipped the phone closed and dropped it into his pocket.

"Dad, what are you going to do to us?"

"Stop calling me that. I'm not your dad any more than that sniveling mother of yours is my wife."

"Wha…what do you mean?" Joel stood beside Derrick, looked at the gun barrel, then back at his father. This was a crazy nightmare. *Crazy*. Would his dad actually shoot Derrick in front of him? Was he next?

"I almost had your mother convinced," said Jonathan. "You were on board from the start. But now..." he waved the gun at Derrick. "My cover's blown because of this moron."

"So...what now?" Even as he asked the question, Joel wasn't sure he wanted to hear the answer.

---

The two spiritual beings faced off, each slowly moving in a slow circle. Abner still hadn't recovered fully after his fight with Pus. Although he healed nearly instantly, the pain lingered to serve as a reminder of his limitations. Teragon put on a menacing face, grinning hideously, as if delighted that he had already defeated Abner. A wide-bladed battle spear, tipped with black poisonous ooze, materialized in his hands. Abner's only weapon was the focused force of his aura. It was sufficient to drive off underling demons, but he had no idea how it would affect the powerful foe before him. Teragon thrust the spear toward Abner several times to test the angel's reaction. Abner calmly continued to circle unflinching. He was not so easily fooled.

With an angry grunt, Teragon hurled the spear at Abner's midsection. Abner bent to one side, but not quickly enough. The blade tore deep into his side, slashing angelic skin. Abner fell on one knee as golden essence poured out of him. Pain, of an intensity he had never known, coursed through his entire body. He could feel energy and life drain from him. Teragon threw himself at Abner, knocking him on his back and pinning his arms apart. Teragon knew Abner could not focus his aura if he could not bring his hands together. Abner struggled, but the demon was stronger than he, a reality exacerbated by his lethal wound. If Teragon held him down long enough, Abner would cease to exist.

"Now," said Jonathan, "we wait until Sal gets here. Then we take a little ride. Sit down you two." Jonathan remained standing. "So, Derrick. I'm curious. What exactly are you doing here and how do you know Joel?"

"Like he said, we were friends back when he lived in the apartment. Joel was a member of my gang."

Jonathan seemed mildly interested. "You were a member of the Blades?"

"Yeah," said Joel sheepishly. "But I'm not anymore. I've changed…I…"

Jonathan rubbed his chin. "Hmmm. Too bad. We might have worked together. You might have even taken over the family 'business' someday."

"*What?*" shouted Derrick. "*This* lowlife? He turned me in. He'd probably turn you in too. His own father. He deserves to die. That's your own rule, remember?'"

"Yes, and unfortunately for you, you've turned me in by telling Joel about me. So you seem to be in the same boat."

"Wait a minute. I didn't know you were his dad until you walked in that door. I was just getting straight with Joel. We're still working together, aren't we?"

"Not any more. You're a loose cannon and I don't like loose cannons."

Fear began to seep into Derrick's face. Joel almost felt sorry for him. "Look, I didn't mean anything by it. You know I wouldn't do anything to hurt you, right? Listen…I'll do anything…please. C'mon, man, *please!*" For the first time in his life, Joel saw Derrick's eyes well up.

"Shut up!" roared Jonathan.

A black windowless van pulled into the driveway. Jonathan waved the gun at Joel and Derrick. "All right you two get up. We're leaving."

Derrick rose unsteadily. Eyes wide and flushed, he turned to Joel. "We get in that van, we're as good as dead. Tell your dad…"

"*Shut up!*" said Jonathan as he slapped Derrick's face hard with the gun barrel. Derrick was sent sprawling awkwardly toward the dining room entrance. Without his hands to break the fall, he shattered an end table and slammed into a corner of the entrance. He lay crumpled against the wall, unconscious. Blood from his temple left a bright red ribbon down the side of his face.

"Great," said Jonathan as if he had broken a shoelace.

"Dad! What'd you do that for?"

"I told you to quit calling me that."

Joel somberly looked up at his dad. "But that's the only thing I know to call you."

"Just get in the van, boy."

"What about Derrick? We can't just leave him here." Joel flashed back to the day Derrick left Eddie bleeding when the Blades' headquarters was raided. Although he wouldn't wish the same fate on anyone, he couldn't help thinking somehow justice had come full circle.

Jonathan's rough voice shook him back to the present. "Move it or you're next."

Joel took a quick look at Derrick then said, "No, I'm not getting in that van."

Jonathan reached to grab him, but only clutched air as Joel twisted out of reach. He ran into the kitchen and grabbed the largest knife from the knife stand on the counter, the one Mr. Thompson kept razor sharp, and pointed it at his dad. Jonathan said, "Now just what do you think you're going to do with that?"

If there was one thing Joel had learned during his time as a Blade, it was how to fight with a knife. Designed to slice large slabs of meat, the knife felt awkward and unbalanced in his hand. He knew he would have no chance to win a fight with his father, even without the gun, but winning was not his goal. Escape was.

He hurled the knife down and it struck his dad in the center of his foot. Jonathan let out an anguished howl then growled, "*Damn you*, kid!"

---

Abner closed his eyes and prayed silently. "Father, if my usefulness to you has ceased, let me be annihilated here. But if not, let me conquer this beast for your glory."

Suddenly, Abner's aura began to gather by itself. As if Abner's hands were brought together, the focused beam became tighter and more concentrated until its streaming pulsations struck the center of Teragon's body. Teragon struggled against the blast of spiritual energy. The beam focused until it covered his upper body. The enormous pressure on Teragon mounted as he fought to hold Abner down. Spiritual skin began to separate from spiritual bone as the beam slowly focused in a tighter and tighter area until it pushed into him. The beam narrowed to a bowl size and began pushing into his chest. Teragon screamed, writhing in pain, but he would not let go. The beam collapsed to a finger width and pushed further into Teragon's midsection. Sharper and deeper it went until it exited out of his back.

Teragon gave a last horrifying, anguished shriek when all at once the beam expanded tearing him into oblivion. Abner rose and placed his hand on his side causing the gash to begin closing. Soon he would be fully restored, but he would always carry the scar, reminding him of the day he was almost defeated by the great and terrible Teragon. Worried that the delay might have meant the difference between life and death for Joel, Abner quickly materialized in the persona of a homeless man.

---

Joel managed to run past his dad back into the living room. He looked out the front window and saw that the van driver, a stocky, muscular man wearing a tight T-shirt, was heading toward the front door. He ran to lock the door just as the van driver reached it, but that gave his dad enough time to hobble over to him.

"You're causing me a lot of trouble, kid," said Jonathan. He put the gun back in its shoulder holster and stretched out both hands as if to plead his case. He limped toward Joel. "Look, I'm not going to hurt you. It's just time to leave. And you need to come with me. Okay?"

Joel had his back against the door. He was trapped. Out of ideas and out of time. The van driver started pounding, pulsating his body. "No. I'm not going anywhere with you."

"Yes you are," said Jonathan, the rage in his eyes quickly returning. In one fierce motion, he grabbed Joel's shirt, shoved him aside, and threw back the deadbolt. He opened the door and Sal came tumbling in.

"Hey boss, what's going on?"

"Take the kid. Put him in the van."

Sal looked at Derrick's crumpled figure. "What about him?"

"He's evidence. Put him in there too."

# CHAPTER 33

Joel sat on the cold metal wheel well in the back of the cargo van. His hands were tied behind his back with a heavy plastic cable tie. Derrick lay at his feet. A trickle of blood ran from somewhere underneath him, down one of the grooves of the corrugated floor. Joel couldn't tell whether he was unconscious or dead. It didn't matter. His breath quickened as he fought off the thought that they might both be dead soon anyway.

He looked through the rear door windows. Gus was following closely in his father's Lexus. The van, driven by his father, rumbled through the city and then turned onto the expressway.

Derrick moaned, slowly blinked open his eyes, and looked up sideways at Joel.

"Derrick! Are you okay? I thought you were dead."

Derrick struggled to a sitting position on the floor. "Where are we going?" he said groggily.

"I...I don't know." Joel tried to sound positive. "My dad is driving us somewhere."

"You know he's going to kill us both, don't you?"

"No, he won't. He's my d..." A sudden sob choked off the last word. The shocking reality finally struck home. He knew now he would never have a father; at least not one that was good and dependable, one who would be a part of the family, a family that was only a fading dream.

"How'd you get mixed up with my dad...with Chameleon?" It was the first time Joel had called him anything other than dad. It tore at his heart, but he let it go.

"He caught me rummaging around in his garbage. He gave me a choice: join up with him or he'd kill me."

"He was going to kill you just for garbage?"

"Yeah. You don't wanna know what that man is capable of."

"What if I pretend I want to join his gang?"

"Won't work. He already knows he can't trust you."

Then another thought occurred. "I made that 911 call back at the house."

"Oh yeah. Like *that's* gonna save us. Face it, man. We're dead meat."

---

In spiritual form, Abner glided beside the van as it turned off the expressway and onto a deserted two-lane road that ran along a row of abandoned warehouses. It was a place far from human observation, and a well-suited destination for evil endeavors.

He could see into the van as if it were made of pure glass and could hear the conversations as if he were with them in a quiet room. And he could feel Joel's spirit. Although desperate and fearful, it was evident he was strongly tuned to Father's Holy Spirit.

Abner knew if nothing changed, the situation would end very badly very soon. Focusing tightly on Joel, he implanted a one-word message: *Pray!*

Joel felt it rather than heard it. *Pray!* Pray for what?

*Pray like you've never prayed before. Pray like your life depended on it.*

Joel felt silly. The thought was so clear, yet somehow he knew it had not come from his own mind. He prayed aloud but quietly, "God, please help us."

*No. Pray specifically, powerfully. Pray hard for your father. Hurry.*

Joel closed his eyes and visualized his dad. Without a shred of self-consciousness, he heard himself praying loudly. "Dear heavenly Father, I don't know what my dad needs, but you do. Help him see you for who you are and what you can do for him. Father, please, turn him from this evil thing."

Derrick stared at Joel wordlessly, his mouth ajar.

---

Under Teragon's command, a minor demon had slowly, over several months, managed to attach itself firmly to Jonathan Somers's soul. It suddenly found itself being lifted away by a force it had never experienced. Against its will, it disengaged and separated from its prey, floating above him. The wide beam of Joel's powerful prayer sent raw spiritual energy through the demon, instantly annihilating it.

---

Joel's dad shook his head as if trying to wake himself up. For several months now, he had known what he was doing, but somehow was not in complete control of his actions, as if watching himself in a nightmare. He was vaguely aware of a voice coming from the back of the van. Was it... *chanting*?

Joel prayed louder. "Heavenly Father, help each one of us get through whatever problems we are facing right now. Help my dad, help Derrick, help this other man, and help me to do the right thing now."

---

Abner watched as Joel's fervent prayer blasted his dad's demon away. He knew this might be his only chance to speak to Jonathan Somers before his own evil predisposition began to rule his actions. *Jon. Stop the van. See yourself getting out. Think about what you are doing. Do the right thing for the first time in many years. Imagine yourself making a change for the better. You know what to do. Look into your soul and see the good that is still there. If not for yourself, do it for your son.*

---

Jonathan abruptly pulled the van over. He found himself breathing heavy, but for the first time in a long time, thinking clearly; without the fog surrounding him.

Sal said, "Boss, what are you doing? You okay?"

Jonathan spoke as if coming out of a dream. "What am I … where are we going … ?"

"You were about to whack these two kids, that's what. Whatsamatta boss? You look kind of … crazy."

Jonathan stared out the windshield at nothing in particular. "I've never been saner. It's like I've been floating in and out of dreams all this time. Ya know what I mean?"

"No. Not at all. Look, we need to get going. You want me to drive?"

"Dad," yelled Joel. "The police are pulling up behind us."

Sal pulled out his gun. "They're not takin' me in. I got too much to lose."

Jonathan held the gun barrel in a powerful grip. In a quiet, fatherly tone, he said, "Sal. We're done. It's time to make amends. We're long overdue."

---

Joel walked up to the officer who arrested his dad. "How did you find us? I never did give all the information to the 911 operator."

"It took us a while, but we finally zeroed in on the full address. Unfortunately, no one was home by the time we got there."

"But, how did you find the van?"

"We got a tip from an eyewitness who saw the van leave the home. Good information, too. Make, model, license plate number. Luckily the van was spotted by a state trooper not long ago. If it wasn't for that witness, we never would have found you."

"So who was the witness?"

"That's the strange part. We were at the Thompson home considering our options—we really had nothing to go on—and out of the blue this homeless guy comes up and gives us all this information. I called it in and then, when I turn around, he was gone. I mean … gone. Like he just disappeared."

Joel spoke more to himself than to the police officer. "Sounds like somebody I know."

# EPILOGUE

Joel sat in his basement apartment alone. The last forty-eight hours were a blur of activity and revelation. Derrick, Sal, Gus, and his father were arrested. His father was charged with a long list of offenses ranging from kidnapping, to obstruction of justice, to extortion. What surprised him was that his father pleaded guilty to every charge, even against the advice of his own lawyer. There would be no trial, and the only thing left for the judge was to determine how long the combined sentence should be. Even though Joel hated the things his father had done, he was proud of him for confessing. Maybe there was hope for him yet...maybe there was hope for them all.

Joel wandered upstairs and out the sliding glass door to the backyard. He looked up at the lazily drifting clouds, and in a whirlwind of thought, visions of all the things that had happened to him paraded across his mind, starting with the night at the sports arena, meeting Beth and Nate, and deciding to leave the Blades. He knew his life was on a new and better path. The words came easy to his mind. *Thanks, God, for everything*!

God smiled. "You're very welcome, my son."